KRISTEN BLC

Cattleman's Club 8

Jenny Penn

MENAGE EVERLASTING

Siren Publishing, Inc.
www.SirenPublishing.com

A SIREN PUBLISHING BOOK
IMPRINT: Ménage Everlasting

KRISTEN BLOOMING
Copyright © 2015 by Jenny Penn

ISBN: 978-1-63259-764-9

First Printing: August 2015

Cover design by Les Byerley
All art and logo copyright © 2015 by Siren Publishing, Inc.

Printed in the U.S.A.

PUBLISHER
Siren Publishing, Inc.
www.SirenPublishing.com

KRISTEN BLOOMING

Cattleman's Club 8

JENNY PENN
Copyright © 2015

Prologue

Sunday, July 20th

Kristen watched the woman cutting through the bakery with a determined stride that had everybody glancing in her direction. It helped that she was tall, well rounded, and held herself with the kind of confidence supermodels strutted with down the catwalk. The woman had it, that thing that only stars had, and Kristen was no star.

She was more like a back-up singer, part of the chorus of crazy people that she was slowly getting to know in her new hometown. Pittsview wasn't like Dothan. It wasn't big, not enough that a person couldn't move around in anonymity, but here…everybody knew everybody. More importantly they all knew each other's business, which was taking a lot of getting used to, especially now that she had some business.

That thought had her warming as her mind drifted toward Brandon and Dylan. The two men had opened her life up to a world of erotic pleasures she'd never dreamed existed. More than that, they'd opened up her heart. That was what she held on to as Wanda Davis finally came to a stop beside her table.

"Kristen Harold?"

"Yes, ma'am." Kristen nodded, feeling strangely small and suddenly quite young next to this woman.

She had to be six feet tall if she was an inch and packed full of the kind of muscles normally only men had. That explained why so many of the men were afraid of her. Kristen had heard the tales and rumors surrounding Wanda and knew that she didn't take shit from anybody.

"Oh, please, call me Wanda." The woman waved away Kristen's response with a warm smile as she plunked her large purse into the seat opposite Kristen and took the one next to her. "And I'm going to call you Kristen. Is that okay?"

"Yes...Wanda." Kristen hesitated as the other woman's gaze narrowed on her for a second before lightening up as Kristen managed to get her name out.

"That's good, honey." Wanda nodded to her, pausing to order a soda as the waitress stopped by before turning a curious glance back at Kristen.

There was something about Wanda's eyes that warned Kristen that she could see deeper than the surface. It was as if she could almost feel Wanda probing at her very thoughts and weighing them. It was quite disconcerting, but no more than the woman's bluntness.

"You look nervous as hell, honey. Something wrong?"

"No," Kristen answered, instinctively going with the polite response, but Wanda's lifted brow assured her the other woman knew she'd just lied. That made Kristen squirm as she tried to backtrack a little.

"It's just that I'm not sure what I can do to help you." Actually Kristen knew what she could do and what she should do. She didn't do either but sat there fidgeting beneath Wanda's studious gaze.

"It's not what you can do for me, honey, but what I can do for you," Wanda finally corrected her as she reached out to cover both of Kristen's much smaller hands with one of her own. "I want to tell you how sorry I am about your cousin."

That, along with the warmth of Wanda's grip, had Kristen stilling as she glanced up at the other woman in amazement. Other than Dylan and Brandon, nobody had expressed their condolences about Gwen's untimely passing. That was because nobody felt bad. Kristen knew how most of the fine citizens of Pittsview had felt about her cousin, knew, too, that whatever sympathy they did express was less than sincere.

Wanda, though, seemed different. She leaned forward, her tone growing somber and the compassion all but shining in her gaze as she gave Kristen's hand a squeeze.

"I know that this has to be a hard and difficult time. The way people are around here..." Wanda sighed and shook her head as she cast a glance over the rest of the patrons. "They have their opinions, don't they?"

Kristen hesitated to answer, licking her lips and following Wanda's gaze to meet the curious looks of the other customers. They were being watched, watched and whispered about. It had been like that ever since Gwen had died.

"Yes," Kristen finally agreed as she turned back to meet Wanda's stare. "Some of them are even entitled to their opinions."

"But none of them had the right to kill your cousin." Wanda didn't even hesitate to lay that down with a firm conviction that touched Kristen.

"No." She straightened up in her seat. "No, they didn't."

She and Wanda shared a look that was broken up by the return of the waitress. She dropped off Wanda's soda and picked up both of their orders before scurrying off. After she left, the mood was different.

Wanda started in about her job, opening up to Kristen in a way that made it impossible for her not to respond in kind. Despite all the rumors and warnings, Wanda wasn't scary in the slightest. She was just a woman, a woman who obviously cared. That was something Kristen could relate to.

Finally when the plates were cleared and the coffee had arrived, the conversation turned back around to Gwen. By then Kristen's guards were all down, and she was certain that she could trust this woman. That really wasn't the question. The question was whether or not she could be of any help.

"I'm not sure what I can tell you about my cousin that you probably haven't heard all over town." Kristen took a deep breath and dropped her gaze, hating to have to admit to the truth. "Whatever rumors you might have heard, they're probably all true."

"I'm not interested in rumors," Wanda assured her, placing her hand back over Kristen's and offering her strength. "I'm here to learn about the other side of Gwen, about what she was like as a cousin."

"As a cousin?" Kristen hadn't ever really thought of it that way. "I guess...she was...giving. I mean, she helped me get my job, let me move in, and even lent me money to buy the things I needed."

"Why don't we start there, then?" Wanda suggested. "Why don't you tell me what it was like to move in with her?"

"Well..." Kristen paused, thinking back all those months to when she'd finally convinced her mother to let her move in with Gwen. "It was like..."

Chapter 1

Wednesday, May 7th

"Are you sure about this, sweetheart?" Marissa Harold looked around the small room Gwen had offered Kristen and frowned, her thoughts clear on her face.

Kristen couldn't blame her mother for them. Marissa Harold was a proper kind of lady. Her skirts never stopped above the knee. Her makeup was always discreet. Her hair came from the 1970s. The only problem with that was it was twenty-first century, and Kristen wanted to wear a mini.

She'd be able to get away with that at Gwen's. Her cousin, Gwen, was a free spirit, living in the moment. She was the rebel in the family, living on her own as single woman, dating more than one man at a time. Most horrifying, she didn't even go to church on Sunday.

Kristen had always sort of admired her for that. She'd been raised with so many rules that she felt stifled by them, but not any longer. She was twenty-two and starting her first real job as a clerk in the City of Pittsview's accounting office. It was a good choice. She'd make enough money to either move out on her own or, maybe, even go to the college over in Troy.

The one place she was certainly not moving back to was Dothan.

"It's going to be all right, Mom," Kristen assured her mother as she offered Marissa a quick hug. "You'll see."

"I don't know." Marissa remained unconvinced, but then she didn't want to be comforted.

Kristen knew what her mother really wanted. How could she not when her mother mentioned it constantly?

"It's just not right, a young lady living outside her parents' house." Marissa glanced around the room. "And, really, look at this room, sweetheart. It's small…and the furniture, I have feeling it came *used*."

Her mother imparted that bit of criticism in a whisper that left no doubt of her thoughts about second-hand goods and had Kristen rolling her eyes.

"There is nothing wrong with this room," Kristen insisted, though, truthfully, it was a little small.

Back at home, her father had converted half the attic into a large bedroom for her. The other half had been her playroom growing up and evolved into her rec room as a teenager and her living room as an adult, and adult women really should be allowed to have a man in their living room, but her parents had a no-men rule.

Hell, they even still had a curfew for Kristen, which probably explained why she'd never had a real boyfriend. Worse, Kristen began to realize that she was boring. That was what had prompted her to finally take that step and apply for a job. She was going on an adventure. Good or bad, it had to be better than boring.

"It'll be all right, Mom. You'll see." Kristen didn't have anything else to offer her mother. There was nothing else, nothing else but listening to her complain.

"What I see is shabby sheets, and not the chic kind you see in the magazines." Marissa froze, her eyes widening. "I bet there are roaches and spiders, and you know how much you hate bugs."

"That's why I have Gwen here, to help me take care of them."

"And that's why I need Kristen here." Gwen stepped into the doorway, obviously having heard her aunt's comment about her house. "Maybe she'll teach me to live bug free."

That obnoxious retort drew a quick frown across Marissa's brow as she turned to offer her niece a look Kristen knew well. Manners, though, had to be maintained. So instead of correcting Gwen for her rudeness, Marissa tried in vain to correct her own.

"I'm sorry, Gwen." Her mother actually apologized, not that it sounded anything but strained. "I didn't mean anything by that. You have a lovely home."

"Yeah, I know." Gwen's smile assured everybody that she knew more than that. "But don't worry, Aunt Marissa. I'm going to take good care of your girl, and we're going to have some fun, isn't that right, Kristen?"

She didn't dare say yes, a little afraid of Gwen's smile and her definition of fun. So, Kristen smiled and allowed that to speak for her as her mother tried to salvage the moment without revealing just how horrified she was by what Gwen would define as fun. They all knew it involved men.

Kristen's mother had always said Gwen's skirt was a little light...and a little short, which was just her way of saying she thought her niece was a slut. While Kristen didn't want to be a slut, she did wonder what women like Gwen found so addictive about sex.

She'd never had sex before, and the few kisses she had shared with men hadn't left her tempted at all. It made her wonder if maybe she wasn't gay, not that she found women appealing in that way, but who knew what she'd enjoy. Kristen was ready to find out. She couldn't do that at home.

"I'm sure everything will work out," Kristen said, interrupting her mother's inane babbling. Her mom was just digging her hole bigger anyway. "Besides, Mom, I'm going to be too busy working to get into any trouble."

"I don't know why you need a job in the first place," her mother muttered, sounding sore and put out by the argument they'd been having for nearly three weeks now. At least her dad wasn't there. He was less polite and more opinionated than her mother.

"Because I need the money to afford school." Kristen recited her line, knowing exactly what her mother would say to that.

"I don't know why you need to go to school."

"Because I can't live the rest of my life in your attic!" Just the idea panicked Kristen, but not more than her mother's suggestion did.

"Oh, sweetheart, you won't live there forever. You'll find yourself a nice man to take care of you and move out." Her mother moved in close to fluff Kristen's hair and smile at her as though she was some kind of doll. "You're so pretty, and there is that nice Kevin O'Leary who has been showing such polite interest in you. I don't know why you always have to be so rude to him."

"Because he's like forty." And bald and fat and he reminded her of her father, which was just disgusting.

"He owns four businesses and a car dealership," Marissa retorted, sounding appalled that Kristen wouldn't take that into consideration.

"I don't need his money because I'm going to make my own." Kristen repeated her position like a mantra.

It had sort of grown into one over the past couple of weeks. Her parents were not adjusting to her plans. They were hell-bent on forcing her into their view of the direction her life should take, which was just why her father wasn't there.

He was boycotting helping her move. Of course her mother hadn't been of any great assistance, but fortunately, Kristen didn't have much to move. It wasn't as if she was going to take all her stuffed animals with her. There was no need. Kristen knew her parents would keep her room as a shrine.

"Hear, hear." Gwen raised her tea in salute to Kristen's determination for independence as she tacked on a political statement that had Marissa's brow furling once again. "It's about time women rose up and took care of themselves. You want to join us, Aunt Marissa? I got an extra bedroom. You can kick my uncle to the curb. God knows, he doesn't treat you right."

"That's enough!" Marissa's mother snapped, showing a rare flare of temper as she turned on her niece. "You will not talk about your uncle that way. He's a good man. He's taken good care of his family, and you should apologize immediately for being so rude."

Gwen didn't respond to that for a moment, just stared down her aunt, and Kristen sensed that something deeper was passing between them. It left her curious, as it always did, just what it was that Gwen knew about her father. There was something there, but Kristen doubted it was anything serious.

Her dad was a good man. A religious man. Devout and loyal to his family. Surely whatever he'd done it couldn't have been that bad. After all, why would Gwen finally apologize if it was?

"Sorry, Aunt Marissa. I was just teasing."

That was a lie. That much was clear from Gwen's tone and the bitter turn of her smile. It would have been rude, though, for her mother not to accept that apology, and Marissa Harold was never rude.

"Of course, Gwen." Marissa heaved a heavy sigh and took one last forlorn look at her daughter. "Are you sure about this, sweetheart?"

Kristen was. This was her future. One day she'd be like her cousin Gwen, with a house of her own and a job that afforded her security and the luxury to do the things she loved, like competing in some of the national quilting competitions. Kristen knew she could. She was good, but she never had the money to attend the quilting conventions. Not to mention her parents didn't approve of her traveling alone.

"Yes, Mom. I'm sure."

Kristen smiled as she began to shepherd her mother back out of the room and past Gwen. Her cousin stepped out of the way, but her smirk didn't dip a bit as Kristen continued to head her mother toward the front door.

"Now you better get back on the road before the sun starts to set. You know how Dad worries about you driving at night," Kristen reminded her, as if that were necessary, but it did help get her mother moving.

"Oh, sweetheart, I thought I might take you out to an early dinner before I left." Marissa stalled out near the door to turn a pleading gaze on Kristen.

Her mother knew how that affected Kristen, knew it made her feel guilty and obliged. Just as she knew that her mother had every intention of using the dinner to nag her and wage one last-ditch campaign to get Kristen to change her mind.

"I've really wanted to try the local bakery. I hear they have excellent sweets." Marissa tempted her with a hopeful smile.

"Fine." Kristen sighed and caved. "Just let me go get my purse."

Five minutes later the two women were packed into her mother's twenty-year-old Buick, which still had less than thirty thousand miles on it. They headed into town, going exactly five miles below the speed limit. That turned a two-minute drive into ten with another three dedicated to parking.

By the time they pushed in through the bakery's front door, Kristen was just glad to have made it there without having anybody shooting them the bird. Her mother tended to get flipped off a lot, which contributed to her view that the world was generally rude.

Manners were a thing of the past, her mother liked to say. Kristen kind of thought that her mother was a thing of the past, but would never have said that. Instead, she turned her attention to taking in the Bread Box.

It smelled heavenly and had a cuteness about it that made Kristen feel at home. Even the woman who came out from behind the counter to welcome them made Kristen feel as though she'd made the right choice. This was the kind of place she could see herself coming to study and get a piece of cake. More importantly, there was nothing her mother could complain about.

Nothing that is but the fight that broke out in the middle of their meal. It built, as most of these thing tended to, with two women at the center and the men who clearly were fighting over them. It started when the deputy sheriff entered and stormed up on the booth the two women were sharing with two men to order one of them to stay away from his woman. It ended when another belted out the most humiliating of all revelations.

"You fucked Hailey Mathews, and *you didn't even share!*"

Kristen's face went up in flames at that language while her mother turned as white as her napkin. Then all hell broke lose, and the two women ran for the door. Kristen envied them the ability to flee. She and her mother still had to pay the check, and that took a little longer than it should have, especially once more deputies started to arrive.

Kristen watched the drama play out as they arrested the first two men, unable to tear her eyes away from the spectacle they were all making. She shook her head, knowing that she was going to be hearing about this once her mother got home and told her dad about what had happened.

It was hard enough to resist the pressure her mother put on her. It was doubly hard to resist her father's lectures. Kristen wouldn't give in, though. She was fighting for her freedom, freedom to do what she wanted, and Kristen kind of thought she'd found what she wanted as she glanced over to find a deputy picking himself off the floor.

He was tall and broad but giant sized. Just the right size to fill out his uniform in a way that made Kristen's blush deepen as she felt the first stirrings of desire. It was a sweet thrill that she savored as she took in the guy's country-boy good looks. He had a little shag to his dark hair and a slightly rounded face that made his smile seem bigger, brighter, and so carefree that Kristen's heart just ached to share that kind of joy in the world, but when he caught her staring, she quickly looked away.

Focusing back on her mother, Kristen was just about to suggest she go wait in the car and let Kristen handle the bill when a shadow fell across their table. It was followed by a deep-toned Southern accent that made each word drawl out in a caress to her senses.

"You ladies doing all right this afternoon?"

Kristen's stomach quivered as she glanced up to find the dark gaze of the deputy twinkling down at her. He might have been good looking at a distance, but he was devastating up close. Up close it was clear that his body was rock hard, flexing with a gracefulness that could have made her sigh with longing if Kristen wasn't already being consumed by a sudden flush of embarrassment she couldn't explain.

Thankfully, she had her mother there to help.

"Oh, Deputy—"

"Deputy Brandon Hammel," the deputy supplied, extending his hand toward her mother and then taking hers, when she offered it up, all the way to his lips to brush a kiss across her knuckles, making Kristen's mom giggle.

"Oh, Deputy, I'm a married woman," her mother informed the big man, as if he couldn't figure that much out. Neither could she resist a little lecture. "It's not appropriate for any man's lips to touch me…but my daughter, here, is available."

Kristen's eyes widened at that ultimately humiliating revelation. Unfortunately, the horror had only begun, and so had her mother.

"Go on, sweetheart, introduce yourself to the nice young man," her mother prodded Kristen as she continued to sit there bug-eyed with her cheeks burning. Then her mother actually kicked her as she nodded to the man, who was clearly biting back his laughter. "Go on."

"Kristen Harold," Kristen mumbled, begrudgingly giving her hand over to the man and then clenching her knees tightly together as she waited for the brush of his lips against her skin.

It was like an electric shot, sending a bolt of pure delight straight up her arms and tingling across her breasts as she felt them swell, the tips hardening in an embarrassing rush. Instinctively, her eyes darted up to meet his, and she felt her breath catch at the interest she saw there.

"It's nice to meet you, Miss Kristen," he murmured, clearly reluctant to release her hand. "I don't believe I've ever had the pleasure."

"That's because Kristen is new to town," her mother volunteered.

The interruption broke the spell that seemed to be twining between Kristen and the deputy, and she quickly pulled her hand back as her mother continued on.

"She's moving in with her cousin, Gwen. Gwen Harold. Do you know her, Deputy?"

Marissa blinked innocently up at the man as if she weren't aware in the slightest that she'd broken up a sweet moment between him and her daughter. That was probably for the best, especially as the man smirked and nodded.

"Oh, yeah. I know Gwen."

Kristen's heart sank because she was sure he was saying that he knew her cousin in more than the passing sense. More like the biblical one, and that was not only gross, but Kristen certainly didn't want to get involved with the men her cousin normally went after.

Her mother seemed oblivious, though, to the obvious. Instead of being indignant, she responded with a smile.

"Well, I'm glad to see my niece has cultivated a few respectable connections." Marissa beamed, her gaze darkening though as it focused once again on the commotion erupting behind the deputy. "But I do think your services might be needed, Deputy."

The big man didn't look impressed by that suggestion but glanced over and eyed the brawl that had now caused half of the diner patrons to evacuate, including the two women at the center of the dispute. Kristen wished she could have joined them, but she was stuck there entertaining one of Gwen's former paramours.

"Ah." The deputy shrugged as he turned back, clearly unconcerned by the fight. "That's Killian's mess. He made it. He can clean it up."

"Excuse me?" Marissa's delicate features pulled tight into a look that Kristen knew well. "I'm sorry, young man, but you are a deputy. It's your job to go over there and put an end to this nonsense."

The deputy's hands shot into the air in a universal sign of surrender as he began backing away. "I'm sorry, ma'am. I thought my services might be needed here. I stand corrected."

"Yes, you certainly do." Marissa waved him away. "Now go on. My daughter and I can handle ourselves."

Kristen couldn't believe her mother. She just wanted to melt right out of her seat and hide beneath it, but there was no escaping the look the deputy shot her. It said it all. He was amused. He thought she was a little girl. God, but she was tired of men looking at her as if she was a child. Worse, she was tired of feeling like one.

"See," her mother started the moment the man was out of earshot. "That's why you need to come home with me. This place isn't safe, and just think of what kind of men must live here if their deputies are so rakish, and don't think I didn't notice you were interested. The way you went all mooneye and mute…it was just embarrassing."

Chapter 2

Brandon watched the little Miss Kristen scurry out of the diner with her uptight and way-too-proper mother. The woman had actually waved him away, and Brandon couldn't deny that he found that kind of spunk a little attractive. The older woman certainly wasn't ugly.

In fact, it was clear from how much she looked like her daughter that the woman had once been a looker. Brandon eyed the sway of Miss Kristen's almost non-existent backside. She was a tiny little thing, and cute as button.

With her hair all done up and her grandma hanging a little too lose on her, Kristen might have easily been looked over by most men, but not Brandon. He noticed the clarity of her skin, all pale and silky smooth looking. Her features were pert and smooth with a perfectly bowed mouth and a set of wide eyes that reminded him of a porcelain doll.

Just like a doll, he was betting she was a virgin.

That thought intrigued Brandon as he wondered just what kind of man Miss Kristen was waiting to give herself to. He was betting he could qualify. Her gray gaze had certainly held the kind of interest Brandon knew well.

The other thing Brandon knew well was Gwen. He had a feeling that wasn't going to win him any points, not unless the good-girl blushes were all just a disguise to mask the woman's true wild and wanton ways. Brandon didn't hold out that kind of hope.

He didn't actually hold out any hope.

He didn't need to. If he wanted a woman, he had a club full of eager applicants willing to do almost anything he commanded. None of them would be as fun, though, as giving Miss Kristen her first climax. He was betting she'd never scored one of those before. Maybe if he made her come, she'd let him a try a few other moves while she returned the favor.

"Are you going to just stand there grinning like a dumbass or help?" Killian snapped at him, drawing Brandon's gaze to where he had Cole pinned to the floor with a knee in his back.

Killian's partner on the force, and in crime, Adam, had Cole's best buddy, Kyle, pinned down against a table. Both deputies already had their cuffs in their hands. So it didn't seem as if there was much to do.

"Eh." Brandon shrugged. "Why get involved? It'll just cause me paperwork. Say, any of you know that Gwen had a cousin?"

Four shocked and outraged stares turned on him as all four men froze for a second, and Brandon knew what they were all thinking, as if he were the improper one. Hell, he hadn't started a fight in the middle of the bakery. Neither had he been the one to horribly embarrass two women in the process. So maybe they weren't the best people to ask for advice.

"Never mind." Brandon shook his head and turned toward the woman barreling at them. "I'll take care of Heather because she looks like she's about to throw a fit."

As if on cue, Heather came to a stop and gaped at them all. "What in the hell is going on here?"

She didn't give anybody a chance to answer before she lit into a lecture that would have done Miss Kristen's mother proud. Heather had spunk, too. Brandon would have made a pass if it wouldn't have landed him on the sheriff's shit list.

Right then Killian and Adam were Alex's current whipping boys, and Brandon wasn't looking to replace them. Actually it was kind of ironic, Brandon thought, given everything that what had landed Killian and Adam in the hot seat with the sheriff was Gwen Harold.

The sheriff and Gwen had a thing for a while. That was until Gwen did Killian's and Adam's things. Not that it should matter. Everybody knew the sheriff wasn't in love with Gwen, but the man was so stubborn he wouldn't go after the woman he was in love with. That was Alex's problem.

Brandon kept a straight face when he got back to the station house and reported to the other deputies on shift what had happened down at the Bread Box. Killian and Adam might have screwed Gwen, but they'd moved on to Rachel. Rachel wasn't half as easy as Gwen, and she was proving to be better at torturing Killian and Adam than Alex ever would be.

"She's got those two idiots tied up in knots." Duncan snickered as they all hung out in the deputy locker room.

Crammed into one of the aisles made by the rows of old lockers, which reminded Brandon of high school, they all clustered around where Brandon stood holding court. That was just like high school, too. High school had been good to Brandon.

He'd been popular, athletic, and had kept up his grades enough to assure that many young women's fathers had considered him an ideal catch. What they hadn't known was that Brandon was wise to the bait. He brought his own condoms and used them religiously because he wasn't ready for that kind of responsibility.

"I don't know, man." Dylan shook his head. "I wouldn't want Cole hanging out too close to my woman."

"Cole, sure," Duncan agreed easily. "Everybody knows that man's got like twelve different women going at once."

"I heard he almost got Patton," Brandon chipped in, sharing a look with Duncan.

"No!" Duncan broke into a big smile. "You don't mean the Davis boys' woman. That Patton?"

"Uh-huh." Brandon nodded. "Apparently, he almost made it all the way to home a while back before them boys caught up with the two of them."

"I don't believe that for a moment," Travis butted in. Hunkered down on the bench that divided two rows of lockers, he was grinning even as he argued with Brandon's suggestion. "If he'd laid a hand on that girl, those boys would have killed him."

"Yeah?" Dylan lifted a brow at that. "Well, I think Cole's lucky Killian didn't do him in. Were you here for the scene that happened earlier?"

"No," Brandon answered, his curiosity piqued. "What scene?"

"Oh," Dylan drew that word out, clearly savoring the moment. "Then you don't know."

"What don't I know?" Brandon snapped, hating to wait for any good gossip. "Tell me."

"Rachel, that girl came storming into the office a while back. Let me tell you, she was lit up like the sun. Pissed as shit." Dylan laughed as if he'd made a joke.

He sort of had. The rest of the men certainly found that revelation humorous, including Brandon. Killian was kind of a dick. He liked to strut around, acting like the big man all because he was a couple years older and a few inches thicker than the rest of them. Not that he'd ever done anything in specific to cause or pick a fight. It was just his attitude.

That attitude came storming into the locker room not but a few seconds later. Killian barely spared them a glance, but his scowl was dark enough to assure that none of them dared to speak up. Instead, they all watched him head over to the sink and start cleaning up. A second later Adam came slamming into the locker room, no doubt looking for Killian.

He paused to shoot them all a dirty look, along with a pointedly challenging question. "Is there something you wanted?"

"Nope." Brandon shook his head but couldn't shake the smile from it. "We're cool."

"Then why don't you be *cool* elsewhere?"

"Come on, boys." Duncan shoved off the locker he'd been leaning against and ambled for the door. "I think we were just dismissed."

* * * *

"Is your mom gone?" Gwen asked that question from behind Kristen as she stood there waving goodbye to her mother.

It hadn't been an easy thing to get rid of her, and really, only the darkening evening sky had finally managed to accomplish what Kristen hadn't. Turning as she shut the door, Kristen shot Gwen a quick smile.

"I think so. She drove off down the street, so as long as she doesn't return for something she might have conveniently forgotten…" Kristen let that comment trail off as Gwen snorted and rolled her eyes.

"It's a good thing you're cutting those cords," Gwen assured her, though Kristen didn't exactly know what that meant. She still got the gist.

"Mom means well, but I do need to claim my own independence." That seemed a much more polite way of saying whatever it was that Gwen was trying to say.

Politeness, though, was pointless when dealing with her cousin, who snorted and rolled her eyes. "Good God, you sound so much like her it's frightening. Tell me, you going to nag me when I light up this cigarette?"

"I didn't know you smoked." Kristen frowned as she stared at the slender object trapped between two of Gwen's fingers.

"Yep. I do a lot things you probably have no clue about, and it's going to stay that way," Gwen tacked on pointedly with a look that said Kristen was supposed to be getting a message, only she didn't understand it.

"What?"

"It's a hear-no-evil, see-no-evil, repeat-no-evil kind of house," Gwen explained, seeming incapable of being direct, but Kristen was finally getting it.

"I'm not here to rat you out to Aunt Harriet," Kristen vowed, referencing Gwen's mother.

Aunt Harriet was married to a minister, who was not Gwen's father and did not approve of Gwen's lifestyle and had driven a clear wedge in that side of the family. Kristen kind of thought that was sad and wouldn't have done anything to aggravate the situation.

"Good." Gwen nodded and turned around. "Then, that case, I'll be out back enjoying a smoke."

Kristen really did want to tell her it was a bad and dangerous habit, not to mention it yellowed teeth, but she held her tongue. Not only was she a guest in Gwen's house, but she also had a feeling Gwen suffered enough criticism. Instead, she returned to her room and began setting about settling in.

It didn't take long. She hadn't brought much, leaving her with little to do and even less after Gwen went out for the night. She cautioned Kristen not to wait up, but she ended staying up until two in the morning, unable to sleep in the strange and too-quiet house.

It was weird, and she found herself wandering around, taking in all of Gwen's possessions. Gwen might have bought her furniture used, but the antique china she had on display had to have cost a pretty penny. So, too, must have the large new TV affixed to the wall on the covered back porch.

The porch clearly served as the main living room as far as Kristen could tell. There was a little mini fridge out there, along with furniture that had to have cost a decent amount of money. Gwen was clearly not hurting for cash, and that gave Kristen a little hope that maybe one day she could have her own covered back porch, though she didn't think she'd put her TV there.

A sewing center, though…that would be a dream come true. She could have a big garden to grow flowers and a sunny room to do her crafts in, and maybe even a cat or two. Kristen was more than aware of how spinstery those plans sounded but couldn't help the way she felt.

She liked crafting, and she liked cats, and she also liked tall, good-looking deputies. It was around midnight when her determination to ignore the embarrassing incident earlier that day wore down and thoughts of the easy-smiling deputy warmed through her. By then she was lying in bed, staring into the darkness and wondering just what it would be like to feel his lips against hers.

The kiss he'd brushed against her hand had been soft and velvety smooth, tantalizing her with feelings she'd never experienced before. Kristen was sure that Deputy Hammel couldn't say the same. After all, just because she didn't have personal experience with men didn't mean Kristen couldn't spot a player.

How could he not be?

With those twinkling eyes and that hard body, the deputy undoubtedly had women throwing themselves at him everywhere he went. That thought irritated her slightly, and Kristen swore she would not become one of his adoring acolytes. After all, she might not agree with her mother about saving oneself for the pleasures of the marriage bed, but Kristen wasn't going to start sleeping with just any man.

She did believe in commitment.

Commitment and respect, the two qualities a man had to demonstrate himself capable of before Kristen gave herself to him. She was certain that man was out there, and she would find him when the time was right. First, though, she had her own future to conquer.

That future would begin tomorrow when she reported to the county's human resources office and got the paperwork started so she could begin her job next week. Kristen was looking forward to working.

More than that, she was looking forward to having the money to buy a car. A car meant freedom. It also meant she'd be able to reach the college when she enrolled. Kristen would need to save up some money first.

That was what she should be focusing on. Kristen didn't have time for crushes, but that didn't stop her from dreaming about the deputy when she finally drifted asleep. He was also why she woke up sweating with her heart pounding and an ache in an unmentionable part of her body.

Confused and embarrassed by the things she'd let the deputy do in her dreams, Kristen tried in vain to push them away, but the need only followed her through her shower. She probably could have taken care of it herself, but she didn't do that kind of thing. It was dirty, and the very idea had her blushing as she scrubbed all the harder at her limbs, pointedly avoiding other parts of her body, but what really needed to be cleaned was her mind.

Singing gospel hymns beneath her breath in an attempt to purify her thoughts, Kristen got dressed for her first day of work, choosing her best Sunday outfit in the hopes of creating a perfect first impression. She wasn't certain she succeeded when Gwen stumbled into the kitchen not five minutes later in an outfit that showed a good deal of leg and a large amount of bosom.

"Good God." Gwen stumbled to a halt to wrinkle her nose at Kristen and give her the once-over. "You're not going to work dressed like that, are you?"

"What's wrong with this outfit?" Kristen frowned, glancing down at her floral print dress and wondering how it could possibly be worse than what Gwen was wearing. "It's my best dress."

"You look like a grandmom!" Gwen shot back. "Take it off."

"What?"

"I'll get you something better to wear," Gwen assured her as she disappeared back out of the kitchen, leaving Kristen far from comforted. She jerked forward, racing out into the hall after her cousin.

"I don't think—"

"Don't think," Gwen cut her off without slowing down a step. "That's a good thing because all you're thinking about is what your mama would say, and she's old. You're not, unless you failed to notice."

Gwen paused to shoot Kristen a pointed look before shoving her bedroom door back open and wading into the clutter as she cut a path through the mounds of clothes and assorted undergarments that littered the floor. Kristen stared in wide-eyed horror at the mess as Gwen kicked a pair of shoes with impossibly long and pointed heels out of her way.

"Now, let's see what we can find."

Gwen ripped open the folding doors to her closet and burrowed into the pile of clothes that damn near fell out on top of her. In short order, things began to fly back out over her shoulder as Gwen muttered and commented to herself, talking about Kristen in a way that she could have found offensive.

"No, that's too short, you'll never agree...you don't have the boobs for that top...and this dress, I'm sure your mother has taught you not to show your arms, too...Here we go! This will do."

"Uh..." Kristen stared in horror at the outfit Gwen selected. "I don't wear pants."

"What are you? In a cult?" Gwen snorted. "Now, unless you want to wear a mini, it's the pants."

"Why do you care what I wear anyway?" Kristen demanded to know, not sure why she suddenly deserved such attention from her cousin.

While Gwen may be helping her out, she rarely actually paid Kristen much mind, but today was different. Gwen wasn't, though. She was still the same vain person she'd always been, and so was her consideration.

"Listen, Kristen, I have a reputation in this town, and you're not going to ruin it with your grandmom dresses. So take it off, or I'll tear it off."

Gwen probably would, too. She was known for her poor impulse control, and Kristen couldn't imagine her reputation was such that she could damage Gwen's good name. Still, she was helping Kristen out, and Kristen did want to change. Pants were preferable to ass-crack-revealing minis.

"Fine." Taking a deep breath and accepting that this was her chance to try something new, Kristen took the outfit from Gwen. "I'll change."

Chapter 3

An hour later Kristen was still fidgeting with her clothes. She felt like a woman in drag and strangely tall, thanks to the too-high heels Gwen had insisted she wear. Gwen had been full-on bossy that morning, taking over not only Kristen's outfit choices and shoes but also doing her makeup and hair.

Now her hair curled in waves that it never had, and she could see the shadow of her lashes thanks to the goops of mascara making them longer than they naturally were. Her lips felt caked with waxy lipstick, her cheeks hot beneath the layers of foundation and blush.

So actually she felt kind of like a clown in drag.

It was horrible, and she swore everybody was staring at her. What the lady at the human resources office must have thought, Kristen didn't know. At least, she'd been polite enough not to comment but hadn't been merciful enough not to send Kristen down the street to the sheriff's office to get fingerprinted.

It was a requirement for the job and a long walk down the busy main street. She got beeped at twice and whistled at once. Kristen didn't take any of those as compliments. She swore then and there that tomorrow she was wearing her own dress and doing her own makeup. That wouldn't save her right then, and as she shoved through the door into the sheriff's office, things grew worse rather than better.

"Oh my God." An all-too-familiar voice called out in a thick a draw filled with amusement. "It's Miss Kristen…and it looks like you grew up overnight."

Kristen stilled at that observation, her gaze cutting across the sheriff's department's small lobby to the large wooden counter that divided the deputies' desks from the public waiting area. That counter was being manned by none other than Deputy Hammel, who cut her one of his big, double-dimple smiles that only made Kristen feel all the more awkward as she hobbled across the floor tiles, not steady in the slightest on her heels. A fact that the deputy seemed to take instant note of.

"You okay there, Miss Kristen?" he asked, quirking up a brow as the mirth sparkled in his mesmerizing gaze.

Kristen found it impossible to look him in the eye and think at the same time. Fortunately, she didn't have to think. She didn't even have to speak. Brandon's buddy said it all as he perked up, popping out of his seat at his desk to pin her with a curious look.

"Miss Kristen? Is this the virgin you keep talking about?"

He said that loud enough to draw just about everybody's notice, and Kristen felt herself flushing hot with a volatile mixture of embarrassment and indignation.

"I beg your pardon." Kristen stiffened up and almost fell over, not fully balanced on her heels.

"Don't pay him any mind." Brandon waved away her perfectly justifiable outrage. "He's just teasing."

"But that doesn't mean I'm lying. He has been talking about you for hours," the other man revealed as he nodded at Brandon, who shot him a dirty look. The deputy didn't seem to care or even notice. He was too busy pointedly checking Kristen out. "And I've got to say I can see why. You're a cute one…except for the makeup. Honey, it's not supposed to be painted on."

"I…I…I…" She didn't know what to say to that. Kristen blinked and glanced down at the card in her hands and decided to simply ignore both men's inappropriate comments.

"I need this filled out." She lifted the fingerprint card toward them and kept her tone as formal and polite as she could. "I don't suppose either one of you could assist me with this, or perhaps there's another deputy available?"

"I'm always available for you, Miss Kristen," Brandon instantly assured her, taking the card from her as he started to nod toward the small gate cut into the counter. "Why don't you—"

"Give that to me." His buddy cut Brandon off, snatching the card out of his hand. "After all, you are assigned to the front desk. You can't leave your station."

"You could cover," Brandon shot back, his tone hardening slightly as he turned on his fellow deputy.

"I could, but I won't." The man stepped around him with that sharp retort and offered Kristen a smile. "Please, come this way, Miss Kristen."

"It's Miss Harold," Kristen corrected him primly, wishing Brandon had won that argument.

Whatever he'd said about her, she felt certain she was in safer hands with him. This deputy, on the other hand, was unnerving with his bluntness and his sparkling blue eyes. He was a handsome fellow, as tall and thick as Deputy Hammel but with a more rakish smile and cut features that Kristen didn't trust.

"I guess I stand corrected." The man bowed formally, earning a round of chuckles from the other deputies, who all seemed to be watching them now. "Please, my lady, would you mind stepping this way."

She would, but Kristen didn't have a choice, and so she stepped through the gate the deputy held open and all but fell over as she missed the step down. Kristen couldn't catch her balance on the heels and went crashing into the deputy, who caught her with one arm and pinned her against his hard frame.

Kristen had never been pressed up against a man so closely or felt him so intimately pressing back against her. Her eyes rounded and darted up to his as her mouth fell open in shock. He was hard. His penis, it was *huge*.

And he was thumping against her!

Kristen jerked back in shock, stumbling over her heels once again. This time there was nobody to catch her. Kristen went down hard, causing about every deputy to leap to their feet. Unfortunately there was only one close enough to scoop her off the ground.

Kristen let out a squeal as she found herself suddenly levitating in a set of strong arms. The deputy's heady, heated scent washed over her, leaving her feeling intoxicated and wobbly on the heels she found herself having to balance on once again.

"I'm sorry about that, Miss Harold. I should have warned you about the step," the deputy apologized as he held on to her arm, keeping her steady as now concerned eyes raked over her. "You didn't hurt anything, did you?"

Nothing more than her pride and dignity.

"Get out of the way." Deputy Hammel came rushing up to shove the deputy's body back, forcing the man to let go and leaving Kristen still in a slight daze as she watched the two bicker.

"Hey, man, don't push me."

"Then don't be getting in my way."

"What the hell is going on out here?"

The commanding tone cut that question through the air with a wealth of irritation that had all the deputies stiffening with a sudden tension. That included the two deputies in front of her. They quickly shuffled back out of the sheriff's way as the man cut across the floor to confront the two of them. Barely sparing Kristen a glance, he pinned the two deputies in front of her with a hard look.

"I asked you two a question. I'd think, between the two of you, one would have an answer."

"I'm sorry, sir," Deputy Hammel quickly answered. "Dylan here was just assisting the lady with a fingerprint sheet when she took a little stumble."

"Is that right?" The sheriff glanced over at her, pinning her with a look that assured Kristen he didn't believe the deputy for a moment.

She could have ratted them both out, could have made a scene, but that was what her mother would have done. Kristen didn't want to end up like her, all judgmental and critical of everything. So, instead, she plastered on a smile and lied, for the first time ever.

"Yes. I'm just…clumsy I guess."

He knew she was lying, and he wasn't pleased, but Kristen didn't crumble beneath his stare. The sheriff might be large and in charge, but he had nothing on her mother when it came to glaring a person into confessing. He figured that out after a moment.

"And you are?"

"Kristen Harold." She extended a hand along with that introduction. "I've just started working over at the city office, and I needed to get fingerprinted."

"Nice to meet you, Miss Harold. I'm Sheriff Krane."

The man took her hand, squeezing a little hard as he pumped it once in a firm shake. She had a feeling it was his routine shake because the man appeared more interested in continuing to stare at her as he held on to her hand for a little longer than appropriate.

"Do I know you from somewhere? You look kind of familiar."

"She's Gwen's cousin," Deputy Hammel offered with a look that told Kristen instantly she was looking at, yet, another one of Gwen's conquests. From the sheriff's frown, things hadn't ended well.

"Is that right?" The sheriff turned a less-than-friendly gaze back on her. "I should have known. Well, come on. Before you cause the kind of trouble your cousin enjoys, let's get you fingerprinted and out of my men's hair."

That explained how the deputies got away with being so brash and insolent with the public. Apparently, it was an office policy to be a prick.

* * * *

"Well, you two certainly know how to shoot yourselves in the feet." Duncan shook his head at Brandon and Dylan, but neither man bothered to respond. They were two busy squaring off.

"What were you doing?" Brandon demanded to know, but Dylan didn't really have an answer. So he came up with the best one he could.

"Following my dick?" That was true, but Dylan didn't know if that was going to get him hit right then. He knew Brandon was thinking about it.

"Why'd you have to be so crass?"

"Oh, come on. That was funny." It was, or would have been if Brandon would lighten up. "Oh, wait…you really like this girl, don't you? It's the whole virgin thing, isn't it?"

"Shut up, Dylan," Brandon snapped, but Dylan was on a role.

"I mean she's cute," he admitted as he followed Brandon back to his seat at the front desk. "I can get why you'd want to do her. Though, she clearly has no sense of fashion or how to do makeup, but who cares about that when you can keep her naked, spread, and at your beck and call, right?"

Despite the fact that Brandon had picked back up his fishing magazine and pointedly lifted it up, Dylan knew he wasn't focusing on any article about lures or bait. He was simmering. Dylan had known Brandon pretty much from the cradle, and he knew that look.

"After all, the woman is Gwen's cousin so you've got to figure beneath that uptight, pinched faced look the woman's got to have a little fire in her, and how fun would it be to pervert a virgin?"

"That does sound like fun," Duncan answered, irritating Dylan by interrupting his attempt to aggravate Brandon. "And it's not like the summer challenge down at the club is a go."

That had Brandon lowering his magazine as both he and Dylan turned slowly to stare across the desks to where Duncan sat. He was leaning back in his chair, his hands crossed behind his head as he appeared to contemplate the matter.

"I mean, after all, since that dipshit Konor got Heather nominated as the prize, he kind of screwed us all out of having any fun this year. Isn't that right, guys?"

There was a chorus of head bobs and "yeahs" that echoed back after Duncan made that observation. He was, of course, referring to the Cattleman's Club. The club catered to some specialized interests, mostly involving naked women at the male members' beck and call, which was just why Dylan cherished his membership as his greatest possession.

"That doesn't exactly seem fair, does it?" Duncan asked, drawing Dylan's attention back to him.

He was still complaining about the challenge that the club put on every year. The game was simple. All a man had to do to win was seduce the woman who was known as the prize. Normally those prizes tended to be less than easy. This time they were impossible because the woman selected, Heather Lawson, was the sheriff's own personal obsession.

Everybody knew how Alex responded when one of his deputies slept with one of his obsessions. If they didn't, all they had to do was ask Killian and Adam how much fun the night shift was. Nobody planned on joining them there, least of all Dylan. He had better things to do with his nights than work.

Better things, like perverting a virgin.

"I think he's right." Dylan knew he was about to piss off Brandon, but he liked to live dangerously. "Perverting a virgin sounds like a perfect in-house challenge."

"Everybody chips in five hundred buckles to the winner?" Duncan suggested, referring to the club's own currency.

"Why should the winner get anything?" Jason spoke up from his desk, joining the conversation while Brandon continued to fume. "Isn't introducing a woman to the world of total pleasure reward enough?"

"No." Duncan snorted. "Virgins aren't any good."

"What do you mean? If they're no good, that means you didn't train them right," Jason shot back, starting an argument that had all the markings of growing bigger.

That was without Brandon's involvement. With his ears red and his face crunched up into a constipated look, Brandon jerked back around and plopped back down in his seat, pointedly ignoring everybody and making it clear he wasn't about to get involved in their bet.

Dylan kind of thought he wouldn't be able to help himself, after all it was clear Brandon was sweet on the girl. Normally whoever caught Brandon's attention caught Dylan's as well, and he had to admit he was interested, especially when she came walking back through the station.

Everybody fell silent, listening in as Alex wished her a good day and sent the woman on her way. It was clear from the way she avoided looking at anybody that she was either embarrassed or annoyed, probably both. She also couldn't walk on those heels and looked absolutely ridiculous in them.

In fact, she kind of looked like a child playing dress-up. A sweet kid, and Dylan felt a moment of guilt for unleashing the dogs behind him on her, but then he forgave himself. After all, he planned on keeping her safe from those dogs because nobody but either him or Brandon would be winning the challenge.

Chapter 4

Kristen breathed a sigh of relief the second she escaped back out into the sunshine. Walking back through the lobby of the sheriff's department had felt like walking through a gauntlet. There had been no denying the eyes tracking her progress or the sense of anticipation that had filled the air. She'd felt like a cat strolling past a long, hungry line of dogs…no, wolves.

That's how they'd looked, hard and tough and so much more knowledgeable of the world that Kristen felt almost like a child by comparison. Hell, she couldn't even dress herself according to Gwen. One thing was for sure. She either had to come up with some money for new clothes or alter some of her old ones because she could not go out like this again.

What she needed were some magazines to point her in the direct path, and possibly a mentor to help her get there. Kristen thought she might have found the latter later that morning as she was introduced to Cybil Bliss. She appeared to be everything Kristen wished she could be.

Well groomed in an attractive but sophisticated manner, Cybil held herself with a confidence that Kristen admired. She gave off a take-no-guff kind of attitude, and nobody gave her any. They certainty didn't tease her inappropriately the way the deputy had Kristen.

She still blushed thinking of the things he'd said. Worse, she couldn't stop thinking about them or how *big* he'd felt. It was embarrassing to admit, but Kristen never had seen a man naked, and definitely never aroused. The closest she had to compare the deputy to was Matt from school, who had an unfortunate habit of growing hard whenever Mrs. Poppy came to teach music class. That was over ten years past.

Kristen kind of thought that was a statement of how pathetic her life was, but then she consoled herself with the reminder that her life had only just begun. So had her job, which didn't turn out to be half as exciting as Kristen had dreamt.

Assigned to assist Cybil with auditing the city's accounts, Kristen found herself sitting at a table reading through an endless list of transactions as she looked for the ones that Cybil needed marked. It was boring and mundane work, and she was thankful when lunch rolled around.

Cybil invited her out with several of the other ladies to go to lunch. Kristen agreed, though she remained quiet as the group moved down the street. They headed straight for the bakery, that being their habit. Apparently, Gwen was not a part of this tradition. Kristen could sense several of the women's hesitation when they were first introduced to her and knew instantly she was not among her cousin's fan club.

The verdict was still clearly out on Kristen.

That made her all the more self-conscious. As her nature was to be quiet, she was damn near silent when nervous. That's pretty much how she stayed as they entered the packed bakery. It was clear from the crush and the way people called out to the different ladies in the group that they shared a lunch time tradition with just about everybody working in town.

That made Kristen feel only more out of place.

It didn't help that the ratio of men to women seemed to be three to one, making the place full of testosterone and, worse, deputy uniforms. Kristen even caught sight of the sheriff, looking irritated as all get out as he sat tracking the well-rounded waitress fluttering from one table to another. It was clear something was going on between the two, and Kristen couldn't help but assume the obvious.

The sheriff was wearing his heart on his sleeve, and the woman was hanging on to just about every other man in the room. She either wasn't interested or was interested in annoying the sheriff. That kind of put Kristen off, her first loyalty going to the only person she knew out of the two. The sheriff hadn't seen that bad earlier. A little gruff and abrasive, but maybe he was just heartbroken and hiding it well.

What wasn't being well hidden was the looks Kristen was drawing from the male population dominating the dining room. It soon became clear, as their pack of women cut across the room, that there were two groups present in the bakery that afternoon.

One was the gaggle of gawking men, who the women pointedly ignored. Then there were the locals, the professionals, the older couples, and all the other, no doubt deemed, acceptable people that the ladies went out of their way to greet. What wasn't clear was what group Kristen belonged to, though she had a feeling she knew where she was being grouped.

It was impossible to miss when every single time she was introduced to somebody as they passed by their table, Kristen could sense an immediate withdrawal the second they realized who her cousin was, making one thing perfectly clear. Gwen was not beloved in this small town.

Just the opposite, but Kristen refused to accept that was based on anything other than a lack of understanding. Sure, her cousin might be a little wild and somewhat bossy, but Gwen wasn't a bad person. In fact, she was generous enough to let Kristen stay with her, and that counted for a lot in Kristen's book.

What didn't count for much, though, were the friends Gwen came strolling into the bakery with not a few minutes after Kristen's group had finally settled down at a table that had clearly been reserved for them. The young set of mostly inappropriately dressed women that accompanied Gwen didn't bother to head in their direction or to speak to anyone at any of tables Kristen and her group had paused at.

Instead, they were greeted by a chorus of welcomes from the men and ended up fitting themselves in among that rowdy, clearly randy, group. Kristen couldn't say she was surprised, but she was a little disappointed when she saw several of Gwen's friends settle down at a table with Deputy Hammel.

His more forward friend was there next to him, greeting the ladies with a smile that assured Kristen he was more than familiar with them. That just went to prove what she'd already suspected. The man was a flirt. He'd just been amusing himself with her.

That was humiliating enough, but he'd done it simply because she was a virgin, a fact that seemed to be apparent to more men than Kristen had ever realized. That was a depressing thought, one Kristen lost herself in as the conversation swirled around her.

It was broken up by the sudden hushed whispers that drew Kristen's attention from her own dark thoughts to the group that was leaning in close as they all tracked the movement of the woman walking in on the arm of a very large, very hard looking man. He was the kind of man who got painted onto a romance cover, and the woman was even better looking.

Kristen couldn't help but gape, feeling small and completely mousy as the tall, auburn-haired beauty swept past their table in a light fragrance of flowers and sunshine. She not only looked good. She smelled even better.

"…can you believe it?"

"*Three men?*"

Kristen didn't know what the ladies were whispering about, but that comment caught her attention. She glanced over to find them all smiling at each other and shooting looks back at the hunk the woman had just walked in with.

"Oh, please, like you'd turn down a single one of the Davises."

"Like any woman would."

That received a round of snickers and agreements that had Kristen glancing over at Cybil with a silent question. She caught Kristen's glance and returned her smile as she bowed in slightly to give her the low down.

"That's Patton and *one* of her boyfriends."

"She dating all three brothers," Cindy, a sweetly round-faced blonde chipped in with a smile that lead to no good thought.

"At the same time." Janice tacked that on, causing the whole table to erupt in giggles and leaving no doubt that what they meant by dating was really sleeping…sleeping with three men at the same time.

Kristen's eyes damn near bugged out of her head as that realization hit, and her face went up in flames a second later. That unleashed a round of laughter across the table as Kristen looked back over at the woman, not certain if she should loathe her or admire her. She was sort of torn between both.

Three men!

Three men that looked like that!

"It isn't fair," Cybil sighed, echoing Kristen's silent thoughts. "I can't even find one man to treat me right, much less one whose back I don't have to shave, and she's got three of the hottest, most devoted men."

"And she looks like that for Christ's sake," Janice chipped in again.

"I hate her." Cybil sighed, revealing that confession without any real emotion behind it, other than a slight tinge of amusement.

Not that she really should complain. Cybil was quite attractive as far as Kristen was concerned. She had a sophisticated kind of air that matched the cut of her dark hair and the seriousness of her green eyes. She could have been an artist's muse.

"Don't we all?" Cindy asked with an outright smile.

"Oh, look at that," Janice whispered. "Patton's headed back into the kitchen with Heather…when did she start hanging out with the A crowd?"

"The A crowd?" Kristen repeated, certain she knew what that meant but shocked to hear that adult women still thought in terms of high school rankings.

"The popular people," Cybil said, helping her as if she needed it before turning to argue with Janice. "And Patton was never in the A crowd. She was too weird."

"And how would you know?" Janice shot back. "You'd already graduated by the time she got to high school."

"Because I know Chase." That had every eye widening on Cybil, who quickly corrected herself. "I mean I knew him."

"*Knew* him knew him?" Cindy pressed as Janice giggled.

"Like bow-chiki-bow-wow knew him?"

"No, you pervert," Cybil shot back. "I tutored him in math."

"Oh." Cindy sighed, her gaze drifting back to the hunk who'd joined the sheriff for what appeared to be an intense conversation. "I would have loved to teach him a thing or two."

"Speaking of a thing," Janice muttered, her tone darkening as her gaze darted over to the deputy strutting across the dinner. "Here comes Deputy *Thing*."

"Oh, please." Cindy snorted. "I wouldn't let him get anywhere near me with his thing. You know he's one of them."

Kristen didn't know and didn't have a chance to ask who they were before Deputy Hammel's buddy reached their table. He cast a smile over them all as he nodded.

"Ladies."

A chorus of murmurs responded without a single hint of welcome between any of them.

"Deputy Singer."

"I wanted to stop by and invite all you lovely ladies to a pool party this weekend."

"Uh-huh." Cybil didn't look impressed by either Deputy Singer's invitation or his smile.

"By ladies, he means you, Kristen," Janice tipped in, casting a dirty glance over at the deputy. "Because the rest of us certainly haven't ever earned such a prestigious invitation."

"I'm offended by that," Deputy Singer shot back, but his double-dimpled grin made a lie out of his words. "I'm willing to ogle all of you in your bathing suits. Just because Miss Kristen is the youngest and prettiest of you all, I don't discriminate."

"You really think you're funny, don't you?" Cindy shot at him, not half as amused.

Neither was Kristen. In fact, she was flaming red and back to wishing this bakery had an escape hatch. The deputy felt no shame in what he'd said, though, and snapped back an answer to Cindy's question in an instant.

"I know I am, gorgeous. So why don't you stop by Duncan's on Saturday afternoon, and I'm sure we'll have ourselves a lot of laughs." Something about the way the deputy spoke made it hard to know if he was being a jerk on purpose or just wasn't aware he was one.

"I hope to see you there."

He aimed a pointed look at Kristen and then strutted off before she could say anything, leaving Kristen the sole focus of the entire table and feeling worse for it. It wasn't as if she'd asked to be the prettiest, or even thought she was, but somehow Kristen felt condemned by Deputy Singer's summation.

"That man is just no good." Kristen spoke that thought aloud and with enough emotion to cause the other women to break out in a round of laughter. She found herself offering up a hopeful smile to the group as Janice nodded.

"You got that right, Miss Kristen. Dylan Singer is a dog...one with fleas. You best stay away from him."

That's exactly what Kristen planned to do until Cybil spoke up, shocking them all with her pronouncement. "I'm going."

"Going?" Cindy blinked as if she didn't know the meaning of that word. "Going where?"

"To the party," Cybil clarified, causing every woman there to blink and stare in utter amazement. "What?"

"You really want to go hang out with those fools?" Cindy pressed.

"I really want to go swimming and eat free food," Cybil corrected her. "And if all of you come, I'll have somebody to talk to."

Janice and Cindy looked at each other and shrugged before Janice answered, speaking for the both of them. "Okay. We're in."

"But I don't have a bathing suit," Kristen spoke up, though not loud enough for any of the women to hear her other than Cybil, who shot her a comforting smile.

"Don't worry, honey. We'll get you one."

"Uh-oh, check it out," Cindy leaned in to whisper as she nodded to the portly waitress who had come storming back out of the kitchen. "Heather looks fit to be tied."

That was an understatement. From where Kristen sat, she would have said the woman looked hurt. There was no denying who had caused her pain. A hush fell over the dining room as she stormed over to the sheriff and gave him a look that assured everybody knew she thought he was the dirt beneath her feet.

"Get out."

A long, tense moment followed before the sheriff scooped up his hat and shoved out of his seat. Without a word, he stormed through the dining room and out the front door, leaving a trail of whispers growing in his wake. Those whispers swirled around the table as Kristen gathered that nobody thought that situation was going to end well.

Kristen rather thought that it was her situation that wasn't going to end well. After all, she didn't not only own a swimming suit. She didn't know how to swim and was afraid there were going to be sharks in the water.

She fretted over the matter the rest of the day and couldn't help but ask Gwen what she thought that night. That was mistake. Before she knew it, they were down at the mall in Dothan with Gwen picking out bikinis that covered less than Kristen's underwear.

"I'm not wearing that." Kristen shook her head, refusing to take the skimpy two-piece from Gwen's hands. "It's inappropriate."

"It's a bathing suit," Gwen corrected, snatching up Kristen's hand and slapping the hanger into it as she imparted even more of her sage wisdom. "It's supposed to be inappropriate, and we're not going to know if you're wearing it until you try it on."

"But...what about this one?" Kristen gestured to a black and white polka-dotted one-piece. "It has a nice little skirt."

"And unless you're forty, hairy, and have a few kids running around, it's inappropriate," Gwen snapped before jabbing a finger toward the changing room. "Now go try on the bikini."

Conditioned to do as she was told, Kristen slowly began heading for the changing room. Once she got there, she moved even slower, feeling completely stupid as she shed her clothes and strapped on the stringy two piece that didn't cover as much as her underwear. In fact, her underwear stuck way out, which Gwen took immediate notice of the second she stuck her head into the changing room.

"Oh God. Look at those granny panties," Gwen groaned, both embarrassing and horrifying Kristen as she declared that new underwear was needed.

Before she could object, much less even stop her, Gwen had bought Kristen not only the bathing suit but also a whole set of lacy thongs that Kristen would never wear. Just the idea of having a string floss her there had her blushing. Her nightmare, though, hadn't ended.

It had only just begun.

That became clear as, instead of heading for home, Gwen headed to an all-too-familiar strip mall and the small salon tucked into it. Kristen stared up at the door Gwen led her to but refused to budge as she read the sign.

"We're getting tans?" She blinked, not certain she wanted to risk her delicate skin in some human glow tube.

"No. Don't be ridiculous." Gwen smirked. "We'll work on those on Saturday at the party, but first…well, I hate to tell you this, cuz, but you are a little hairy."

Gwen imparted that news in a hushed whisper as she pointedly glanced down. "You know, down *there*."

Kristen felt her face go up in flames as the truth of what Gwen was implying hit her. As if that humiliation wasn't enough, the truth of what Gwen intended hit her, and Kristen dug her heels in.

"No. No way. I'm not getting…"

"Waxed?" Gwen provided when she couldn't seem to get the word out. "Don't be embarrassed. Be thankful we caught this before any of the guys found out you're bush. Now come on."

With that blunt summation of the situation, Gwen latched onto her arm and began dragging Kristen toward the door.

Chapter 5

Saturday, May 10th

Brandon woke up early Saturday to go for his ritual run. Dylan wasn't anywhere around, but he hadn't expected him to be. Alex had decided to punish the man for picking on the little Miss Kristen, assigning him the night shift all weekend and assuring his buddy wouldn't be able to enjoy the party that afternoon for more than a few hours.

Brandon, though, was free and clear with the whole day to himself. He had a full day planned. Those plans started with jogging all the way down to Gwen's street and then past her house in the chance he might catch Miss Kristen out and about.

That had been his hope for the past several days, but Miss Kristen had yet to show her pretty face or to admire Brandon's sweaty physique, which was just why he'd taken to running without a shirt.

That was okay. He'd catch up with her later at Duncan's party. Brandon had it on good authority from Gwen that she was bringing her cousin, and he couldn't wait to see what kind of bathing suit the woman owned. Brandon was betting on something with a skirt.

That is if Gwen didn't dress her. It had become clear over the past two days that Gwen had taken to dressing her cousin up like some deranged doll. It hadn't helped that she was pulling from her own wardrobe, which was clear from the horrible fit of Kristen's clothes. Gwen was built like a playmate, a surgically enhanced one, where Kristen was more petite and delicate, even fragile looking.

She was clearly way too shy to put up with the games that Dylan liked to play, but that was okay by Brandon. He wasn't looking forward to introducing Kristen to the exotic world of erotic delights because he wanted to win some bet. He was just looking forward to the fun.

Fun was the last thing Dylan looked like he was having by the time Brandon made it home. He entered through the garage, coming into the kitchen to find Dylan bent over the coffee maker as he watched it drip looking haggard.

"Rough night?" he asked, though that much was already obvious.

"Floyd and Frank Young got into it again," Dylan muttered, offering no further explanation because none was needed.

When it came to the title fight of town drunks, the two brothers could throw down and often did. With Floyd tipping the scales at three hundred pounds and his brother being bigger than that, it normally took a good four to five deputies to separate them and a few extra to pin them. That wasn't anybody's idea of a good time.

"You still thinking you're going to make it to the party this afternoon?" Brandon wouldn't be disappointed if the answer was no, but it wasn't.

"Of course, I'll drop by for a while." Dylan glanced up from the coffee pot to shoot Brandon a smirk as he pulled out the milk from the refrigerator. "Can't miss the sight of Miss Kristen in her bathing suit, can I?"

That drew a sour look from Brandon as he slapped the refrigerator door closed. "Why do you have to be like that? Huh? You know I'm sweet on the girl."

"Which is just why I've got to be like this," Dylan shot back. "Wherever you go, I shall follow."

That stopped Brandon dead in his tracks as he realized just what Dylan was thinking, but he was crazy to think it. Too crazy, even for Dylan.

"You don't actually think we're going to share her, do you?" Brandon gaped at Dylan as his buddy snickered.

"Why not? Why should Kristen be any different?"

"Because she's probably never been kissed!"

"So she's a late bloomer." Dylan shrugged, seeming completely unaware of the ridiculousness of his comments. "That doesn't mean she can't bloom."

"No!" Brandon shook his head. "I'm putting my foot down."

"Oh, are you?"

"Yes, I am."

"Well, then," Dylan drawled out as he turned around to confront Brandon and warn him that he'd made a mistake in challenging a man who loved to take on any dare. "If it's not united we stand, then you know how it's going to fall."

"Damn it, Dylan, this isn't a game," Brandon argued. "I'm serious."

"About the girl?"

"Yeah." Actually he didn't know if he was. The only thing Brandon knew was that he couldn't stop thinking about her, which was kind of insane.

"She hasn't even spoken two words to you." Dylan snickered.

That was actually part of the allure in a weird way. It was the mystery of what was really going on behind those cloudy gray eyes that had Brandon wondering just what she was really thinking. Who knew?

She'd covered for them with the sheriff, which had shocked Brandon outright. He hadn't expected that at all given her mother's disposition. It left him wondering if maybe Dylan wasn't right. Kristen was cutting ties and just starting to bloom.

"Hello? Earth to Brandon." Dylan snapped his fingers at Brandon, jarring him out of his thoughts and back to the argument they'd been having.

"Hello, it's Uranus calling to tell you to get your head out of your shithole and stop being a dick," Brandon shot back, going with as juvenile a response as Dylan deserved.

Dylan knew it, too, which was probably why he laughed instead of taking offense at that observation. Of course, that's because Dylan excelled at juvenile behavior. Brandon was playing on his home turf.

"You know what's grosser than gross, man?"

"I'm going to go get a shower," Brandon stated, not about to engage Dylan at this game. Instead, he headed for the door, taking the milk with him as Dylan called out after him.

"A man so pathetic he can't even get up the nerve to talk to the girl he likes!"

* * * *

Dylan laughed as Brandon slammed the bathroom door loud enough to echo down the hall and into the kitchen. His buddy was in somewhat of a temper. He had been these past few days, ever since Duncan and Dylan had agreed to make Kristen the prize of the Deputy Dawg Challenge. They'd named it after Killian just to irritate him, not that the man needed help with his brooding.

God help them all. There wasn't a man on the force who didn't pray daily for Rachel to take Killian and Adam back and save them all from the two deputies' dour moods. They were grumpy and distracted because that's what women like Rachel, like Kristen, did to a man. Whether Brandon wanted him to or not, Dylan was going to save his friend from that fate.

That is if it wasn't already too late.

There was a frightening thought. Brandon was Dylan's wingman. He couldn't lose his wingman. That was what was really motivating Dylan. He knew it was selfish. He didn't care. He didn't worry either that he'd end up hurting Kristen. In fact, that thought was unfathomable.

Dylan had known and been with a lot of women. Not a single one of them had a bad word to say about him, except maybe that he was brash, but he didn't see any reason to either bother lying or disguising his intent. Those were two lessons Miss Kristen was soon to learn. It was a lesson that Brandon already knew, which probably explained why he didn't bother arguing over the woman.

There would be no point.

Brandon could make his choice to aid Dylan's cause or be prepared to battle. He hadn't made his decision. That much became clear as they headed out for Duncan's party several hours later. They were some of the first guests to arrive, most of the women choosing to show up late.

He had to admit he was surprised when Cybil and her gang showed up at all. Duncan was clearly caught off guard, too, but he was gracious enough not to let it show as the woman picked up drinks and then pointedly distanced themselves from almost every other body there. They took to the loungers on the far side of the pool, which was just where Kristen headed when she showed up an hour later, following behind Gwen and her friends.

Dylan noticed her right off, mainly because Brandon's attention suddenly shifted from talking about going fishing the next day to the women at the back. Otherwise, Kristen was easily missed in the bevy of beauties stripping down to next to nothing. Within a minute the gaggle of scantily clad, nicely endowed, half-naked women were swarming around them.

That was normally when things got fun and, better yet, interesting, but Dylan kept glancing back at Kristen. She'd seated herself on the foot of a lounger and was quietly listening to the other women. Occasionally she'd smile or nod, but damned if he ever saw her actually speak.

That began to bug Dylan as he wondered if she had nothing to say or was afraid to say what she thought. One meant she was boring as dirt. The other intrigued him, making Dylan wonder what she was thinking that couldn't be said. There was somebody who might know the answer to that.

Dylan glanced over at where Gwen was hanging off of Duncan's arm, pointedly pressing her generous bosom into the man's side. She was on the make, as usual, and she normally got what she wanted. Not that she was that good looking, but she was that well rounded and easy to boot, which explained why, when she noticed Dylan staring, she immediately abandoned one mark and latched onto him.

"Was there something you wanted?" Gwen all but purred as she pressed her big tits into his side. They were soft, and he knew not real. Not that it mattered. Not then. He had other interests at that moment.

"Yeah, I was wondering about your cousin."

"Oh, her." Gwen sighed and stepped back with a look of disappointment. "Yes, she's probably a virgin."

"What?" Dylan blinked, unsure of where that had come from.

"She's a virgin," Gwen repeated without any sense of shame. "That's what you were going to ask, right? I mean that's what everybody has been asking."

"Actually, I was just wondering what was up with her."

"What?" Gwen glanced over at where Kristen sat before making a face and turning back to Dylan. "Nothing is up with her."

"Does she speak?" Dylan pressed, only appearing to confuse Gwen all the more.

"Huh?" Gwen frowned. "Of course. I mean, sometimes. Why? What do you care what she's got to say?"

"He cares about the competition," Duncan butted in, carrying two plastic cups full of beer and passing one over to Gwen. She took it, though she appeared more interested in what Duncan had said than the drink he offered her.

"What competition?"

"The deputies' competition," Duncan elaborated, going into greater detail as Gwen prodded him along.

It would have been appropriate, if not expected, for Gwen to get indignant on her cousin's behalf when she found out the deputies had turned her virginity into a prize, but Gwen had never cared about appropriate. Instead, she laughed and shook her head.

"You idiots." Gwen snickered and shook her head. "Isn't it obvious? Nobody is going to pop that cherry until they put a ring on that finger."

"There is no such thing as the un-seducible," Dylan insisted. "It's not even a word. So watch and learn."

Snatching Gwen's beer out of her hand before she even took a sip, he headed off around the pool that had already started to fill up with people splashing all about and hollering. Somebody cranked up the music, and by the time he made it over to the old lady group, the sound was deafening.

Dylan shot an annoyed glance back across the pool where Duncan was grinning at him from the stereo before plastering a smile on his face and approaching Miss Kristen.

"Excuse me?" Dylan spoke up, interrupting the conversation, only nobody heard him or responded. So he tapped Kristen on the shoulder, making her start as she turned.

"I'm glad to see you made it," he began again but didn't think she heard him as she shook her head.

"I'm sorry. I...drink...you."

Dylan didn't catch everything she said, but the way she smiled, nodded, and turned her back, he knew he'd been dismissed. Everybody else knew it, too. Their howls of laughter echoed across the pool, but Dylan wasn't so easily turned off. Just the opposite. He was kind of turned on.

So he tapped her on the shoulder again, this time drawing a frown from the woman, but Dylan wouldn't relent. He just spoke louder.

"I'm glad to see you made it."

Kristen's frown deepened, and she shook her head. Dylan knew she hadn't heard him. So he spoke even louder.

"I'm glad to see you made it!"

The music clicked off halfway through his practiced line, leaving him yelling like a fool and drawing every eye in his direction. Kristen blushed, clearly embarrassed by the sudden attention, but Dylan wasn't. Instead, he silently promised to get Duncan back as he reached out and latched onto her hand.

"Come on, let's get you some food."

"But I'm not hungry," Kristen responded as he began dragging her back around the pool.

"Well then, you can watch me eat," Dylan offered.

"I can?" Kristen blinked.

"Yeah, and while I'm chewing, you can tell me about yourself." Dylan shot her a smile. "I'm interested in hearing everything you have to say."

Kristen frowned at that. "Everything?"

"Yes." Dylan pulled to a stop near to the buffet of chips and sub sandwiches. He paused to release Kristen and hold his hands up in surrender. "Go on and hit me with what you're thinking right now."

"You're very rude."

"What?" Dylan hadn't expected that.

"You're very rude," Kristen repeated, slower this time as if he was a little slow himself. "You didn't say hello to my friends. You dragged me over here without actually asking me. You humiliated me the other day at the station house, and you were lewd at the bakery. I think you're very rude."

"Well…shit." Dylan wasn't sure what to say to that, but Kristen clearly knew what to say.

"You shouldn't cuss around women."

"I shouldn't?" Then he probably shouldn't laugh at her, but it was hard because she was really beginning to sound like a true, blue spinster from a century or two back.

"It's inappropriate to use such colorful language around women. You should apologize."

"Well then, I'm sorry, my lady." Dylan stepped back, considering that he really had to recalculate his approach. Obviously he was striking out.

"It's not me you should apologize to," Kristen informed him with a lofty distain that made his balls ache.

The woman was so damn proper. He'd make her cuss. He'd make her beg, but not today. Today he had to regroup. So, he let her go and watched as she sashayed all the way back around the pool without ever looking back.

* * * *

Kristen breathed deep and told herself it was all right. She was right to stand up for herself and her new friends. Still, her stomach was rolling, her pulse racing, and her knees quaking beneath her with every step. It was exhilarating, and the look on Dylan's face had been priceless.

She'd left him staring after her, a fact that Kristen didn't need to look back to find out. Cybil was waiting to fill her in on the details.

"Oh my God, honey. You should see the look on Dylan's face." Grinning from ear to ear, Cybil shook her head at Kristen. "It's priceless but don't look. It'll ruin the moment."

"I think I'm going to be sick," Kristen admitted as she settled down on the foot of Cybil's lounger. "I've never been that...that honest before."

"It's liberating, isn't it?" Cybil asked with a knowing look.

Over the past two days, the older woman had taken Kristen in under her care, helping her relax at her new job and settle in enough that Kristen considered Cybil a real friend. That was something else Kristen had never had before.

"Oh, my mother would be so ashamed," Kristen whispered, wondering if that were true. After all, her mother never hesitated to stand up for what she thought was right. That, of course, led to an even more horrifying thought. "Unless, of course, I'm turning into her!"

That had Cybil laughing once again. "Oh, please. You are way too young to start worrying about that. Besides, Dylan Singer is a player, and it's about time a woman told him no."

That might be true, but Kristen still didn't feel like a woman. She felt like a child. That was what came from keeping her clothes on. While she might have let Gwen force her into wearing a bikini, Kristen had sworn there was no way anybody would get to see her in it, but as the day warmed up and everybody else stripped down, including her friends, she began to feel a little like a sore thumb sticking out sitting there in an oversized T-shirt and shorts that went all the way to her knees.

That, of course, might have been a justification for the tempting little voice whispering through her head, leaving her wondering what it would be like to be so unclothed around so many people.

Chapter 6

Brandon smirked as he watched Kristen all but dismiss Dylan. The woman had some spunk in her. More than that she was the first woman to ever turn Dylan down, which explained the boner tenting his swimming trunks. That was bad news, but mostly for Dylan unless he actually figured out he needed to lighten up his approach.

Brandon had already figured that out, and he was plotting his move when Kristen surprised him. After exchanging a few quick comments with the older lady Brandon recognized as one of the clerk's down at the city offices, Kristen stood up and finally reached for the hem of her shirt.

Silently placing a wager on a one-piece with a skirt, Brandon felt his breath catch as her shirt slid up to reveal a creamy, smooth stomach and unleash a set of breasts bigger than he'd imagined, barely contained by the two tiny cups strung together with a whole lot of string.

His Miss Kristen had been hiding a whole lot in those oversized outfits she'd been wearing. Hiding a whole lot, and Brandon's mouth was beginning to water. There was no way a woman who looked that good should be saving herself for anybody but him. Something primitive and possessive stirred within him as he watched Kristen accept a bottle of lotion from her friend.

That was his woman…and Duncan was making a move.

Without paying any attention to the woman sitting beside him prattling out some boring story, Brandon just got up and started around the pool. He hadn't even made it halfway through the throng growing bigger by the minute when Duncan lifted her right off her feet and sent her flying, screaming, into the pool.

She hit with a splash, flailing about while everybody laughed as she went under. Brandon wasn't laughing. He didn't think Kristen would be either when she came back up…if she came back up. It hit him after about ten seconds that she probably didn't know how to swim, and then he was moving on instinct, diving into the pool and going down after her.

The chlorine stung his eyes, but he could see Kristen clearly still kicking and fighting to make it back to the top. Her motions were like that of a deranged animal, desperate and panicked. She wasn't going to make it. Not without his help.

In an instant, Brandon was on her, wrapping an arm around her waist and hoisting her back to the surface. He got kicked and hit for his effort but barely took note of the blows. Kristen didn't have the strength to do any real damage. Neither did she have the breath left to fight as they finally broke through the water to a circle of concerned faces.

Everybody had caught on that there was trouble, just not as quickly as he had. That was particularly true of Duncan, who he would be dealing with later. Right then, Brandon's first priority was to get Kristen out of the water. She was clinging to him now, coughing up water as she still fought to clear her lungs.

She was so small and frail in his arms, and Brandon's anger grew with every painful-sounding retch coming from her lips. By the time they made it to the edge, where Dylan waited to help haul Kristen out of the water, Brandon was fuming.

He didn't say a word, though, simply allowed Dylan to take Kristen's wrists in his hands and lift her straight out of Brandon's arms. He followed her right out of the pool and had her back in his arms before Dylan could object, and then he was cutting a path through all the concerned looks and questions that started to circle around him.

Brandon ignored them all, not even bothering to talk to Kristen as he carted her into the house and cut through the kitchen to aim for the bedrooms down the hall. He'd been to Duncan's rental enough to know the layout. There were four bedrooms, but Brandon carried Kristen into Duncan's, figuring she at least owed him the wet sheets.

Kristen didn't ask where they were headed, didn't make a single sound as she buried her head in his neck and clung to him. She didn't say a word. The way she was trembling said it all. She was in shock. He set her down on the bed gently, only to turn around and realize he'd picked up a trail.

Kristen's friends, along with Dylan, Duncan, and several of the other guys, crowded around, flowing past Brandon as he headed toward the bathroom to collect a towel. By the time he got back, she was surrounded, flanked on either side by two women with Jimmy Mathews kneeling before her, taking Kristen's pulse.

A paramedic by trade, he checked Kristen completely over before declaring she'd be fine. As he rose up and stepped back, Duncan stepped forward to offer an apology.

"Listen, Kristen, I'm sorry." Duncan sounded and looked sincere, but that didn't buy him a pass in Brandon's book. "I didn't know you didn't how to swim."

"Well, maybe you should have asked," the dark-haired woman sitting beside Kristen snapped back before Kristen could say anything.

Coming off the bed, the woman actually poked Duncan in the chest, backing him up toward the door as she lit into him. That didn't buy Duncan a pass in Brandon's book either. They'd be having their own words later.

Right then, Brandon took advantage of the situation to sit down next to Kristen and wrap her up in the towel he'd brought back. He wrapped it around her and left his arm slung across her shoulder. Without a word, he tucked her into his side, and they sat like that in a silent moment of perfection.

Words weren't needed. Brandon just knew. This was where he belonged, by Kristen's side watching the world with her as everybody started to slowly migrate back outside. Eventually even Kristen's friends left her with her assurance she was all right, but Brandon could hear the lie in her tone. He waited, though, until they were completely alone before finally speaking.

"Want me to take you home?" Brandon glanced down as he asked that question, struck by how clear and smooth her skin was as she lifted sad gray eyes up to meet his.

Kristen hesitated for a moment to lick her lips and draw his gaze down to their perfectly arched bow before whispering an answer that about broke his heart.

"I don't want to go back out there...but I have to get my stuff."

"Don't worry. I'll go get everything," Brandon assured her but didn't make a move to leave.

It was almost impossible to tear himself away from her side, a part of him needing to feel her warm and safe and tucked into his side.

Brandon didn't question the needs swirling through him. He simply accepted them. After all, how could anything that felt this good be wrong?

It couldn't be.

Kristen shifted beneath his arm, lifting her head finally to gaze up at him with such longing Brandon felt his heart quiver and clench. Her words about broke him. They came out with a soft, whispery voice filled with shame and embarrassment.

"I made a fool of myself, didn't I?"

"No," Brandon answered instantly, irritated that she would even think such a thing. He put the blame exactly where it should have been placed. "Duncan was being an ass."

Her cheeks pinkened slightly at that word, and Brandon knew instantly he should have chosen another word.

"Sorry," he apologized. "I just get a little worked up when jerks pick on such pretty girls."

Kristen blinked, and he expected her to take the compliment with a soft smile, but her brows gathered in a look that was more disapproving than pleased.

"So, if he'd thrown an ugly girl into the pool, you would have let her drown?"

"No! Of course not." The suggestion was insulting, but Kristen didn't back down. She just sat there staring up at him, waiting for an explanation he really shouldn't have to give. "It was just an expression."

"Then you don't think I'm pretty?"

"Yes, of course I do. I think you're very pretty. The prettiest girl here."

"Now you're lying."

Brandon felt himself growing red as she flustered him with her blunt honesty. He wasn't lying but knew he sounded it as he tried desperately to convince her of the truth. "No. I am not. You are the prettiest girl here, to me."

"Really?" Kristen blinked, and he sensed her doubt. It had him smiling as he lifted a hand to brush a stray strand of hair that had curled and stuck to her cheek.

"Really."

Their gazes caught and locked, and he felt hypnotized almost instantly. Despite the fact that the time and location were all wrong, Brandon couldn't resist taking a little taste of the paradise that awaited him. When his head dipped, he felt Kristen shift a little closer, her own chin lifting so that her lips met his for a gentle brush before starting to pull back, but Brandon wasn't ready to let go.

He tightened his arm around her, letting his hand slide down over the smooth curve of her shoulder and glide across the graceful arch of her back. He pulled her in closer as his mouth broke open over hers. The tight purse of Kristen's lips gave away beneath the strength of his own, and before she could respond, his tongue swept out to claim possession of her mouth in a carnal mating that only fueled Brandon's desires.

He wanted her. He needed her. Right then and there.

He'd never been hit so hard by a bolt of lust, and he lost all control, knew that he was scaring her. Brandon felt Kristen tremble against him and expected her to push him away when suddenly her arms were twisting around him as her tongue finally began to lift and twist against his in a duel as old as time.

* * * *

Only it was all new to Kristen. She'd never felt anything like this. The feel of the deputy's warm, callused palms sliding up and down her back set off sparks of pure delight that had her squirming against him. Each motion ground the naked skin of her upper torso against the hot, hard cut of his chest, unleashing a searing heat that had her going up in flames in the deputy's arms.

A voice deep in her head screamed that this was wrong, but Kristen didn't care. This felt too good for right or wrong to matter. He tasted too good. She was drowning in the intoxicating flavor of his kiss. He was like the shot of pure molten whiskey she'd once tried but without the after burn.

At least, her throat wasn't on fire. Other parts, though, were warming in ways that she'd never felt before. A restlessness filled her that had Kristen lifting and grinding against the deputy in a wanton invitation that would have shocked her if she'd been thinking clearly. She wasn't.

She was just loving the thrill, especially when the deputy growled and yanked her right up onto his hard lap. He turned with the motion, pinning her to the bed as he tore his mouth free of hers. Leaving Kristen gasping for breath, Brandon began to suck and nibble his way right down her jaw and over the sensitive arch of her neck. Kristen flexed into the tender pleasure, her breasts swelling, her nipples hardening in a rush of excitement as the deputy's big hands lifted to cup them.

The thin scrap of fabric of her bikini top offered protection against the hard, rough caress of his fingers as they rolled her tender tip, making Kristen cry out with the pleasure growing so intense it was nearly painful. Then his mouth was there, his fingers pulling her bathing suit out of the way as his lips closed in over her nipple in an electrifying kiss that had her jerking hard and bucking beneath him hard enough to send the deputy flying over the edge of the bed.

Kristen heard a loud crash followed by an even louder expletive.

"*Shit!*"

The deputy's hard curse awakened her to the realization of what had just happened, or had been about to happen, and suddenly, Kristen was horrified.

"Fuck, man...*damn!*"

Time to go.

Without even looking back to see what had the deputy cursing, Kristen leapt off the bed and went racing out the door, only to almost slam into Cybil.

"There you are. I was coming to see...oh, honey. What happened?"

* * * *

Brandon gripped his head and curled into the fetal position as the pounding cutting straight out of the back of his skull made him feel as though he was getting hit with a hammer. That was where he'd clipped the corner of Duncan's nightstand when Kristen had chunked him onto the floor. He should have seen that one coming.

He'd really blown it.

He'd moved way too fast, but in his defense, he'd been completely blindsided. Brandon had fucked his way through a lot of women and a lot of good times, but none of that compared to the all-consuming heat that had seared through him at the first taste of Kristen's kiss. The pleasure, the want, the need, had all been beyond words.

He wanted more.

He wanted it all, and he was going to have it.

He just needed to move a little slower, and maybe strap Kristen down. That thought brought a smile to Brandon's face and an even sharper pain to his head. He was definitely going to strap her down, tie her up, and then have some real fun.

That is if he managed to catch her. While Brandon knew he hadn't been alone in the fires that had sprung out of their embrace, he'd also suspected that a virgin as sweetly untried as Kristen would bolt at the very first electric touch of lust. So, she had, and he wasn't the least bit surprised to find her missing when he finally managed to drag himself off the floor.

His legs held, though they weren't complete steady beneath him. That was the leftover effects of Kristen's escape, and so was the room that felt as if it was spinning around him. It took a moment for the world to right around him, and still, when he took that first step, it started to spin again.

At least he didn't throw up, and he kind of wanted to by the time he made it all the way to the back door. The sunlight was too bright for him to make it out past the awning that covered the small patio off the kitchen. He didn't have to go much farther, though, to draw attention to himself. In fact he didn't have to take another step before his friends were starting to buzz around him.

"What the hell happened to you?" Dylan scowled as he took in Brandon's condition. "You're bleeding."

He hadn't known that, but it explained a lot. So did his answer. "I made a move."

Dylan instantly snorted over a laugh and turned to the side as Jimmy shoved his way forward. He was scowling, and that couldn't be a good sign.

"Jesus, look at you. You guys aren't going to let me take a single day off, are you?" Jimmy bitched as he latched onto Brandon's arm and all but shoved him toward a lounger. "Now sit down before you fall down and let me see if you need stitches."

* * * *

"I should have known never to go to Duncan's stupid party," Cybil muttered as Kristen sat silently in the seat beside her.

She was still trying to come to grips with what had happened to her, but there was simply no explanation for it. She'd lost complete control. She'd allowed the deputy liberties no man should have unless they were involved in a serious relationship. What was even worse, she wanted more.

"Of course, I'm the idiot who insisted we go," Cybil raged on, seeming completely unaware of Kristen's impending breakdown.

She was wanton, and definitely not gay.

"I don't know which one of that makes us the bigger idiot."

Kristen did. She was the big idiot...maybe she was in love. That would certainly explain a lot, but wouldn't she know if she loved the deputy? How could she love him when she didn't even know anything about him?

"And then he had to go throw you into the pool. And all for what?"

What? That was the question. What was wrong with her? Kristen wished she knew.

"To make me jealous." Cybil snorted and braked hard for a stop sign. "I really don't know why I love him."

Kristen blinked, coming out of her thoughts to turn and blink in stunned amazement at Cybil, who was looking back at her with just as shocked an expression.

"You're in love with Duncan?"

"No."

"But you just said—"

"That he's an immature asshole. Yes." Cybil turned back to the road to stare out at it forlornly. "And I have bad taste in men."

Kristen didn't know why, but she giggled at that. The light, airy sound deepened into true laughs as Cybil joined her. In that moment of misery disguised as hysteria, their friendship was bonded. It ended as it began with an abrupt blare of a horn as the driver behind Cybil honked at her.

"Oh, honey, we are a pair." Cybil sighed and eased up on the brake to finally roll through the intersection. "Though, you haven't told me what idiot you fell in love with, but I bet I can take a guess. Deputy Hammel?"

Kristen blushed and glanced down at her lap as she confessed to the truth. "He kissed me."

"Hmm."

"And I liked it." Kristen peeked up to see if that had shocked her new friend, but Cybil's smile was nothing but warm and full of understanding, emboldening her to expand her confession. "A lot."

"You've never been kissed before, have you?"

"Not like that." Kristen sighed and shook her head. "It isn't right, but…I wanted him."

"There is nothing wrong with that," Cybil quickly assured her. "You're a pretty woman with healthy needs."

"But I always thought that those…healthy needs would be…"

"Saved for marriage?" Cybil supplied, a hint of amusement sounding in her tone.

"For love." That's what Kristen really wanted.

"Well then, you need to give it time and room to grow," Cybil suggested as she pulled into Gwen's drive. She brought her car to a stop and pulled up the hand brake before turning to pin Kristen with a pointed look. "And who better to give that to than a man who makes you lose your head?"

"I just don't understand." Kristen really didn't. "The deputy is not my type."

"You have a type?" Cybil lifted a brow, clearly doubting that Kristen did. "I don't mean to offend you, honey, but you don't seem to know what you like. After all, you keep letting your cousin pick your clothes."

Cybil had a point. One that bothered Kristen as she finally said her farewells and headed into the house. It was time. Time for her to get her sewing machine out and start looking online. She might not have money for a new wardrobe, but Kristen had the talents to make one out of her old clothes.

Chapter 7

By the time Gwen got home that night, Kristen had already decided what her new style was going to be—retro. She'd spent a good part of the afternoon on the Internet, purposefully avoiding thinking about both her near drowning and the passionate embrace that followed. The two were impossible to ignore, though, and her thoughts led her to a shocking realization.

She wasn't really living. Kristen was only existing.

Sure, she had plans and dreams, but for some strange reason, she seemed to be waiting for life to happen. Well, no more. She hadn't moved out of her parents' house and gotten a job because she needed somebody tell her what to do. That included everything, including how to dress.

So, with renewed determination, she began pulling out her clothes and figuring out how to alter them so they were more modern but yet still in the stylish fashion of decades gone by. She worked late into the night until she was just too tired to continue on. By the time she went to sleep, it was well after midnight, and Gwen still hadn't come home, leaving Kristen lying in bed exhausted but too unnerved to pass out until she heard her cousin finally stumble in through the front door.

By noon the next day, Gwen still hadn't appeared from her room, and Kristen had grown tired of waiting for her to wake up so she could ask her cousin for a ride. Instead, she called Cybil, who immediately agreed to take Kristen down to Dothan to see if she could get a haircut.

More than that, Cybil knew just the place to go and offered to shell out for the facials and pedicures that came with the new, more sophisticate hairstyle Kristen had selected the previous evening. The length didn't shorten by much, but this time she got layers and highlights, red ones, the same color they painted her toenails. Her mother would have been so scandalized.

That was just why Kristen didn't mention the idea of going to her normal hairstylist, Mrs. Hankon. Not only was she as old as the moon, but she was also the biggest gossip and would have told Kristen's mother everything. Then the questions would have come, along with a full-on panic attack, no doubt, and Kristen didn't want her mother to worry.

Though, it was her who worried when she got back and Gwen's bedroom door was still shut, the house quiet. Too quiet. It was nearly evening, and Kristen had a sick feeling something was wrong. She creeped down the hall to press an ear to Gwen's door but couldn't catch a hint of sound.

That left her worried. Of course, she could be overreacting. She didn't know, and she didn't dare knock or enter. Instead, Kristen went back down to the dining room, where her sewing was set up. She hadn't even made it through her first seam before Gwen came stumbling in, grumbling about all the racket.

"What are you up to?" Gwen scowled as she shuffled into the room dressed in a pair of men's boxers and a tank. "Sewing? What the hell are you—oh God. What is *this*?"

Gwen held up one of the dresses Kristen had already finished altering so that it now cinched in better at the waist. She'd also removed the high-neck collar for a nice large square one and cut the cap sleeves back into thick straps. It was absolutely adorable as far as she was concerned, and she even had material left over to make herself a matching hairband.

"Are you making clothes for the poor?" Gwen glanced over at her hopefully, but the depression returned to her gaze as Kristen shook her head.

"No. These are for me. I'm modernizing."

"Uh-huh." Gwen's frown deepened as she studied Kristen. "Well, that explains the 1990's hairdo, but not the 1960's wardrobe you're creating."

"I like it." Kristen stuck her chin in the air, pulling on every bit of confidence she had to stand up to her cousin. "And I'm going to wear it."

"Where? To church?" Gwen snickered.

"I didn't go to church today."

That was another thing her mother better not find out about. She'd called and invited Kristen to church and lunch last night, but Kristen had assured her mother that she wanted to start going to church in Pittsview as a way to get to know the town, but instead, she'd spent the morning getting to know herself.

"Oh, wow. Somebody is about to be struck by lightning." Gwen rolled her eyes and chunked the dress back onto the table before turning to head into the kitchen.

Feeling compelled to follow, Kristen first paused to straighten the dress back out so it couldn't wrinkle then she headed into the kitchen to find Gwen pulling the coffee pot out of its maker and beginning the process of brewing up a new pot.

"So…did you have fun yesterday?" Kristen started, not certain how to ask what she really wanted to know but sure she didn't want to come right out with it.

"Yeah." Gwen shrugged. "I got burnt. I got drunk. I got laid. Just another Saturday."

Kristen stared, reeling between each one of those revelations and not certain on how to respond to any of them. So, she chose to ignore them all and plastered a smile on her face.

"I had fun."

"Yeah?" Gwen quirked a brow at her as she paused to snicker. "Nearly drowning is your definition of fun?"

"No." Kristen almost laughed at that bit of absurdity before shyly adding on. "But after…"

"Oh, you mean cracking Brandon's head open." Gwen laughed outright at that as she turned back to her coffee. "I warned those boys that you were a good girl."

"Excuse me?" Kristen blinked, not completely certain by what she meant but sure that it wasn't good.

"You know, a virgin. Oh, there is no need to blush over it," Gwen tossed over her shoulder as Kristen felt her face go up in flames. "Virginity is a rare and very precious commodity in this city."

"I…I…"

"And I told those boys none of them would be claiming any prize until they put a ring on your finger," Gwen assured her, but Kristen did not feel comforted in the slightest.

"That…that…"

"But you know, men will be men, and they've got their stupid competitions, so you'll probably have to crack a few more heads open until they get the message."

"I have no idea what you're talking about." Kristen finally managed to latch onto a thought and get it said. "What competition?"

"The deputies' challenge." Gwen turned around as she rested back against the counter to offer Kristen a smugly amused smile. "They've got a competition going to see who can pop your cherry first."

Kristen felt sick. Instantly sick at that revelation. It had all been a game. What had happened between her in the deputy had been nothing more than him trying to win some stupid bet? She'd never been so crushed. It was as though the joy and possibility that the day had held had suddenly soured into a nightmare, and all she wanted to do was flee from the memories of how stupid she'd been.

They were impossible to escape. So was Gwen's laughter. It followed Kristen into her bedroom, where she slammed the door and fell across the mattress before bursting into tears.

* * * *

Brandon found himself whistling while he worked. It was a beautiful day, full of possibilities. It didn't even matter to him that his head still hurt or that he probably had a new scar and tiny little bald spot. That was what hats were for. Besides, his hair would grow back, though he was betting Miss Kristen would feel horrified when she heard what she'd done to him.

Guilt was going to be his weapon, and Brandon planned on using it to talk the little miss into a date. He even had the plans made. They included flowers, a romantic dinner, a stroll by the lake, and then he was going to kiss her again. This time he wasn't going to lose all sense of self. He would stay in control.

After all, he was a Cattleman. Cattlemen were all about control.

They were also all about getting the girl, but his plans got put on hold when the sheriff called to ask him to fill in for Byron, who had come down with a serious stomach ailment they called "drinking too much." That didn't mean he didn't intend on stopping by Miss Kristen's place and giving her the flowers, at least.

He already had them picked by the time the sheriff called, and he took enough razzing from the guys when he came in carrying the fragrant bouquet. He ignored all their jokes and Dylan's glare as he got a glass of water to keep the pretty petals plump and attached to their stalks.

Then he sat down at the front desk and began twiddling his thumbs until his dinner break finally came and it was time to go woo his maiden. He went whistling past Dylan once again, knowing he was irritating the hell out of the other man. Dylan was just sore because he didn't have his own maiden.

Actually, Brandon knew that wasn't true. His friend was worried, worried that Kristen was going to tie Brandon around her little finger and turn him into a well-whipped man. That wouldn't happen. Not now. Not ever. It was Kristen who was going to be wrapped around his finger.

Brandon's optimism continued right up to the moment that Gwen answered her front door. She took one look at him and the flowers and started to laugh. She was such a bitch, but Brandon didn't have time to get into it with her. She didn't give him the time. Gwen stepped back and called out to Kristen that she had an admirer at the door.

Then Gwen waltzed out of the way to let Kristen shuffle past. She looked like hell. Her hair was a mess, her cheeks all red and raw looking, and her eyes puffy. Brandon knew instantly she'd been crying. He would have demanded to know why if she hadn't spoken up first.

"Hello, deputy." Kristen looked disinterestedly at the flowers clutched in Brandon's hand and asked without a single hint of enthusiasm, "Are those flowers for me?"

"Yes." He thrust them forward proudly. "I just wanted to stop in and see—"

"If I'm as gullible today as I was yesterday?" Kristen said, cutting him off and confusing Brandon with the amount of bitterness in her tone.

"Pardon me?"

"I know about the competition," Kristen stated simply, confusing Brandon all the more. She didn't explain, though, simply told him how it was. "And I'm not interested in being your prize. Good day."

With that, Kristen slammed the door, the heavy wood banging into his flowers and crushing them. Brandon stood there staring down at the crumpled mess as his fist tightened over the flower stalks. His mind was catching up, and he knew who to blame for this disaster. Unfortunately, Gwen was out of reach right then.

But Duncan wasn't.

* * * *

Dylan sat with his feet up on the counter and his nose buried in the listing of college courses as he tried to decide what to pick from for the upcoming semester. The county offered to pay for one class a semester as long as a B average was maintained. Dylan normally got A's.

Brandon was the B student. He was also grumpy as shit as he came storming back into the station house, assuring Dylan that his buddy had gotten shot down. Normally that would have drawn a smile and a joke from him, but he could tell that Brandon wasn't in the mood.

"Where's Duncan?"

"In the back." Dylan jerked a thumb over his shoulder as he eyed Brandon. "You okay, man?"

"No."

"Then I guess you don't want to discuss what course to take this semester?" Dylan offered up hopefully, but Brandon was already storming around the counter.

"No."

"That's what I figured," Dylan muttered to himself as he turned his attention back to the course listings.

He was leaning toward a women's lit class. There would be women in it, no doubt. Women who would think he and Brandon were so civilized and evolved for taking an interest in such a subject. That would be a great lure to getting laid all semester. Unless the women turned out to be lesbians.

A commotion in the back drew Dylan from his thoughts as almost every deputy there jumped up and rushed toward the sound of a fight breaking out. Dylan didn't move that quickly. He knew what was going on. Kristen was already twisting Brandon into a demented man.

That was what women did.

If he had any doubts about his conclusion, they were cast aside as he shoved open the locker room door to find Travis restraining Brandon and Dale holding Duncan back while the two men continued to holler and cuss.

"You screwed me!"

"What the hell, man? I didn't do anything!" Duncan spat back as he wrestled against Dale's hold.

"Bullshit!" Brandon stretched and reached but couldn't break Byron's hold. "I have bad news for you, you idiot. Kristen knows about the competition."

"Well, I didn't tell her."

"Did you tell Gwen?"

That had Duncan stilling as he appeared to settle down. From the way he went silent, the answer was obvious, but it was too late to avoid the wrath of the sheriff, who shoved past Dylan and stormed into the locker room.

"What the fuck is going on in here?" Alex held up a hand before anybody could say anything. "No, wait. I don't care. It just has to stop, and now. Got me?"

"Yes, Sheriff." A chorus of agreements echoed through the room as Alex nodded.

"Good. Now break it up and get back to work." Alex paused to stare at Brandon for a second. "Except for you. You better go get that head wound checked out. Dylan, cover the desk."

Duncan followed Alex out the door, mostly because Dale kept shoving him. Travis trailed behind him as Brandon collapsed onto the bench seat, looking more dejected than Dylan had ever seen him. He couldn't leave his best friend like that.

"Hey, man." Dylan dropped down onto the bench across from Brandon. "You want to talk about it?"

"No."

That didn't mean he didn't need to. Dylan knew Brandon well enough to push. "This about Kristen? I take it she turned you down."

"She slammed the door in my face," Brandon muttered.

"Well, that's not that bad. Last time she brained you," Dylan pointed out with a small smile that got him one in return as Brandon snorted and shook his head.

"I just…really like her, you know?"

Actually, Dylan didn't. He'd never really liked a girl before. They were fun, momentary distractions, nothing more. He wished Brandon would agree with him, but he could tell that it was a lost cause. Despite the fact that it made no logical sense to Dylan how Brandon could be so attached to a girl he hadn't even talked to for more than five minutes, the truth was right there in Brandon's sad gaze.

"When I kissed her, it wasn't like anything ever before."

Dylan doubted that, too, but what mattered was that Brandon believed it. "Then you try again, right?"

"I don't know."

"You're giving up?" Dylan asked, appalled by the very idea. As much as he didn't want Kristen turning his best friend into a milquetoast, he didn't want her defeating him either.

"What am I supposed to do? She thinks I'm total scum."

"Then prove that you're not." Dylan shrugged, as if it were that simple.

"How?" Brandon demanded to know, putting Dylan on the spot.

"I don't know." Dylan frowned as he studied Brandon. "But I know sitting here moping isn't going to win you any favors, so why don't you go on over to the fire station and see if Jimmy can fix you up again? You're bleeding."

"Fine." Brandon heaved a big sigh and dragged himself off the bench. "Just tell Duncan to stay out of my way. I'm still pissed at him for throwing Kristen into the pool."

Dylan watched Brandon shuffle out of the locker room and shook his head before following. His buddy had it bad and clearly needed help. That was where Dylan came in, and he had an idea, one that took him only about five minutes of researching before he was on the phone with Kristen's mother.

"Good afternoon, the Harold residence." That polite greeting made Dylan smirk as he guessed exactly what kind of people he was dealing with.

"Good afternoon, is this Kristen Harold's mother?"

"Why yes it is, and who is this?" There was a proper kind of demand in that response.

"I'm Deputy Dylan Singer of the Pittsview Sheriff's Department."

"Oh no. Did something happen to my baby? Is she all right?" Panic and a frantic sense of fear filled those rapid-fire questions and had Dylan quickly rushing to assure the woman everything was fine.

"Your daughter is fine, ma'am. In fact, she is quite lovely."

"Oh thank God." Mrs. Harold breathed a heavy sigh of relief before appearing to take notice of what else Dylan had said. "Did you say she was lovely?"

"Very lovely," Dylan repeated. "And I was hoping to court her, but I know she's a very proper kind of lady and thought I should seek your and Mr. Harold's approval first."

"Why yes. Yes, you should, young man, but that will require more than a phone call," Mrs. Harold responded primly. "It would require you to come down here so that we might meet you in person."

"I was expecting you would say such and would be happy to meet with you at your convenience."

Chapter 8

Monday, May 12th

Kristen woke up the next morning as miserable as she'd gone to bed. She brushed her teeth and showered as she silently lectured herself on allowing the deputy to have so much impact on her life. After all, he didn't really mean anything to her.

It was definitely not love. Kristen had come to that realization after she'd slammed the door on the deputy's face. Why, it was so obvious she didn't know why she hadn't thought of it before. What she did know was that she'd had near-death experience and been in a vulnerable condition.

Deputy Hammel had shamelessly taken advantage of that condition, which just went to prove what kind of man he was—rotten. She didn't have the time to waste on rotten. She had a pretty dress, a pretty hairband, and put on only enough makeup to enhance her natural look.

Kristen looked at herself in the mirror after she'd slipped on her sensible pumps and smiled, liking the image that stared back at her. All she needed was a light sweater to cover her arms through the day, and she looked just like a good girl. Kristen's smile dipped at that thought, knowing that it made her a target now.

It didn't matter. She wasn't going to let anybody pressure her into anything. She looked like a good girl because she was one, and there was nothing wrong with that, Kristen told herself as she stuck her chin up, forcing herself to move with a confidence she did not really feel.

Fake it until you make it. She knew that was what Cybil would say. Cybil had a lot more to say, too, when Kristen finally made it to the office that morning to find her desk surrounded by a veritable forest of flowers. Flowers and co-workers, who were all giggling and whispering but fell silent as Kristen walked up.

"What is this?" She blinked, taking in the little cubicle she'd been assigned. The sight was overwhelming. "Who did all this?"

"The deputies," Janice quickly informed her, biting back a smile. "Apparently, you're popular. Real popular."

"But...but, this is about that stupid challenge." It clicked in an instant what was really going on, but she shouldn't have spoke aloud. It was too late, though, to take the words back or avoid the questions they caused.

"What challenge?" Cybil eyed her with a curiously amused look, and Kristen knew she was trying not to laugh. Well, it wasn't funny.

"The deputies' challenge," Kristen snapped, allowing the anger she was feeling to show in her tone for the first time ever.

That was how far those damn men had pushed her. Toying with her affections and reducing her down to a symbol to be conquered and discarded, they should all be ashamed of themselves.

"They challenged each other to what?" Janice blinked, watching as Kristen began gathering up as many of the arrangements as she could. "Smother you in flowers?"

Kristen paused to shoot Janice a frown for making a joke out of this. "Seduce me. Now somebody tell me where the dumpster is."

It took three trips, and Kristen had begun to sneeze by the time she'd finished, but she managed to throw everything away. Everything that was but the cards they'd sent. Those she kept and carried with her to the Bread Box when they all went out for lunch.

Just as she'd expected, the sheriff was at his table, glaring down the brunette waitress Kristen had learned owned the place. The woman was pointedly ignoring him, which, according to Cybil, was the normal state of their relationship. That made Kristen feel sad for the two of them but didn't stop her from intruding.

Ignoring the deputies, who called out greetings as she stormed past, Kristen marched right up to the sheriff and pointedly cleared her throat. The big man's gaze lifted slowly until his eyes locked with hers. Then he frowned.

"Miss Harold."

"Sheriff Krane." She nodded her head slightly with that greeting before whipping out the stack of notes she had stored in her purse. "If you don't mind, I would like to have a word with you."

* * * *

"One sugar or two?" Mrs. Harold asked, hovering over the pot of tea she'd carried in on an ornate tray.

She set it down on the coffee table that fronted the couch. A couch that had plastic on it. Actual plastic. Dylan couldn't believe it. He felt as if he'd walked into a TV set back from before he was born. It was surreal but totally fitting.

After all, he was playing a role. To that end, he leaned forward to answer politely. "Two, thank you."

"You're very welcome."

Mrs. Harold smiled at him, and Dylan could see that she'd once been a pretty woman. Kristen clearly had inherited her clear and perfect skin from her mother, along with those gray eyes. Thankfully, she hadn't inherited her father's nose hairs.

"Now, I told Mr. Harold about your interest in our daughter, and he was quite concerned, wasn't that right, dear?" Mrs. Harold directed that question toward her husband, who roused himself in the large recliner Dylan had a feeling he spent a lot of time in.

"Yes. Yes. Quite concerned." He nodded as Mrs. Harold passed a very small and delicate looking teacup over to Dylan. He murmured a soft thank you and got another smile as she began serving up her husband a cup.

"Well, I certainly don't want you to worry," Dylan stated as he settled back against the crinkle of the plastic and offered the other man a pointed look. "Your daughter is very lovely, and I would never do anything to disrespect her."

"Hmm." Mr. Harold breathed deeply and studied him for a long moment before finally responding. "Kristen is our daughter, our only daughter, Deputy Singer. I'm sure in your profession you've seen enough to understand that parents have a right to worry over their girls."

"Of course." Dylan nodded instantly in agreement. "I'm well aware of the horrors that await a young lady out in society. That's just why I think a lady as special and sweet as Kristen should be well-protected by a man who knows how to handle that world."

"I'm assuming you know how to handle it," Mr. Harold filled in, accepting his tea and immediately turning to put it down on the side table next to a TV remote that looked shiny and new. In fact, everything kind of had a sheen to it, including Mr. Harold's bald head.

"It's my job." Actually, there were no real horrors that happened in Pittsview, but he didn't think that needed to be pointed out. "I've been a deputy with the department for four years now."

"And that would make you how old?" Mrs. Harold asked rather baldly as she settled down onto a small, floral print chair that Dylan doubted he could fit in.

There was a second one right beside Mrs. Harold and suspected it belonged to Kristen. Poor girl. He couldn't imagine how many teas she'd been subjected to.

"Twenty-four," he answered, knowing that was a mark against him by the way Mr. Harold shook his head.

"So young," Mrs. Harold murmured. "Are you certain you know what it is you really want out of life, Deputy Singer? Aren't you just beginning to enjoy it?"

"How can I?" Dylan responded smoothly. "I'm all alone, and I was raised in a big family."

"Do you want a family?" Mrs. Harold pressed, and Dylan knew better than to hesitate.

"Yes. A big one." That was actually true, but that didn't mean he wanted it then. "Big enough to keep a woman at home."

"Oh, well." Mrs. Harold sighed, surprising him when she didn't immediately leap to the question of whether he had enough money to afford that dream. He didn't, but he would have lied.

"I'm sorry to hear that, Deputy Singer." Mrs. Harold shook her head at him. "Because our Kristen is determined to work."

"She is?" That actually shocked him. Given this show, he'd figured Kristen was looking for home and babies. Apparently not.

"Yes, sir." Mrs. Harold nodded before poking up with a small amount of pride.

"Women shouldn't work outside the home," Mr. Harold instantly interjected. "It isn't right. Her going off to live with that—"

"Henry!" Mrs. Harold fluffed her hair as she shot her husband a pointed look. "I don't really think we need to get into all that."

"It's okay, Mrs. Harold," Dylan assured her. "I'm aware of Gwen's reputation, but it's Kristen I'm more concerned about."

"Kristen?" Mrs. Harold blinked that in, looking suddenly alarmed. "Why? What has Gwen gotten her into?"

"Well, I understand that you are faithful people, and I'm sorry to inform you but your daughter…she missed church on Sunday." Dylan knew that was true because Gwen had told him. She'd also told him that if Mrs. Harold found out she'd flip her lid. Two useful pieces of information right then.

"Oh, do you hear that, Henry? Kristen's being led astray."

"Hmm." Mr. Harold made that strange grumbling noise that Dylan was beginning to suspect was an agreement. "We'll have to have a talk with her."

"Now I didn't come here to get Kristen into any trouble," Dylan warned him, inflecting enough distress in his tone to have Mrs. Harold reaching out to pat his knee.

"Don't you worry, Deputy. You didn't do anything wrong," she stressed, making it patently clear who she thought had done wrong.

"Yes, well, church is important."

"Do you go to church?" Mr. Harold asked, eyeing him with a look that assured Dylan he was being measured and tested once again.

Thanks to Gwen, though, he knew all the right answers. "Certainly, sir. I attend First Christian Baptist."

"Do you hear that, Henry? He's a Baptist." That had Mrs. Harold smiling, but Mr. Harold was studying him with a narrowed gaze.

"I've heard of First Christian. Reverend Hampton runs the show up there, no?"

"It's Hapton, sir." Dylan smiled, not about to be tripped up on details. "Reverend Hapton."

"Hmm."

"And I hear good things about your church, First United." Dylan easily turned the conversation back toward his ultimate goal. "Though I've never had the pleasure of sitting through a service."

"Well, you should join us this weekend." Mrs. Harold immediately leapt to the invitation Dylan was fishing for. "It would be the perfect first chance for you and Kristen to get better acquainted."

"I couldn't agree more." Dylan smiled.

* * * *

Brandon sat at the front desk, staring at his magazine without actually seeing anything on the high-gloss pages. His mind was caught and stuck by the memory of how good Kristen had looked in her dress that afternoon. She'd waltzed into the Bread Box at lunchtime looking as if she'd walked right off the set of an old sitcom.

Her slick dark tresses had been lightened with a hint of red and curled around her headband in a cascade of waves that framed the perfect curve of her heart-shaped face. Those wispy curls had highlighted the soft arch of her brows and the shine of her brilliant eyes. With her nose, her lips, the way her chin stuck ever so slightly out, she looked like an angel…and dressed just about as modestly as one.

That was all right with Brandon, especially if it helped keep the other men at bay. Like that was going to happen. Those idiots had screwed him completely over, and Brandon knew that was the point. It had become clear that the stupid competition was really about him.

After all, most of the deputies liked their women full-figured and fresh. Normally so did Brandon. Why work for it when easy came so…well, easy? Kristen was anything but easy, but she was worth the work. The way she'd strutted past them with her head held high that afternoon at the bakery had proved it.

Kristen had class. She might have been a little quiet, but it had been clear when she'd dumped all the letters the other deputies had sent her on Alex's table that she also had a backbone. Nobody was going to mess with her. Nobody better or Brandon would be taking care of them.

"Hamilton, Hammel, Young….and where the hell is Singer?" Alex stuck his head out of his office to call out those names. Thankfully for Dylan, he was just walking in the door.

"Right here, sir."

Alex grunted and shoved the door to his office farther open. "I want to see all of you. Now!"

"You're in trouble," Travis sang softly as all four deputies treaded slowly past. "Enjoy the night shift, guys."

"Screw you, Travis," Brandon shot back, miserable already because he knew the bastard was right.

Nothing was going his way these days. Fate hated him. That was clear enough when he walked into the sheriff's small office and found both extra chairs already occupied by Duncan and Dale. Brandon realized in that moment he was not going to catch a break. Not today.

"Shut the door, Singer," Alex snapped as Dylan crowded in behind Brandon. "I want to talk to you idiots because I'm sure, between the four of you, I'm talking to the mastermind of some stupid deputies' challenge."

Brandon, Dylan, and Dale all looked over at Duncan, who managed to look almost innocent in that moment. The sheriff wasn't buying it, and neither was anybody else.

"That's what I thought." Alex snorted as he settled down behind his desk. "Well, it ends now. Understand me?"

Alex pinned each man with a pointed look until every one of them had nodded.

"Good," he grunted. "Because Miss Kristen Harold is aware of your juvenile attempt to make her into some stupid prize. She's threatening to go to the mayor *and* the paper."

Brandon couldn't help but smirk at that. The little miss had the brains to know just what to threaten to make Alex squirm. He didn't like the mayor. Nobody really did. The man was pompous and annoying. Whenever he got involved with the sheriff's department, it was an utter disaster, which reflected in Alex's tone.

"None of us need that kind of attention. Understand?"

Another round of nods met that question, leaving Alex sighing and nodding himself.

"Good. Then stay away from the woman. If she ends up talking to the mayor and he ends up talking to me, I'm not going to waste time talking to you. Got it?"

That they certainly did. To a man, every one of them understood exactly what the sheriff was saying. If he had to suffer the mayor's displeasure, then all four of them would be suffering his. Nobody wanted that. Alex could get creative with his revenge.

"Now get the hell out of my office…and, Singer, I'm docking your pay for that extra half hour you took at lunch." Alex pinned Dylan with a hard look as Dylan hesitated with his hand on the doorknob. "Don't be making it a habit."

"Yes, sir." Dylan waited to roll his eyes until he'd gotten out of the office.

Travis sat his desk snickering as he watched the four of them tromp back past. It didn't take but seconds before Duncan was asking what he was looking at and an argument to follow, which was mostly just insults being passed around. Brandon ignored them all to take up his station at the front desk.

He'd be glad when his tour of duty sitting up there ended and he was back out on the road. He enjoyed patrolling, and nobody enjoyed the front desk. That was why they all took turns unless, of course, Alex was ticked at somebody.

Brandon was kind of pissed at Killian and Adam right then, but those two idiots were in such bad shape over Rachel picking on them, that it would have been kind of like picking on a sick puppy. Nobody was that cruel, even the sheriff.

"So aren't you going to ask me where I was?" Dylan came to lean back against the counter as Brandon picked up his magazine.

"Nope."

"Oh, come on," Dylan cajoled. "You're not still mad at me about the Kristen thing, are you? You know I didn't have anything to do with that."

"And you certainly haven't been of any help, either," Brandon muttered, knowing that he was being a dick.

The hole he found himself in wasn't Dylan's fault, but he still couldn't help but feel as if the other man was set against him. He knew how Dylan felt about relationships. He was allergic to them and considered love like a disease. How then could he even begin to understand what it was like to fall so hard, so fast, and end up so miserable?

"That's where you are wrong, my friend." Dylan turned to lean in closer and drop his tone, assuring nobody else heard him. "I just had the most enlightening cup of tea with Mr. and Mrs. Harold."

"You what?" Brandon froze, feeling his heart seize, his lungs following suit and making it almost impossible to even get out a whisper. "What did you do?"

"Had an enlightening cup of tea," Dylan repeated before correcting himself. "Actually it was a horrible cup of tea. Hot. Who drinks tea hot? I'll tell you who, people who put plastic on their seats."

"Dylan." Brandon was breathing hard now, hard enough that it was still hard to speak.

That was okay. He didn't know what the hell he would say. He really just wanted to hit Dylan, but his limbs felt too heavy, and his mind was still reeling with shock.

"And I scored an invite to church." Dylan grinned, an evil, mischievous twist of the lips. "Wanna come?"

Brandon keeled over, hitting his head against the counter three times before letting it rest there as he focused on taking several deep breaths. He couldn't kill Dylan. Not at a police station. Maybe later.

"What?" Dylan blinked at him innocently as Brandon turned his head to glare up at his best friend. "I'm helping."

"You're being a dick."

Dylan paused as he seemed to consider that before heaving a heavy sigh. "Look, man, you know how I feel about relationships and women like Kristen, but it's clear you feel differently. So, if this is your play, then I've got your back."

That had Brandon straightening slowly up as he studied his friend. "What's the catch?"

"There's no catch," Dylan assured him, a faint hint of insult sounding in his tone, but Brandon knew Dylan better than that.

He knew better than to believe the innocent look Dylan was trying to sell him. The bastard had joined the high school drama club just to get chicks and then ended up learning a whole new set of skills that had allowed him not only to bluff well at poker but to also lure girls to the dark side.

"Oh, there is always a catch." Brandon was certain of it.

"Well, I mean, wherever you go, I go, right?" Dylan blinked over at him, clearly biting back a smile and leaving no doubt as to what he was thinking.

"You have got to be kidding me! Are we back to that?"

Brandon said that a little too loudly, drawing the attention of the other deputies as they all eyed them suspiciously. He lowered the volume as he leaned in to whisper furiously at Dylan.

"You can't really think we're going to share Kristen."

"Why not?" Dylan shrugged. "We've shared everybody else."

"Nobody like Kristen, though," Brandon insisted. "She's different."

"Maybe. Maybe not." Dylan smiled. "We won't know until we try."

"Dylan—"

"Look." Dylan cut him off, his tone hardening into a sound of serious intent. "You can work with me or against me, but I'm not stopping."

"Didn't you hear the sheriff?"

"Fuck the sheriff." Dylan snickered. "And don't even play that line with me because I know you're not stopping, and you know together we are undefeatable. So you coming to church, or not?"

Chapter 9

Wednesday, May 14th

"Are you sure about this?" Gwen frowned as she stared at the small moped Kristen was admiring. "Wouldn't you rather get a new one? I already told you I could float you the money."

"Yes, but I would rather be in debt for only five hundred dollars instead of a few thousand. Besides, this one is already painted pink." Pink was Kristen's favorite color.

She and Gwen had, at least, that much in common. They had a little more than that, actually, because Gwen had showed the true kindness of her heart when Kristen had mentioned the idea of getting a scooter to get around. The idea had come to her after enduring one of her mother's long lectures about the sanctity of worship.

Apparently, she'd heard that Kristen hadn't gone to church on Sunday. This Sunday she was going with her mom and dad. If she didn't want to get stuck spending Saturday night at their house, she either had to come up with a ride or get herself a set of wheels.

Kristen really didn't want to spend Saturday night playing gin with her mom. Cybil had already invited her to go dancing down in Dothan. Kristen didn't know how to dance, but Cybil had assured her they'd all be lined up in a row and she would be able to easily follow along.

That meant she needed a set of wheels, which she needed anyway for school. While she'd been thinking about a car, the idea of a scooter felt so much more her. It even came with a pink helmet.

"I want it." Kristen smiled at the man who stood on the other side. His name was Petey, and he smelled kind of funny. "I'll give you three hundred dollars."

"Five." The man held firm.

"Don't you think you should try driving it first?" Gwen suggested.

"Four," the man readjusted instantly.

"What if it doesn't even run?"

"Three fifty and only if it rides out of this drive."

"Three seventy-five and it's in perfect shape."

"Three seventy-five." Kristen nodded, holding out her hand to shake Petey's as Gwen sighed.

"Your mother is going to blame me if you get hurt."

"That's probably right." Kristen agreed, not even wanting to consider her parents' reaction when they saw her new ride. Instead, she threw her arms around Gwen and hugged her tight. "Thank you. Thank you. Thank you! You're the best cousin ever!"

"Yeah, yeah, yeah." Gwen squirmed out of Kristen's hold. "Let's not get like that, okay? I've got a meeting to attend later, and I don't need to go in all messed up."

Kristen released her to step back, not even perturbed by Gwen's complaints. She knew what a meeting meant. Gwen had a lot of meetings, but that was none of Kristen's business. Instead, she focused on trying on her new helmet as Gwen pulled out a wad of cash and started counting out the hundreds.

The sight didn't bother Kristen in the least. Neither did the fact that she was now in debt. Gwen clearly made good money, and Kristen was expecting that her paycheck would be nice enough to afford her to pay off her cousin in just a few months. It would be worth it for the freedom she was purchasing.

"You want instructions on how to ride?" Petey offered as Kristen tucked her skirt between her legs and stepped on to her new scooter.

He didn't wait for an answer but quickly went through the controls before sending her on her way. Gwen headed off, too. She had a meeting to attend, and Kristen was headed to the bakery for a little celebratory dessert. She was skipping dinner that evening and going straight to the pie.

* * * *

"You got me stuck on the night shift," Brandon sulked as glared across the table at Dylan.

"I didn't do anything," Dylan said, defending himself, not about to take the blame for Brandon's bad turn of luck. "Go blame Charles for getting sick."

"I'm blaming you because otherwise Killian or Adam would have been chained to that damn desk. It's so God-awful boring."

What was boring was listening to him complain. That was getting old fast as far as Dylan was concerned. If this was what Brandon was going to be like without Kristen, then Dylan really had to rethink his stance on his friend being better off without her.

As if summoned by his very thoughts, the woman making Dylan's life hell puttered past the Bread Box's front window. Dylan's eyes widened as he took in what she was riding.

"Oh no."

"What?" Brandon frowned and turned to follow Dylan's gaze.

"No, don't look," Dylan warned him, but it was too late. Brandon was already flushing red.

"What the fuck was that? Was that Kristen? Was she on a motorcycle?"

"It was a scooter," Dylan corrected him, not that Brandon was listening.

He was already out of his seat and storming toward the door. Dylan sighed, certain that the mayor would hear about whatever scene Brandon was about to cause. He was just as certainly not going to let his best friend get into trouble without him. Dropping a few dollars on the table to cover the coffee Brandon hadn't drunk, Dylan hopped out of his seat and went chasing off after Brandon, who was already storming into the Main Street parking lot.

"What the hell is this?" Brandon came to a stop right before Kristen and splayed his arms to include the scooter she was hopping off of. Her answer came quick and with enough sharpness to impress even Dylan.

"Well, it's certainly not the proper way to greet a lady."

"No." Brandon shook his head.

"No?" That had Kristen pausing with her fingers on the buckle of her helmet. She blinked in honest, sweet confusion, but Dylan felt certain he knew what Brandon had meant.

"No," Brandon repeated himself, crossing his arms over his chest. "You're taking this thing back."

"I am not." Kristen puckered up so cutely Dylan couldn't help but smile. She was actually kind of entertaining, especially when she was pissing off Brandon.

"Yes. You are." Brandon tried his best to intimidate the little woman, but she just sniffed and turned her back on him. "Kristen—"

"I'm not talking to you." She cut him off without even sparing Brandon the respect of glancing back at him.

Instead, she focused on hanging up her helmet and removing her purse from where it was strapped down on the back seat. Only then did she turn and meet Brandon's simmering gaze.

"You, sir, are rude and boorish." She couldn't have said that in a prissier tone if she'd tried. "Now if you will excuse me, I don't have time to waste listening to your pointless commands."

With that, Kristen proudly stuck her chin in the air and walked right around Brandon. Dylan could only imagine the thoughts running through his head. He bet they were similar to the ones running through his own. They all featured Little Miss Bossy strapped down and naked, begging for more.

Just the thought had him smiling as Kristen sashayed past, and Dylan couldn't help but turn his head to admire the sight of that prim little ass swinging beneath the heavy folds of her grandmom skirt. He was going to fuck that ass. Then they'd see how she walked after that.

"No!" Brandon's abrupt outburst had Dylan glancing back over at his friend, who was still standing there fuming. "No!"

"Who are you talking to, man?" Dylan asked. "The woman went that way right after she dismissed you, so maybe you ought to think about lightening up your approach. Huh?"

Brandon shot Dylan a dirty look and took off after Kristen, leaving Dylan sighing and muttering to himself.

"Or maybe not. Let's just go dig the hole deep enough to bury both ourselves in it." Because Brandon was not going down without him.

Turning to follow Brandon back into the Bread Box, Dylan strolled back into the heavenly smelling shop. It was pretty busy, but then again, it normally was. Still, they didn't want to be causing a scene with this many witnesses. Especially not in uniform.

Unfortunately Kristen and Brandon were already making spectacles of themselves, even if it was a silent one. She sat there in her booth with Brandon across from her, glaring hard enough to set fire to the menu Kristen held up like a shield. The sense of tension and growing expectation of an explosion already had people glancing in their direction.

It was time to diffuse the situation.

Of course, that wasn't Dylan's specialty. Normally he caused the situation, and Brandon diffused it. He figured he owed it to his best friend, though, to try. So Dylan joined the couple, choosing to sit next to the pretty lady instead of his steaming best friend. Kristen ignored him, too, but she didn't manage to ignore the arm he threw over her shoulders.

"Excuse me, Deputy, what do you think you're doing?" Frosty gray eyes turned on him with a cold blast that strangely warmed him.

She had pretty eyes and smelled like the flowers covering her skirt. Dylan could certainly see why Brandon was attracted to the lady. He surely was.

"I'm helping." Dylan finally answered, unable to control the smile as Kristen's frown furled with a cute look of distaste.

"Helping? And how would you be doing that?"

"By explaining a few things to you," Dylan stated patiently before nodding toward Brandon, who looked as if he was ready to pop a vein. "See, my buddy over there, he's an idiot."

"On that, at least, we can agree," Kristen shot back, but Dylan had noticed that she hadn't shrugged his arm away or told him to move it. That had him wondering if the flush coloring her cheeks was all irritation.

"Yep." Dylan sighed. "And he's done something stupid."

"He has?" Kristen raised a brow at that.

"He's fallen for you," Dylan confessed, receiving an instant kick under the table.

"Oh please." Kristen rolled her eyes, appearing completely unaware of the look Brandon was now shooting Dylan.

"And when an idiot falls in love, they grow even dumber," Dylan continued on, ignoring both Brandon's and Kristen's attempts to deter him. "Which is why he can't seem to say what he's really thinking. So, when he says no, what he's really saying is he's concerned."

"Concerned?" Kristen repeated back frostily, but Dylan caught the shift in her gaze and knew that she wasn't as cold as she wanted them to think.

She was bluffing.

"He's afraid you're going to get hurt. Isn't that right, Brandon?" Dylan threw it back to his friend, hoping he could manage a decent response. He kind of did.

"You're going to kill yourself," Brandon barked, still seething but at least he looked more worried than mad now. "Motorcycles are dangerous things."

"It's a scooter." Kristen turned the argument on him. "It doesn't go over forty miles an hour."

"You can still kill yourself," Brandon insisted.

"It's mine, and I'm not taking it back." There was the universal tone that all women seemed born with. Kristen had just put her foot down. There would be no winning this battle. "Besides, it none of your concern…either of your concern."

Kristen shot that at Dylan as she turned those mesmerizing eyes back on him. Dylan was wondering if they'd go clear or cloudy when she came. He'd love to see those puckered little lips gasping for breath as he made her come again and again. Once he had her limp and completely at his beck and call, he was going to take that little pout for a ride. She was so little, though, he didn't know if she'd be able to swallow him whole.

"Why are you looking at me like that?" Kristen asked, her gaze narrowing on Dylan.

Brandon knew why, and it earned Dylan another kick as he shifted uncomfortably in his seat, suddenly too hard and big for his britches. That hadn't happened in a while.

"No reason," Dylan said smoothly as he pulled his arm back and put some distance between him and Kristen.

He needed the moment and the fresh air to get control of his unruly body, but that control escaped him. For the first time in a really long time, he couldn't seem to will his dick down. It was rebelling.

It wanted Kristen. Normally it wasn't so picky, which made this moment kind of alarming. Was Brandon contagious? Was he coming down with the same virus? No. That would not happen to him.

"Are you okay?" Kristen asked, her gaze suddenly sweetly concerned, and Dylan felt his heart pound.

"Oh shit." This could not be happening. Not to him. "I gotta go."

* * * *

With that, Dylan left. Brandon watched him go with a scowl, wondering what the hell had just gotten into him. Whatever it was, it was probably nothing. He was probably just playing, making a grand exit that left Kristen staring after him with a frown.

"I think something is wrong with your friend," she suggested, seeming momentarily distracted by Dylan's rapid retreat, which was probably the point.

"I'm sure he'll be all right." Brandon was certain of it.

He didn't know if he could say the same about himself, though. Not with that damn pink scoter sitting outside. He took a breath and forced himself to sound reasonable instead of incensed as he tried to pick up on the bridge Dylan had built for him.

"And he wasn't wrong. I am concerned."

"I don't understand why."

"And that scares me even more." It really did. "You shouldn't ride that thing until you understand the dangers."

"That was what I was thinking about believing you," Kristen retorted tartly. "This is another setup, isn't it? I'm supposed to melt with tender feelings because you care, aren't I? Then you'll sweep me up into an embrace that leaves me forgetting all good sense."

"No, it isn't," Brandon insisted, refusing to allow himself to be distracted by the suggestion that he could make her lose all sense. He already knew that.

"Look." He stretched forward, trying to will her to believe him. "I didn't start that stupid competition, and I wasn't a part of it, and it wasn't even really about you."

"It wasn't?"

"No. It was about me." He knew how that sounded and wasn't shocked that she doubted him.

"I find that hard to believe."

"Don't. The guys, they know that I've got this thing for you, and they were just taunting me is all. You have to believe me," Brandon pleaded, never having found himself in the position of having to beg for anything but willing to lower his pride for her.

"I would do anything to prove it to you," he swore and knew he'd just caught a break when Kristen straightened up and eyed him curiously.

"Anything?"

"Anything."

"Then you won't mind attending church with me and my parents this weekend." Kristen smiled brilliantly, but Brandon suddenly saw a trap widening beneath his feet.

"Uh...yeah, about that." Brandon breathed out a deep breath and silently cursed Dylan. "I've already been invited."

"What?" Kristen frowned.

"Dylan, he...uh, kind of met your parents for tea and—"

"He did *what?*" The force of her indignation had Kristen actually lifting out of her seat. "How dare he!"

"He was just trying to help me out," Brandon tried desperately to explain.

"You don't understand," Kristen snapped as she fell back into her seat, her elbows hitting the table and her hands catching her head as she moaned. "My mom's going to have me engaged to that jerk by the end of the week!"

Brandon blinked in that complaint and, for some reason, couldn't help smiling. That would teach Dylan to get involved in his business. Brandon could almost see it now, and it was funny as hell.

"Well, I'm glad to see my impending doom amuses you," Kristen muttered as she glared balefully across the table at him.

"No." Brandon shook his head. "But Dylan's impending doom does."

That had Kristen's head lifting out of her hands as she straightened up, a hint of hurt glinting in her eyes. "You consider marriage to me to be impending doom?"

"No, but I consider being henpecked by your mother to be a nightmare that Dylan roundly deserves to suffer." Brandon met her gaze with a snicker. "Don't you?"

For the first time, they shared a smile. Then Brandon dared to press his luck and reach out to cover her small hands with his as he sobered up.

"I really am sorry about what happened at Duncan's party. I didn't mean for things to get that out of control, but you just have this effect on me."

Kristen blushed, a hopeful glimmer rekindling in her eyes. "Really?"

"Really, but that's no excuse." Brandon took a deep breath, willing himself to relax, as it seemed he was finally making progress. "You deserve better, and I would be honored to escort you to church."

Kristen blinked and shyly looked down at the table as she began in a hesitant voice. "You know, some of my friends and I are going dancing on Saturday down at the Strut in Dothan. Have you ever been there?"

"No, I can't say that I have, but I love to dance." Especially if that meant having a chance to hold her close once again.

"Maybe you'd like to join us, and, um, we could even get some dinner first." Kristen glanced up from beneath her lashes to offer up that hopeful sounding suggestion, and Brandon felt his heart melt. She really was sweet, and so much fun to tease.

"Why, Miss Kristen, are you asking me out on a date?"

Chapter 10

Saturday, May 17th

Kristen was still blushing two days later as she stared at herself in the mirror. She couldn't believe she was going on a date. An actual date! And *she'd* been the one to ask the guy out. It was as if she was a whole new woman.

A whole new woman that had a date with a very attractive deputy.

Kristen couldn't help but sigh as her thoughts turned back to Brandon. She called him that in the privacy of her own mind, daring to dream of him in ways that were all too sinful to be repeated. That didn't stop her from quivering with a rush of delight as she thought one day, maybe, they might come true. One day she just might let him kiss her again.

Not tonight, though. That would be moving too fast, and Kristen had already decided she wasn't going to make that mistake again. That reserve got tested when Deputy Hammel arrived looking fresh, pressed, and bearing flowers. His shaggy hair was combed and the smooth line of his jaw completely hairless.

He was a handsome devil with that sparkle in his eyes and the grin that assured her he was liking what he saw, too. Kristen didn't dare to allow her gaze to wander, not like he did. She blushed as he took a slow, long look. The warmth in his gaze made her stomach quiver as a rush of pleasure flooded her senses, and felt more than her cheeks heating beneath his look.

"You sure are beautiful, Miss Kristen," the deputy drawled out as he shook his head and lifted his smoldering gaze back up to meet hers. "And I'm going to be the envy of every man we pass tonight."

"Why, Deputy Hammel, I do believe you are trying to sweet talk me," Kristen teased him, unable but to melt beneath his praise.

"I think you can call me Brandon tonight," he stated with a heat in his tone that sent a shiver down her spine.

Kristen swallowed hard and nodded. "Okay. Brandon."

"Very good. Oh, these are for you." He thrust the flowers clutched in his fist out to her, and she could tell they were freshly cut and couldn't help but cast him a quick smile.

"They're lovely," Kristen assured him as she took the unwrapped stalks from his hand. "But I'm wondering if there is there some old lady out there you sweet talked into letting you pluck her garden?"

"No old lady," Brandon swore. "These came from my own garden."

"You grow flowers?" That had Kristen pausing to glance up at him in surprise. She never would have thought of him as the type.

"I prefer to say I enjoy gardening and keeping a well-kept lawn." Brandon's grin grew as he cast a wink at her. "Sounds a little more manly, don't you think?"

Kristen laughed at that and nodded. "Definitely more manly. Why don't you come on in while I go put these into water?"

"Thank you." He accepted her invitation, following her into the house and shutting the door behind him as Kristen headed for the kitchen and a vase.

There were no vases, only glasses, but they'd do. Kristen pulled one down as Gwen appeared, dressed for one of her meetings. She scowled at the flowers lying on the counter as she pulled open the fridge to pull out the six-pack of hard cider she had stored there.

"Where did those come from?"

"Deputy Hammel," Kristen responded primly. "We're going on a date."

She hadn't told her cousin about her date and hoped to avoid her altogether tonight, not wanting to be reminded of why this was a bad idea or how gullible she might be. Kristen had a made a choice. She was going to give the man and these feelings a chance. She owed that much to herself.

Thankfully, Gwen didn't have anything rude to say. Not to her. She just snorted and headed out to the living room as Kristen fluffed her flowers up in their new makeshift vase and began filling the glass with water.

The rumble of the faucet couldn't drown out the conversation taking place in the living room, and Kristen couldn't help but cock her head and listen in, even though she knew it was wrong to eavesdrop.

"Gwen." There was distinct distaste in the deputy's tone.

"Brandon," Gwen shot back just as sharply. "What's with the look?"

"You tried to screw me over." Brandon didn't hold back, and Kristen found herself drawn to the kitchen door as she strained to hear every word.

"What are you bitching about?"

"You knew I had nothing to do with that stupid competition. That was all Duncan, and you just had to go and run your mouth, didn't you?"

"Kristen had a right to know."

"Bullshit," Brandon shot back before shocking Kristen with the accusations that he laid at her cousin's feet. "You're just jealous, aren't you? You know Kristen is a true diamond, and all you are is a sack of well-used coal."

"Jealous?" Gwen sounded honestly outraged by that suggestion. "Please. I haven't got the time to waste."

"Not even for the sheriff?"

"Screw you, Brandon."

"You know he's in love with Heather Lawson."

"That pudgy stick in the mud won't be able to keep him."

Gwen attacked, proving that Brandon had hit the nail on the head. She was in love with the sheriff. Who would have ever figured wild-child Gwen would fall for a straight arrow?

"She already has him…and he's already had you. Guess you just weren't worth keeping, huh?"

Kristen frowned, unnerved by the harshness of Brandon's tone. If her cousin was in love and heartbroken, then it was a sad state of affairs, and nobody should taunt her over it. That wasn't right.

"That's quite enough out of you, Deputy Hammel." Kristen stepped around the corner and stepped up for a very shocked Gwen. She wasn't any less surprised than Brandon, who reddened, hopefully in shame.

"Kristen—"

"I'm sorry, sir, but I can't allow you to continue to belittle and insult my cousin."

"I didn't mean—"

"You most certainly did." Kristen cut him off as she stormed across the room to latch onto the front door handle and wrench it open while both Brandon and Gwen continued to gape at her. "Now, I think you should leave."

"But…but…our date?" Brandon sputtered, sounding suspiciously panicked.

"Is over," Kristen told him definitively and then nodded toward the outside. "So go on. Get."

* * * *

"Get. She told me to *get!*" Brandon looked across the bar at Riley, who stared back without a single hint of an expression. "And dumbass that I am, I got! What the fuck is with that? I mean, really, I'm letting this woman turn me into a complete pussy. Dylan's right. I'm not in charge here, am I?"

The big bartender sighed.

"And, God help me, if the guys down at the station house ever hear about this, it'll be get, get, get, get, all damn fucking day long. They'll never shut up. Do you know what it's like to have to listen to same damn story over and over again?"

That had Riley smirking.

"Yeah, I know, you've probably heard it all before. So, you got any advice?"

"Yeah. Order something."

Brandon shot him a dirty look for that uncompassionate response and reached for his wallet.

"Beer me. No. Never mind that. Whiskey me." Brandon slapped a fifty onto the countertop as he met Riley's gaze. "And leave the bottle."

That had the man rolling his eyes, but he did as told, snatching up the fifty and making no change. Brandon didn't care. He didn't even notice. He was still stuck on shocked.

This was supposed to be a perfect night. He was going to charm Kristen, dance with her, and then, at the very end, go in for another kiss. Instead, he had to call Dylan and confess that he'd screwed everything up again. It hadn't helped that his friend hadn't seemed surprised.

He hadn't volunteered to come hang out with Brandon either, which left him sitting there alone drinking until all three Davis brothers piled into the bar, leading a small group of hands in. The boisterous group took up position at the pool tables in back while Devin, the youngest of the Davis brothers, cut a beeline for the bar.

"Hey, Brandon." Devin greeted him a hard slap on the back. "How's it going?"

That had Brandon turning his brooding gaze from the bottom of his glass up toward Devin's questioning gaze. "I'm sitting here drinking whiskey by myself. How do you think it's going?"

"That bad, huh?" Devin asked as he nodded to Riley. "Three pitchers, man, lots of cups."

"Sure thing," Riley nodded before pausing to look pointedly at Brandon's whiskey bottle. It was almost half gone, and he wasn't relinquishing the rest of it. Brandon made that clear as he reached out to pull it closer.

"So..." Devin plunked down in the seat beside him, not taking the hint when Brandon returned his gaze to the bottom of his glass. "I'm going to take a guess and say this is about a girl."

"Kristen Harold." Brandon nodded, knowing there was no point in staying silent. Devin wasn't one to let up.

"Never heard of her."

"She's new in town." Brandon glanced over at Devin. "She's Gwen Harold's cousin."

"Gwen Harold. Oh, man, you are in trouble." Devin shook his head sadly as Riley began to pile the pitchers up on the bar.

"Don't I know it." Brandon sighed. "I was supposed to go to church with her and her parents tomorrow. Going to make a good impression and all that, and then I blew it by running my mouth at Gwen. Jesus, I'm an idiot."

"Aren't we all at some point?" Devin countered. "And really? Church?"

Brandon understood the doubt in the other man's tone and shared a look with him. "Kristen is a good girl."

"Is that right?" Devin seemed to consider that for a moment. "Okay, here is what you do. Show up for church. If she's that good, she won't make a scene there."

That was a good point, but Brandon didn't know where it was going when Devin pulled his stool up a little closer and breathed a little too near Brandon's ear.

"Then you make sure you get seated next to her, real close, and take her hand and just gently rub her palm with your thumb and—"

"Dude!" Brandon leapt backward, coming off his stool the second Devin tried to take his hand and show him what he meant. "What the hell do you think you're doing?"

"Giving you good advice and getting your sorry ass out of that seat," Devin shot back as he slid off his own stool to pick up the pitchers Riley had slid in front of him. "Now grab the cups and come join us. Moping and drinking alone isn't going to do you any good."

* * * *

Dylan certainly wasn't moping around or drinking alone. He had no interest in joining Brandon for either of those events. Instead, he headed out to Dothan to right the ship Brandon had tried to sink once again. The man was on a roll, a downward slide, and Dylan wasn't going to take that trip.

Whatever had happened in the bakery, he was sure it had been a fluke. He had his head right on his shoulders now, Dylan assured himself, as he turned into the Strut. He was early, but he figured Kristen couldn't accuse him of following her if he was there first.

Taking up a spot at the bar, he waited damn near two hours for the place to fill up and Kristen and her friends to show up. During that time, Dylan received quite a few invitations from the young and the available, but he passed them all by, remaining rooted in his spot.

He wasn't about to screw things up by having Kristen walk in and find him dancing with another woman. He knew he'd made the right call the moment he saw Kristen come through the door. Damn but she looked pretty tonight.

She was dressed, as always, in a modest outfit that complemented her slender frame. Dylan admitted that she wasn't really his type as he sat there studying her. He liked big boobs, a round ass, and legs that made a man weak, but for some reason, he couldn't seem to tear his gaze away from Kristen.

She moved with such grace and smiled with such joy it was like watching a bolt of sunlight drift through a room, and he just wanted to reach out and be warmed by that heat. Dylan's heart began to do that strange thing again where it pounded a little too hard. Damn if his hands weren't growing damp. He was nervous and about to break out in a sweat.

How very unattractive was that?

He needed to get a hold of himself. He was here on a mission. To that end, he stayed seated, giving himself the time to study his prey and manage his reaction to her. That last one was harder than the first. Dylan's gaze tracked Kristen's every movement, and he found himself smiling when she smiled, feeling lighter when she laughed and annoyed when men came up to hit on her.

With her light-colored sundress and her hair all curled, Kristen was attracting every lowlife in the bar. Thankfully, she was also turning them all down, dancing only with her friends. Kristen really was a good girl, and God how Dylan ached to corrupt her.

Physically ached. He couldn't remember the last time he'd been so aware of his balls, but they were boiling, and his dick was throbbing. It was just lust he told himself, just lust, and the sooner he got Kristen naked and moaning beneath him, it would done. He could fuck this need right out of himself and go back to being happy.

Right then Dylan was far from happy. In fact, he was downright miserable, and he knew the cure. Finally lifting off his seat, he carried his beer and cut across to the table Kristen and her friends had taken. They'd settled back down when the music had turned from an upbeat honky-tonk rhythm back to a slow melody that invited the warm press of two bodies. Dylan knew who he wanted to press up against.

"Ladies." He nodded to the table at large, casting quick glance across the group that fell awkwardly silent as his gaze finally landed on Kristen. "You're looking lovely tonight."

"Hmm." Kristen eyed him, making that same non-committal sound her father had and addressing him with a good deal of similar skepticism. "Deputy Singer. What a surprise."

"Hopefully a pleasant one." He offered her a little smile, daring her to be rude and tell him it wasn't.

"That remains to be seen," Kristen murmured less than charitably. "What can I do for you, Deputy?"

"I'm just looking for a dance."

"Hmm."

"I swear," he vowed as he held out his hand to her. "Just one dance and you'll be done with me."

"Somehow I doubt it."

But that didn't stop her from putting her hand in his or allowing him to lead her out to the dance floor. Dylan was vainly aware that he was the first man she'd said yes to. The only man. That thought filled him with a strange warmth that only bloomed hotter as he turned to sweep Kristen up in his arms.

She was such a little thing and tucked in perfectly against him as he wrapped his arms around her waist and lost himself in the smooth perfect sway of her body against his. Nothing had ever felt so right before, and he was in serious trouble.

* * * *

Kristen knew she was in trouble the moment Dylan wrapped his arms around her. She'd assumed he'd wanted to talk about Brandon, but Dylan didn't say a word. He just tucked her against the hard length of his body and started moving in a slow circle that was lulling her into melting all over him.

God but he smelled good and felt even better.

Kristen couldn't fight the pull to snuggle deeper into Dylan's arms. The music, along with the voices raised in conversation, faded away as her world narrowed down to the heady scent of soap and musk, a distinctively masculine scent created to intoxicate a woman's senses and leave her drooling and too weak to do anything other than sway to the rhythm he set.

Kristen breathed in deeply and sighed, letting go of her worries and her concerns as she simply enjoyed the moment. It didn't even dawn on her to object when Dylan slid those big, broad palms of his over the slight curve of her ass and pressed in, leaving her in no doubt as to what he was feeling.

He was hard, and Kristen knew she should have been scandalized by the feel of his large erection pressing up against her, but right then, she couldn't work up the energy to do anything more than sigh. Besides, he was hard all over.

Beneath the soft fabric of his T-shirt, Kristen felt the strong wall of his chest flexing ever so slightly with each slow shuffle of their feet. More than that, she could hear heavy thud of his heart beneath her ear. It matched the pounding of her own.

It was like a magical web wove around them. That magic shattered with the blare of an upbeat tempo that came roaring out of the speakers overhead, jarring Kristen back to reality. The reality was she was a little too hot.

Kristen blinked, taking in the world around her to realize that Dylan had danced her over to a dark corner. They were well out of everybody else's sight, locked in their own private shadows. Those shadows held a tense sense of anticipation as Kristen raised her eyes up to meet Dylan's.

He was staring at her as though he was seeing her for the first time, and before Kristen guessed his intent, Dylan latched onto her hand and started dragging her down a dark hall. That brought her all the way back to reality and the realization that she might be in true trouble now.

"Hey, wait." She tugged on her hand but only ended tripping over her own feet as Dylan continued to drag her into the darkness. "Where are we going?"

"To have a long, overdue talk," Dylan snapped back, sounding upset as he shoved through a door that led straight out into the bar's back parking lot.

"Is this about Deputy Hammel?" Because honestly, Kristen couldn't think of anything else they had to talk about.

"No." Dylan spun her around and up against the rough, brick wall and pinned her there with the heavy weight of his own body. Only then did he bother to explain the situation. "This is about us."

"Us?" He couldn't have shocked her more if he tried. "There is no us."

"There will be," Dylan vowed. "And the first thing you've got to understand about me, honey, is I don't waste time asking."

"Asking? Asking wh—"

Kristen's question was cut off by Deputy Singer's answer as his mouth crashed into hers, stealing the words right from her lips.

Chapter 11

Dylan didn't know what he was doing. All he knew was that he was running on emotion. Emotion and need. Right then he needed Kristen. That didn't make what he was doing right. It also didn't mean he wouldn't get slapped, but he didn't.

Kristen's hands came up, no doubt to shove him away, but as Dylan's tongue sank into the sweet ambrosia of her mouth, her fingers, instead, curled around his shirt as she clung to him. For a moment, she stood just like that, stiff and uncertain. Then a second later she was melting against him just like she had on the dance floor, and all of Dylan's control shattered in an instant.

It left him stunned and weakened, at the mercy of primitive needs that drove him to want more. Like a hot lance, that need seared through him as Kristen's tongue began to duel with his, her fingers burying themselves in his hair as her body lifted toward him in open invitation.

Dylan growled, reveling in Kristen's surrender. The soft feel of her breasts swelling against his chest, along with the sweet scent of a cunt warming for his touch, fueled the feral desires raging through him. They demanded ever more, and he ground back into her soft curves until they molded against his body, caressing him from chest to knee as they began to sway just as they had on the dance floor—back and forth in a rhythm as old as time.

Kristen whimpered, her body moving with his and proving that beneath all that prim prissiness was a hot little vixen waiting for a man to awaken her to the erotic world of ecstasy. Dylan wanted to be that man.

Flexing against her and silently cursing the clothes in his way, Dylan dug his hand into the heavy cotton of her skirt and began dragging it up until his fingers brushed against the soft, velvety silk of her skin. Kristen broke free of his kiss at that first electric brush and began gasping for air as Dylan rained suckling little kisses down the graceful arch of her neck.

He felt the hard points of her nipples pressing through her dress. They ground against him, leaving him desperate for a taste as hungry, little moans fell from her lips, cheering him onward as he gripped her thigh and jerked it high up along his hips. Her knee bent, her leg wrapping around him as her skirt fell back, allowing him full access to the pussy weeping for his touch.

Dylan brushed the backs of his fingers against the wet crotch of her panties, nearly losing it at the feel of her cunt so soft and ready for him. Impatient now, he thrust his fingers beneath the elastic edge of her panties and split the plump, swollen folds of her pussy wide open. Kristen squealed and jerked hard at his invasion, but Dylan wasn't about to be bucked off like Brandon had.

He held firm, keeping her pinned beneath the wall and whimpering with a need he planned on conquering. Kristen was his. Dylan didn't fight the truth of that thought as it hammered through him. Instead, he trapped her clit beneath his thumb and began twirling the little bud, even as he nuzzled aside the collar of her dress to lap at the nipple still trapped beneath a thick cotton bra.

"Oh God," Kristen moaned as she began to gulp for breath, her entire body tensing beneath him, and Dylan knew she was coming close to a release.

He was almost certain it would be her first. He wanted to give it to her, to feel her come apart in his arms if not all around his dick. That he could not do. Despite the inferno consuming him, the need he had to protect Kristen overrode everything. She deserved better than having her first time up against the back of a bar.

That didn't mean he couldn't take a taste.

Dylan was already sinking to his knees as that thought hit. Above him Kristen leaned against the wall, lost to all reality and allowing him to take every advantage. Dylan wasn't known for letting those kinds of opportunities pass him by.

* * * *

Lost in a sensual swirl of delights she'd never imagined, Kristen couldn't even believe this was real. It had to be a dream. A wonderful, amazing dream that only kept getting better. Smiling at that thought, she let her head roll back as the ecstasy twining through her grew tighter with every roll of Deputy Singer's thumb.

"Again. Please."

That wasn't her voice. She didn't sound like that. Whoever had moaned that plea had sounded like a sensual vixen calling out to her lover in honeyed, husky tones. Kristen didn't have a lover. Just a fantasy…a really, really good fantasy. One that had her twisting and flexing as the liquid heat of desire flooded through her body.

She was hot, wet, and so damn needy it took her a moment to realize it was the heated breath of the deputy fanning across her intimate flesh, causing her to feel as if the sun had opened up all around her. While a voice in the very back of her head screamed out a warning, it was drowned out by the rush of rapture that rocked through her at the very first velvety brush of his tongue lapping over her clit. Then there wasn't the time to care about anything other than how good it felt to be kissed in such a way.

Deputy Singer certainly knew how to kiss.

Kristen's eyes nearly bugged out of her head as the deputy devoured her molten flesh with a hunger that had him thrusting that wicked tongue of his right up inside of her. His fingers followed, stretching her untried muscles delightfully wide. She felt so full, so deliciously full, and then he added motion to the sensation, and Kristen was lost.

The pressure built rapidly inside of her until she felt as if she couldn't even catch her breath. Then, like a bubble, she popped, shattering into a dizzying burst of frenzied delight. It was like pure sunlight shined right into her soul, leaving her melting downward against the brick wall. Thankfully, Deputy Singer was there to catch her.

He rose up to hold her tight until the world started to reorder itself around her and the reality of what had just happened. Kristen blinked, taking in a world gone crazy but couldn't muster the energy to feel the least bit of shame. That was probably what she should be feeling, what she might feel later, but right then, she could only smile.

That had been wonderful.

She wanted to do it again. Apparently, that was going to cost her. Deputy Singer made that clear as he finally stepped back to meet her gaze. Kristen knew she was blushing, but it wasn't from embarrassment. She was still just a bit hot. Hot and feeling a sense of freedom that she'd never felt before. That was what gave her the confidence to meet his gaze.

"Well, look at you," he whispered softly, reaching up to brush a thumb across her cheek. Kristen caught the scent of her own arousal as his voice washed over her like a hypnotic lure. "All rosy and flushed, and ready for more, aren't you?"

Kristen swallowed back the yes that wanted to fly from her lips and refused to answer, not wanting to break the spell. It was as if the deputy sensed her thoughts. He smiled slightly.

"Yeah, you've had a taste of something you like, so let me now explain to you my terms."

"Terms?" That didn't sound good, and Kristen felt a frown begin to mar her bliss.

"I'm going to give you the gift of a pleasure so great that you can't even conceive of how wonderful it will be, and you? You're going to give me total control."

Something about his tone warned her he wasn't playing a game. The deputy had plans, and just the thought of what they might be made her shiver. It was Pandora's box, and she knew she shouldn't open it, but she was tempted. Really tempted.

"I'm not giving you anything more tonight." Kristen gathered what strength she could muster and straightened up. "Nothing more than the promise that I'll think about it."

"I know you will," the deputy all but purred as his smile widened. "And think about this. It doesn't have to be love to be good. The kind of lust we share, that's special, too."

Kristen frowned, fundamentally disagreeing with him. Arguing would be pointless, though, given what had just happened. He'd proved his point, but she still couldn't help but wonder if it wouldn't all be better if it were love.

Kristen put that question to Cybil as she drove her home later that night, though she didn't get the answer back that she was expecting.

"Oh, honey, I wish I could tell you that was true, but..." Cybil sighed heavily and shook her head sadly. "It actually very rarely works out that way."

"Really?" Kristen frowned.

"The hotter something burns, the faster it burns out," Cybil stated.

The grim solemnness in her tone had Kristen falling silent as a darkness began to creep into the light that had been her soul ever since Deputy Singer had given her a taste of all she'd been missing.

She watched the large town of Dothan slip past as she considered that Cybil very well might have a point. Deputy Singer was certainly not the type of man she'd have chosen for herself. He was too good-looking, too arrogant, and too rude, and none of that mattered when it came to how it felt to be touched by him.

Maybe he was right. Maybe that alone was special enough. After all, what if she never fell in love? Or what if she fell in love and it wasn't as good as it had been tonight? Would she always wonder what might have been?

Kristen frowned at all those questions as Cybil brought her car to a stop at a red light. She'd been lost in her thoughts as the world whipped by, but now as it came into focus, she found herself staring into the parking lot of a cheap strip motel. Kristen knew the place only from having seen it from the road and would never consider even pulling into, but there sat Gwen's car.

Kristen blinked and frowned, but there was no denying it was Gwen's car, especially not when her cousin came dancing out of a room wearing some lacy bit of lingerie to meet a man who looked just like Mr. O'Leary, the man her parents were intent on marrying her off to. That was because it was Mr. O'Leary!

Kristen's gasped and quickly looked away, both horrified and embarrassed at the very idea of what the two of them were doing. She certainly didn't want to end up like that, but neither did she want to end up saving herself for a man like that either. She really did have some serious thinking to do.

* * * *

Dylan couldn't stop smiling as he drove home that night, and he knew who to thank for the rush of anticipation making him grin like a loon. Little Miss Kristen might like to dress like an uptight prig, but she came apart like a true creature of sensual beauty. Better than that, she'd been tight, real tight, and he couldn't wait to feel that cunt clinging to his dick.

Dylan was pretty damn sure he was going to get to see that dream come true. After all, she hadn't turned him down. He had her hooked. All Dylan had to do was reel her in. Reel her in and then figure out what he was going to do about Brandon. That idiot clearly needed help, but did Dylan want to help him?

The answer had always, instantly, been yes. That was until he'd tasted the sweet, intoxicating cream of Kristen's release. That shit was like gold, worth coveting and even considering betraying his best friend. Of course, if he did that, then that would be all but admitting this was love when it couldn't be that.

This was lust, and men didn't turn traitor over lust. That was probably a lie, but Dylan didn't care. He didn't betray his friends. Not over any woman. Dylan clung to that conviction, even as he felt the doubts brewing. He refused to entertain them as he finally turned into the driveway that twisted around a large, old Southern white-planked wood house that he'd bought with Brandon.

It had been in a state of desperate repair, but they were slowly bringing it back to life. Brandon had already blessed the yard with his green touch. The grass was lush, the flower beds full and perfectly weeded. There was even a vegetable garden growing in the backyard. It was that stupid garden that kept Dylan from having the room for the pool he wanted.

That was an ongoing battle he had yet to win. One he grumbled over to himself that night as he pulled his truck to a stop beneath the carport they'd built out back. The backyard was actually a perfect oasis except for that stupid garden.

They'd landscaped in a massive cobblestone patio just off the back porch. They'd built up a fire pit, an outdoor kitchen, and even had some room for horseshoes. Now all they needed was a pool. Still grumbling, Dylan mounted the back stairs and headed in through the always open back door to find Brandon standing at the refrigerator, swaying on his feet.

"Hey, man," Dylan called out and knew instantly by the amount of time it took for Brandon to turn his head and respond that his buddy was drunk.

"Hey."

Dylan bit back a smile as Brandon turned slowly back toward staring into the refrigerator. Brandon was a funny drunk, or at least he was fun to mess with. He was the kind of drunk that could be dressed up like a woman and convinced to go ring the high school principal's doorbell at three in the morning. He could also be heavily relied on to vomit on the man's slippers.

That thought had Dylan eyeing Brandon with some worry. He didn't want his buddy to vomit into the refrigerator. They'd just bought the thing.

"Hey, man, you looking for something?" Dylan asked as he came over to assist, but there wasn't anything he could do apparently.

"Nope."

"Um, then why don't we close this?" Dylan suggested as he pulled the door free of Brandon's hold. The man almost went down before Dylan could catch him. "Oh, I see."

Dylan caught on almost instantly to what the game was and only had one question as he began helping his buddy down the hall. "Who left you like that?"

"Devin." Brandon stumbled over his feet, even though he was carrying very little of his own weight. "He said I needed to cool off."

"Is that right?" That sounded like Devin. The man had a twisted sense of humor. "And how long have you been standing there?"

"I don't know." Brandon smiled, clearly not offended by the joke Devin had played. "But I think the milk went bad."

"Brandon, man, *why* did you let them get you drunk?"

"Because Kristen was mean to me." Brandon pouted, reverting as he often did when drunk to a child-like voice that just invited other men to pick on him. "Gwen set me up."

"Gwen's a bitch." Dylan had come to that conclusion at Duncan's pool party. He hadn't failed to notice that the one person who didn't seem concerned with her cousin's near drowning was Gwen.

"Yeah…but she's smart." Brandon sighed as Dylan lugged him up the stairs to the bedroom. "Smarter than me."

"It'll be okay, man." Dylan would make sure of that.

"No it won't," Brandon insisted as they finally made it to the top and turned into his bedroom. "Kristen will never forgive me. She thinks I'm a jerk."

"Here's a clue. Next time just kiss her."

Chapter 12

Sunday, May 18^{*th*}

Sunday morning, Kristen got up early and dressed in her nicest, most demure outfit. It was a small gift to her parents, though she doubted they would even take note of her clothes. They were going to be too busy wigging out over her scooter. She didn't let that stop her from strapping on her helmet and pointing the front of her pink princess toward Dothan.

Normally it was just a half-hour ride down to Dothan, but Kristen's little scooter couldn't go that fast, so the trip took the better part of an hour. She'd planned on that and spent the time marshaling her defenses.

They took a serious hit, though, when she putted into the parking lot of the First United Baptist Church. The crowds had already begun to gather for services outside the church. Kristen could feel the gaping stares as she circled around to park in an available space. While she'd fully expected that kind of attention, she hadn't actually been prepared for her mother to come crying down the path.

"Kristen!" She all but launched herself at Kristen, engulfing her in a massive hug before jerking Kristen back. "Are you all right? Let me see you? What is going on here? What is that thing that you rode up on? Is it a motorcycle? It is! That's what I thought. Oh…oh!"

Her mother reeled back, fanning herself rapidly as if she feared she might faint at any moment. Kristen wasn't buying it. Her mother had never suffered from a weakness of nerves but tended to overreact to things.

So did her dad.

"What is going on here, young lady?" he demanded to know as he came storming up, drawing even more attention toward them. Her father didn't care. He had eyes only for her scooter. "What is that thing?"

"It's my scooter," Kristen began, only to have to pause to wait for her mother to get another overly dramatized gasp out.

"*A scooter!*" Her mother's hand slapped against her chest as she gazed in horror at Kristen. "You're going to kill yourself."

"I am not going—"

"No." Her father cut her off with a shake of his head. "I'm sorry, honey, you are going to have to take that thing back."

"I can't. I bought it used."

"Used?" Her mother's eyes rounded as if Kristen had confessed to wearing dirty underwear. "A *used* scooter? Oh, sweetheart, no."

"Hmm." Her dad nodded along with her mother. "I'm sorry you wasted your money, sweetheart, but I can't allow you to ride around on that thing."

"Dad—"

"Good morning," Deputy Singer cut in, drawing all of their attention to him as he came strutting up in a suit and a tie.

Kristen could do little more than gape in shock at how fine a figure he cut when he did himself up. That didn't explain what he was doing there, but she had a pretty good guess. He was pretending to court her when really he was on a mission of seduction. What shocked her even more, though, was he was not alone.

"Morning," Deputy Hammel mumbled. He'd dressed up, too, but looked a little green around the gills and far less chipper.

"Are we interrupting something?" Dylan asked politely as he came to a stop on the sidewalk, forming a half-circle around Kristen, along with her parents, and making her feel somewhat cornered.

She'd spent the better part of the night lying in bed thinking about Deputy Singer and his wicked offer, only to come to no conclusion except the obvious one—she wanted him.

"Deputy Singer." Kristen nodded toward him, letting her cool tone mask the warm rush of pleasure that whipped through her as their eyes met. For a moment they were back there behind that bar, sharing a memory.

Then her mother ruined it.

"Deputy Singer, you have got to do something about this," her mother demanded before pointing to Kristen's pink princess. "Do you not see what my daughter drove up on?"

"It's not his job to do something," her dad cut in before Dylan could respond. "It's mine. My foot is coming down. Do you hear me, Kristen? I have put up with enough of this insanity, and I will not stand idly by why you kill yourself on this suicide vehicle."

Kristen felt her cheeks redden under that reprimand, but this time, anger was mixed in with the humiliation of having her dad speak to her in such a way. This time Deputies Singer and Hammel were witnessing her father treat her like a child, when she really wanted at least one of them to see her as a woman.

"Now give me the keys," her father commanded, holding out his hand.

Kristen looked down at the keys in her hand and watched as her fingers curled into a fist around them. Then her chin was coming back up. "No."

That hit the air, and everybody stilled as if they were all shocked by her response, but it didn't take long for everybody to recover. Her mother did with a gasp. Her father did with a gape. Dylan grinned.

"You shouldn't speak to your father that way," her mother chastised her, casting quick glances at her father, who still seemed to be having trouble accepting that she'd defied him.

"And he really shouldn't speak to me that way," Kristen countered before turning pleading eyes on her father. "I love you, Dad, and want to respect you, but I'm not going to live my life at your command. The scooter stays. I like it."

Nobody seemed to know what to say to that. There wasn't time left to argue. The church bell rang, calling everybody inside, leaving her parents little choice but to lock arms and follow the herd. Not that Kristen fooled herself into thinking the battle was over, but she still felt strangely lighter and free as she allowed Deputy Singer to take her arm and lead her all the way to the pew.

He stepped in front of her at the last second, though, taking the seat next to her mother and forcing Kristen to sit between him and Deputy Hammel, who she was pointedly trying to ignore. The man might be rude, but he could also be sweet, and she felt slightly guilty for the embrace she'd shared with his friend.

She hadn't even considered that element last night, but sitting there with both men's thighs pressed up tight against hers, Kristen realized she had a choice to make. Deputy Hammel didn't make it an easy one when he slid his hand down around hers and began to gently rub his thumb across her palm.

Delightful little thrills shot up her arm, sending a spider web of warmth racing across her chest until her heart pounded with a heavy beat, making her think she might have been a little hard on him last night. But how could she possibly even accept an advance from him when she'd already lost her head in the other deputy's arms?

Those probably weren't the kinds of problems she should have been bothering the Lord with, but given they were at church, Kristen couldn't help but offer up a small prayer for a little divine intuition. It didn't shock her when none came. Neither did it surprise her, when the service ended, that her parents went right back to their argument.

They'd barely made it outside when her mother suggested she say goodbye to her friends because they needed to have a little family discussion. Kristen knew what that was code for. Her mom wanted to nag, and her dad wanted to lecture, but it was too beautiful of a day to be cooped up in their house listening to an argument that wasn't going to change her mind.

So, Kristen dared to defy them once again. She announced with great aplomb that she couldn't make it to tea that afternoon because she'd already agreed to go to brunch with the two deputies and then silently prayed that neither one would object. Thankfully, they didn't, but that didn't mean her parents were easily dismissed.

"Maybe we should join you for brunch," her mother suggested with a worried glance at the two deputies before dropping her voice to a whisper. "I'm not sure it's appropriate for you to go out with men on your own."

If only her mother knew what she'd done on her own, she would understand just how laughable that comment was, but Kristen didn't dare to smile as she assured her mother everything would be fine.

"There are two of them, Mom," Kristen pointed out. "One would be an inappropriate date. Two is a chaperoned meal."

"And five is a group," her mother countered, but Kristen had seen that coming.

"I'd invite you, Mom, but we're headed back to Pittsview first. They have the greatest bakery in the world," Kristen informed her mother before offering her a quick hug and a kiss on the cheek. "It will all be okay, Mom. Try not to worry.

"And I love you, Dad." Kristen turned her attention to her father, who was standing there stiffly, clearly still insulted.

She hugged him anyway and dropped a kiss on his cheek as well before turning to find her bike levitating in the air. Her mouth dropped wide open as she stared at the two deputies who were carrying her scooter away. She couldn't believe they'd lifted it up at all.

Their muscles flexed and bulged, cutting through the clean lines of their suits and making Kristen's heart do a double beat. They were both such good-looking men and so strong. If she were a vain woman she might find a bit a pride that they were both clearly pursuing her.

Kristen might not have been vain, but she was a woman and couldn't help but be impressed with her two suitors, even if they were carrying her scooter away.

"Hey!" Kristen blinked, finally realizing she was smiling at them when she should have been frowning. "Wait! Where are you taking my scooter?"

"We're going to load it into the back of the truck," Deputy Singer tossed over his shoulder as he came to a stop by a large pickup.

At least it wasn't jacked up and chromed out. Kristen would hate to think she was being courted by men who were frivolous with their money. No, she was being courted by men who loved to fish. The tinted back window was littered with fishing stickers and the hitch sticking out of the bumper had a small propeller attached to it.

"You want to get the tailgate?"

Deputy Hammel shot her a look, jarring Kristen out of her thoughts and prompting her to dart around both men as crowds started to gather to gawk. She was definitely going to be the topic of gossip that morning. That would be a first for her. Kristen was kind of proud of that.

"Are you going to lay it down?" Kristen asked as she popped the back gate to the truck down, blushing slightly at all the attention. "I don't want it to get damaged."

"We'll strap it down," Deputy Hammel assured her with a quick smile. "Don't worry. We've got it covered."

Kristen still worried until they'd secured the scooter well enough to assure her nothing would happen to the pink princess as they headed back to Pittsview. Then it was time to leave, and Kristen found herself offering her parents another round of kisses and hugs before allowing Deputy Hammel to assist her up into the truck.

It wasn't that high off the ground, but she figured he wanted to make up for his rudeness last night, so she didn't object. Then it was too late to object as she found herself tucked once again between the two deputies. It was in that moment that Kristen realized she might have made a tactical mistake.

As they shut their doors, she found herself caught in a cocoon of warmth, strength, and a strangely intoxicating scent of leather, men, and musk. It did funny things to her insides and made her all too conscious of the heavy press of their legs.

"So we're off to the bakery." Deputy Singer shot her a quick smile as he started up the engine. "You realize it's going to be mobbed. Sunday being a good day to eat sweets."

"Oh, you don't have to take me to the bakery," Kristen assured him, realizing she'd done it again. She'd asked a man out, technically two men at the same time. Gwen would be so proud, but Kristen wasn't as comfortable with the situation. "I was just…"

"Trying to get away from your parents?" Deputy Singer began easing the truck back out of its spot.

"No, of course not." He made it sound so rude when Kristen's intentions were much more noble. Weren't they? "They just need some time to adjust to my new life, and allowing them to get worked up as they talk it through won't help."

"Yeah," Deputy Singer drew out that slow agreement, making sure she knew he wasn't buying her excuse. "That and your mother's tea is terrible."

Kristen froze, her eyes widening at that honest admission. She knew once again she should probably have taken insult, but instead, she couldn't help but giggle. Her mother's tea really was bad.

"Wait a minute." Deputy Hammel injected himself into the conversation. "Last night you threw me out of the house for being rude, and you're laughing now when Dylan insults your parents?"

"Deputy Singer—"

"Call me Dylan."

"—was sharing an honest opinion." Kristen continued on without pausing as she turned to meet Deputy's Hammel's frown. "You were just being mean to my cousin."

"Yeah?" The deputy quirked an eyebrow at that, and she could tell he was still a little sore about her slamming the door on him again. "Well, let me tell you, *honestly.* I don't like your cousin."

Kristen considered that for a moment before nodding. "I can accept that, but you'll still show her proper respect in her home, or I'll throw you out again."

That got a laugh from Deputy Singer and a begrudging smile from his partner. Then he put her on the spot.

"Does that mean if I ask you out you might actually say yes?"

Kristen's eyes widened as she found herself suddenly trapped in an uncomfortable moment as Deputy Singer pulled up to a stoplight and turned to wait for her answer. Surely if she said yes to his friend he would withdraw his own offer.

Was she ready to turn it down? No. She wasn't ready to let go of the kind of pleasure he had introduced her to, but then Deputy Hammel had given her a taste of the same. She might be able to find something more than just lust with him? But what if she didn't? What if she chose wrong and never had a chance to feel the exhilarating rush of feelings she'd drowned in last night?

"He didn't ask you to solve the world's problems," Deputy Singer prompted her as she sat there torn by her choices. "It's a yes or no answer."

"How about a wait and see answer?" Kristen countered, seeing a glimmer of hope in salvaging the moment.

"Honey, you can answer any way you want," Deputy Singer assured her as the light turned green and he eased up on the brake. "That isn't going to change much of anything."

That sounded ominous, and Kristen shot him a quick look, wondering if she'd somehow managed to hurt his pride. Deputy Singer didn't look distressed, though. He was smiling as he stared down the road, so she decided he was just mouthing off. Kristen had a feeling the deputy did that a lot.

"Don't pay him any mind." Deputy Hammel drew her gaze back to him as he waved away the other deputy's comments. "I'm going to count this as our first date, even if he is here to chaperone."

The way he dawdled over that last word assured Kristen she'd amused the deputy with her explanation to her parents. She could easily guess as to what he was thinking. Even if she couldn't, he betrayed his thoughts when he asked her outright if she'd never been on a date before.

"Of course I have. I went to prom twice and to homecoming." That had the two deputies exchanging a look that Kristen could easily read, and she puckered up indignantly. "What? Those dances count."

"Of course they do," Deputy Singer assured her. "But you're what? Twenty-one?"

"Twenty-two, thank you."

"And been on like three dates," the deputy concluded, making Kristen want to stick her tongue out at him.

"I don't know why the two of you keep harping on my lack of experience." Kristen huffed. "Has it ever dawned on you that you might have *too* much experience? Hmm?"

"Honey, there is no such thing," Deputy Singer informed her with a slight hint of condescension that did have her sticking her tongue out at him. "Don't tempt me, honey."

Deputy Hammel instantly came to her defense. "That's enough, Dylan."

"Oh, it speaks." Deputy Singer snickered as he cast his buddy a wicked kind of smile. "If you want to change the subject, why don't you tell Miss Kristen how you drowned your broken heart in too much beer last night?"

"Well, I think you just did," Deputy Hammel snapped back as a touch of red colored his cheeks. She didn't have to wonder where his embarrassment grew from. Deputy Singer was all too eager to enlighten her.

"You should have seen him. Devin Davis left his ass standing in front of the refrigerator, unable to shut the door without fear of falling over."

Kristen couldn't help but giggle at that description, though she tried to smother it because Deputy Hammel certainly didn't seem to share her amusement.

"Shut up, Dylan."

But Deputy Singer wasn't shutting up, and neither was he trying to hide his laughter. "He was all mopey, too, because you'd been, and I quote, mean to him."

"Dylan!"

Kristen took instant offense at that. "I wasn't mean to you."

"Uh-oh," Deputy Singer murmured. "She's puckering up, Brandon. You better kiss her."

"Excuse me?" Kristen did pucker up at that. "I don't—"

Kristen forgot what she was about to say, too stunned by the feel of Deputy Hammel's lips closing over hers. They were as soft and firm as she remembered, and he tasted just as good. In an instant, Kristen forgot about everything, including Deputy Singer, as she leaned into the strong, broad palms that came up to cup her face and hold her still for Deputy Hammel's kiss.

Chapter 13

Brandon knew he should stop. Dylan had, no doubt, set him up to get slapped, but Kristen wasn't going tense in his arms. Just the opposite, she was melting into him. More than that, she was kissing him back.

Kristen twined her arms around his neck, and her mouth clung to his as her tongue rallied to battle with his. All too quickly things started to spin back out of control, and just like the first time he'd kissed her, all reason and thought were ripped away beneath the inferno blast of molten lust consuming him.

Kristen was so sweet and giving, two things that stoked the fires of his more feral lusts, and he couldn't help but slide his hands down to her hips. He was about ready to lift her right onto his lap when Dylan braked hard, making the truck jerk hard enough to break them apart.

"That's enough of that, or you'll make it hard for me to concentrate on the road," Dylan warned them with a smile in his tone.

Brandon snorted as he released Kristen, allowing her to settle back down in her seat. She was clearly flustered and embarrassed, casting quick little glances at Dylan, and Brandon could easily read her thoughts. She was worried, worried about what had happened last night with his best friend.

Dylan had told him all about their heated embrace, along with the ultimatum he'd laid down. Kristen hadn't shot him down. That alone had shocked Brandon, but now he understood what his friend had been saying about just kissing her.

It did really work.

Kristen seemed to have completely forgotten about their argument. Actually, she settled down quite nicely, all too eager to move on past their kiss and the embarrassment it clearly caused her.

"So, Deputy Hammel—"

"Brandon," he corrected her, having a feeling he'd be doing that for a long time to come and not surprised in the least when she ignored his correction.

"You said something yesterday about enjoying gardening."

"Oh God, don't encourage him," Dylan groaned.

"Why do you have to be like that?" Brandon shot back. "You like our yard."

"Your yard?" Kristen blinked as she glanced between the two men. "You two live together?"

"Actually, we bought a house together," Dylan informed her, shooting a dirty look over Kristen's head at Brandon. "One, I was assured we could fit a pool into the backyard, but *somebody* has taken it over with his stupid vegetables."

"Don't somebody me." Brandon wasn't about to let that one lie. "And you like those vegetables."

"I'd like a pool more."

"I like vegetables," Kristen chipped in softly, drawing both Dylan's and Brandon's gaze down to where she sat between them, still blushing like the virgin she was. "Actually, I used to have my own little garden. Mom and I grew herbs."

"Your mom cooks with herbs?" Dylan sounded doubtful, and Kristen seemed to understand why.

"No." She smiled. "But they smell nice on the porch."

"On a porch," Dylan latched onto that comment. "That's a great place for a few pots and great way to make room for a pool."

"Oh, shut up about the pool," Brandon groaned. "If we took out the garden, what would you cook with?"

"I'd go to the supermarket and buy something," Dylan shot back.

"You cook?" Kristen injected herself into their argument once again, blinking up at Dylan with an expression full of surprise.

"I dabble." He shrugged. "Dad used to be a cook in the army, so he taught me a few things."

"I bake," Kristen declared, blushing over that admission, as if there were any reason to be embarrassed.

"Well then, maybe we should get together and make a meal," Dylan offered with enough of a suggestive hint for almost any woman to take his double meaning. Any woman that was but Kristen, who beamed proudly up at him.

"What a wonderful idea."

Brandon rolled his eyes and bit his tongue as Dylan snickered and finally turned down Main Street. They were almost there, which was a good thing because it was becoming harder and harder not to give into the urge to kiss Kristen again.

The light, floral fragrance that seemed to be distinctly hers filled the cab, making it hard to concentrate. It didn't help that he felt the soft plushness of her thigh pressed up against his. It had him overheating in inappropriate ways and shifting in his seat as he tried to get comfortable with the ever-growing erection beginning to tent his slacks.

He wasn't alone in that. Brandon couldn't help but take note that Dylan kept fidgeting down at his end of the bench seat. He could guess what had his buddy all itchy. So would most women, but Kristen seemed completely oblivious to the effect she had on either of them as Dylan pulled into the Main Street parking lot and started looking for a spot.

There were none, and the search cost precious seconds that allowed the temperature in the cab to rise another couple degrees. Brandon needed to get out of the damn thing before he turned and ravaged Kristen right there in her seat. Thankfully there was a spot on the side of the road, and seconds later, Brandon was all but leaping out of the truck, gulping in the fresh air.

It didn't really help.

Not with Kristen following him with that sweet smile still tugging on her lips. Boy but she was pretty, and so damn sweet a man could get more than a toothache. Brandon would suffer all the aches just to have the pleasure of escorting her into the bakery and knowing that every man there was jealous because Miss Kristen was with him...and Dylan.

* * * *

By the time Deputy Singer and Deputy Hammel dropped Kristen off that evening at her house, she was all but quivering with excitement. It had been a wonderful day. They'd had a big brunch and been joined by several other people, who had also shared their opinion on the pool versus garden debate.

Kristen feared Deputy Hammel's garden was endangered and had insisted on seeing it herself. She'd expected something small, something like what Gwen had with a little yard and quaint old home, but it was much more like an old farm, with a long, sweeping drive and a massive backyard overtaken by rows and rows of garden beds overflowing with produce.

The flowers...Deputy Hammel grew the most beautiful ones. They attracted bees and butterflies and even a humming bird that she'd watched buzz all around. It had been an exciting moment.

So had seeing their house first-hand.

They'd bought one of the old, white-clapboard homes that rose up tall and proud and was banked by a nearly wrap-around porch that Deputy Singer had already restored back to its former glory. The latticework was ornate, the railing spindles hand-spun by Deputy Singer himself.

He had a workshop set up in the old garage. He was using it to build new, custom kitchen cabinets. Kristen had been suitably impressed. Deputy Singer clearly took a lot of pride in the house and had big dreams. What Kristen couldn't figure out was how Deputy Hammel played into those dreams.

The two men had bought a forever home, one that had enough bedrooms for a whole brood of children, but whose children? *Their* children? Like Deputy Hammel and Deputy Singer were a couple?

That made little sense, but it also made sense of other things, like why Deputy Singer hadn't been jealous when Deputy Hammel had kissed her. Of course, Deputy Singer hadn't confessed to feeling anything other than lust for her, so maybe he was just not honestly jealous.

That still didn't explain the house. Kristen couldn't escape her curiosity or her need to find out just what was up with the two friends because they were clearly very, very close. There was one person she knew who would know. Gwen.

Kristen found herself staring into the bedroom Gwen had turned into a den. It housed Gwen's precious computer and even more coveted large screen television, but she wasn't busy using either. Instead, she was sitting at her desk staring down at something and looking completely lost.

"Is everything all right?" Kristen asked as she came to a pause in the doorway, not sure if she should intrude.

"What?" Gwen sniffed and blinked as she looked up.

"You look upset. Did something happen?"

"Nothing you can help with," Gwen assured her, recovering her normal hard, brittle tone. "Is there something you wanted?"

"No. I just..." Kristen didn't even know how to ask what she wanted to know, and Gwen wasn't patient enough about how to get the words out.

"Is this about Brandon and Dylan?"

"How did you know?" Kristen blinked, shocked by her cousin's perception.

"How do you think?" Gwen snorted. "You showed up for church on a scooter and you don't think your mother is calling me up and reaming me out for letting you buy the thing?"

Actually, Kristen had expected her mother to do something like that. She'd just forgotten that she had expected it. She'd been having too much fun that afternoon to be worrying over her parents, but now she felt a twist of guilt as she smiled sadly at Gwen.

"I'm sorry. She shouldn't have done that."

"Don't worry about it." Gwen shrugged and shoved away from the desk. "She didn't say anything she hasn't said before."

"Still…" Kristen stepped back as Gwen tried to brush past her and then followed her cousin into the kitchen. "It wasn't your responsibility to let me do anything. She should know that."

"Well then, tell her. Doubt it will make any difference," Gwen muttered as she headed for the refrigerator. "So what is it you want to know about your boyfriends?"

"Boyfriends?"

"The two deputies." Gwen paused to remind Kristen of what she'd interrupted her for. "You have a question or not?"

"Well, it's just…they're not my boyfriends." Kristen felt compelled to correct that misassumption. "But they have both showed interest in me, and I was just wondering…I mean…"

"It's not either-or." Gwen cut her off, wrenching open the refrigerator. "Whatever has you stuttering over there, I can guess they both made a pass, and you're wondering who to choose, but the great thing about Cattlemen is you don't have to. You can have them both."

Kristen blinked, not following that explanation. "What do you mean *both*?"

"I mean at the same time." Gwen shot her a knowing little smile as she began to pull the beer out of the refrigerator. "Front and back, there is nothing like that ride."

"You mean both," Kristen repeated, having trouble computing that crude thought. "At the same time?"

"Oh, yeah." Gwen took a deep breath and let it out slowly, clearly savoring some kind of memory. Kristen was horrified to think of what it might be.

"I...I...but that's wrong!"

"Nothing is wrong when you're naked and having fun," Gwen assured her as she began popping every can of beer open and pouring it down the drain. That seemed peculiar, but Kristen was still stuck on shocked to pay her cousin much mind.

"Well then, my answer is no, absolutely not!"

Kristen was half tempted to ride back over to the deputies' house and tell that to their faces, but she didn't want to give them a chance to kiss her again. Their kisses were potent, making her want to agree to almost anything.

No, she'd tell them off in public. It would be safer.

"What are you doing?" Kristen frowned as she finally focused back in on Gwen, who had now emptied a whole twelve-pack down the sink.

"Going on an alcohol-free diet," Gwen tossed back, leaving the cans to drain as she turned and headed back toward her bedroom. "And I have a friend coming over. Let him in when he knocks."

That drew Kristen's eyebrows up. Normally, Gwen's friends didn't come by the house. She wondered if this man was special, but she somehow doubted it when he arrived not ten minutes later. Kristen answered the door with a smile that dimmed slightly as the tall gentleman waiting on the other side frowned in response.

"I'm Kristen, Kristen Harold, Gwen's cousin," she explained as she held out a hand that he just looked at. "And you are?"

"Gwen didn't tell me her cousin was in town," the man responded with a hint of accusation in his tone. It reflected the sudden sense of animosity she felt seeping from the man.

"Yes, well...she told me you were coming over." Kristen wasn't sure what else to say.

If this was her house, she might have told the rude stranger off and slammed the door in his face, but this was Gwen's guest, and she had little choice but to step back and allow him entry.

"She's in her bedroom. I'll go get her."

"Don't bother," the man grumbled as he brushed past Kristen to storm off down the hall toward the back bedroom.

"Excuse me." She raced after him, leaving the front door wide open. "I don't think it's appropriate for you to announce yourself in such a manner."

"She won't mind."

"But—"

"Gwen!" he hollered as he banged on her bedroom door. "Open up."

"Dean." Gwen threw the door open to latch onto the man and jerk him forward. "Get in here."

A second later the door slammed in Kristen's face, leaving her beyond curious and feeling a little torn. Whatever was going on in there wasn't her business, but Kristen was sort of instinctively nosey and couldn't help but lean slightly as the murmur of voices grew until the man was storming.

"*How could you let this happen?*"

"*Shhh!*"

Gwen shushed him as the patter of footsteps raced for the door. Kristen jerked back instantly, ducking into the den as she heard Gwen's bedroom door open. It slammed shut a second later, and that should have been her cue to flee, but Kristen's attention caught on the page still lying on Gwen's desk.

It wasn't a paper after all, but a picture. Several of them, in fact. They were all of a fetus. Kristen's eyes rounded as she shuffled over to stare down at the printed sonogram results and the name clearly typed beneath them.

Gwen was pregnant!

Kristen couldn't help but wonder if the man Gwen had pulled into her bedroom was the father and then, uncharitably, wondered if Gwen knew who the father was. That was wrong of her, but then so was pressing her ear back up to the wall and eavesdropping on their conversation, but Kristen was curious, and, she reasoned, her cousin might need her help. God knew Gwen would never ask for it.

"That is the stupidest thing I have ever heard," the man snapped, sounding very angry. "You should get an abortion."

"That's the stupidest thing you ever said," Gwen snapped back. "Do you know how much this baby is worth?"

Kristen frowned at that, not liking where that question led at all. Her opinions didn't count for much, though. She couldn't even share them. She had to bite them back as she continued to strain to catch every detail.

"You can't do this, Gwen. It's too dangerous." Beneath his anger, the man sounded honestly concerned.

So was Kristen because, while she could agree that Gwen's words lacked wisdom, they hadn't struck Kristen as dangerous. She was clearly missing out on something here, something she probably didn't want to know the details to, but she couldn't seem to stop herself from trying to gather them.

"It will work out," Gwen assured him. "But I need your help, and you know you owe me."

"Fine. What do you need me to do?"

"Help me convince the sheriff the baby is his."

"*What?*" The man sounded just as horrified as Kristen felt, but obviously for very different reasons. "You can't blackmail a whole bunch of men into thinking they're each a daddy when you're trying to convince the one man you're certain isn't that he is. *That's insane.*"

That certainly was. Gwen was blackmailing somebody, from the sound of it more than one person. Suddenly Kristen couldn't help but wonder if maybe Gwen could afford a house and fill it with such nice things because she had a second source of income. That was an unnerving thought.

"Are you going to help me or not?"

"I don't even know what you're trying to do here because Alex will demand a blood test."

"Who cares?" Gwen spat. "By then Heather won't want anything to do with him."

"You need to give up this obsession and focus on the problems at hand," the man insisted.

Kristen couldn't have agreed more. All these silly games Gwen was playing seemed pointless and a way to avoid the real problem of what she was going to do with a baby.

"What I need is for you to help me. Now are you going to or not?"

"I said I would. Just tell me what you want me to do and don't blame me when this all blows up in your face."

"It's not going to blow up."

"Of course, it is. Alex *hates you.* You slept with two of his deputies."

Kristen's heart froze at that as her thoughts turned immediately to Deputies Singer and Hammel. The way Brandon had spoken to his cousin would be easily explained if he were some kind of scorned lover. It would also explain why he thought Gwen would be jealous over her, because he wanted her to be.

Maybe the two of them were just using her to get back at her cousin. That thought cut deep, and she didn't want to hear any more. Everything was all messed up. Gwen was pregnant and blackmailing people. She'd probably slept with the two men Kristen had actually thought were taking an interest in her.

It was all just so confusing that it gave her headache, and she went to lie down.

* * * *

Dylan didn't normally whistle while he cooked, but that night he was just full of songs. Brandon watched him, wondering if his friend even knew how happy he sounded. That was Kristen's effect, and Brandon was not immune.

He found himself wondering if he wasn't being kind of dick about the pool. Dylan really wanted one. It had been something that he'd rejected houses over until Brandon had sworn they could put one in. That was really why they'd bought a house with a big backyard.

Four years ago Brandon hadn't known he'd turn into such an avid gardener. That was his grandmom's doing. She'd come over to help with the yard, and he'd been hooked. That didn't mean he couldn't share the yard.

"You know, I'm thinking if we put in maybe a round pool, not too big," Brandon tacked on quickly as Dylan spun around at just the word pool. "I could rearrange the gardens so they surrounded it."

"That's a brilliant idea." Dylan nodded, looking like a kid who'd just heard Santa Claus was real. Brandon couldn't help but laugh.

"Yeah, but we need to get some real designs together."

"Of course, but if we got a pool, we would have an excuse to teach Kristen to swim."

"Naked?" Brandon perked up at that idea.

"What other way is there?" Dylan shot back, sharing a laugh with Brandon before turning back to flip the chicken breasts over in the cast-iron skillet.

He then picked the heavy pan up and slid it into the pre-heated oven. Slapping the oven mitts down on the counter, he picked up his beer and joined Brandon at the table.

"You really think we're going to have an opportunity to teach Kristen anything?"

"As long as you don't do something stupid and screw it up." Dylan snickered. "Just remember the rule I told you about this morning."

"If she starts getting prissy, just kiss her," Brandon repeated, amazed that it had actually worked.

"That's right." Dylan tipped his beer back, taking a long gulp before smacking his lips and glancing back over at Brandon. "You really like this girl, don't you?"

"And you don't?" Brandon shot back, feeling no need to admit to what was obvious.

"I'm hoping a good fuck will set my head back to rights," Dylan admitted before frowning. "But something tells me it's not going to be that easy."

"I don't think it's going to be possible." Brandon took a deep breath and knew that he was risking making a fool of himself as he continued on. "I'm thinking maybe we ought to start picking out baby names and deciding on where to honeymoon."

Dylan didn't respond to that for a long moment before pointing out the obvious once again. "We haven't even slept with her."

"Do you really think that will change anything?"

Dylan frowned and slowly turned toward Brandon. "I'm not ready to get married and have babies and all that. I mean, one day, sure, but right now, I just want Kristen and a pool."

Chapter 14

Monday, May 19th

It was Brandon who found himself whistling Monday morning as he selected only the prettiest flowers from his garden. He had the day off and planned to surprise Kristen with a fresh cup of coffee and a cinnamon curl from the Bread Box, along with his perfectly arranged bouquet.

He meant to leave them on her desk but ran into Kristen in the hall. She looked as pretty as the sunshine in a form-fitted yellow dress that matched her headband. With her hair brushed to curling and her lips glistening with a little bit of gloss, he was struck by the overwhelming urge to kiss her right there and then in the busy hall.

Quickly stashing his gifts behind his back, he waited for her to reach him as he offered her a giant smile. "Good morning, Miss Kristen, you're looking lovely as always."

"Hmm." She paused to give him a disapproving look that warned Brandon things had soured once again between them. Only this time he had no clue as to what he had done.

"Is something wrong?"

Kristen glanced around to assure nobody could hear her before she hit him with her bombshell. "You slept with my cousin."

Brandon flushed instantly, feeling his cheek heat with guilt that left him no other option than to try to explain. "That was a long time ago."

"Was it?" She lifted a brow not looking as if she believed him at all. "Long enough that you've gotten over it?"

"Yes!" Hell, he'd been over Gwen less than five minutes after he'd been done with her. She was just that kind of woman.

"Hmm."

"I swear." Brandon brought his hands around front to cross his heart, completely forgetting he still had hold of his gifts. Kristen's eyes lit on them immediately.

"Are those for me?" She perked up slightly before her frown returned and she pinned him with a suspicious look. "And are they from you or Deputy Singer?"

"Does it matter?" Brandon scowled, wondering at the point hidden in that question. He didn't have to wonder long. Apparently, Gwen had gotten chatty.

"Only if you *share*."

"I...uh..." Brandon didn't even know what to say to that. He didn't need to say anything to cause Kristen to gape up at him.

"Oh my God! *It's true*! Front and back, just like Gwen...oh, oh, oh..." Kristen began to fan herself as she grew redder with each breath. "You shared Gwen! That... That is so gross! Ew! Ew, ew, *ew!*"

Kristen waved her arms in the air as her nose wrinkled as if she'd smelled something foul. Apparently, it was him. She danced around him, shaking her head and storming off, leaving Brandon standing there hold his flowers and wondering how the hell the conversation had gone that wrong.

It was supposed to have gone totally different. She should have said the flowers were beautiful, and then he could have said not as beautiful as her. Kristen would have blushed demurely, and he would have gotten that rush he did whenever he made her smile.

"Ew!"

Kristen spat back at him, pausing to shoot him one last dirty look before she stepped into the accounting offices. Brandon stared at the doorway she'd disappeared through and wondered what he was supposed to do now.

The sane thing would be to leave, but his feet turned in the other way as his mind began to churn. Kristen could say ew all she wanted. He knew the truth. Soon, so would she. With that determination fueling him, Brandon shoved right into the accounting offices and walked past the receptionist, who glanced up.

"Can I help you?"

"Nope. I know where I'm headed," Brandon tossed back, making a beeline for where he saw Kristen settling down at her desk.

Her ass never touched the seat. Brandon caught her before it did. Plopping the flowers, coffee cup, and bag containing her breakfast treat down on her desk, Brandon latched onto her elbow and jerked her back up.

"We need to have a little talk," he stated before she could reprimand him. "And we can do that here or some place private."

"Is everything all right, Kristen?" the receptionist asked. She'd hurried after Brandon and looked concerned enough to call the cops. That was until Kristen told her Brandon was the cops.

"It's all right, Cindy. Deputy Hammel and I just need to have a moment."

"Okay." Cindy glanced at him, and he read the uncertainty in her gaze as she slowly retreated.

"Come along."

Kristen jerked out of his hold and turned to lead the way back out into the hall and across it to the walled-in stairwell that bought them a measure of privacy after the door had banged closed behind him. Almost instantly Kristen turned on him and began wagging her finger at him.

"You have thirty seconds and—"

Brandon did exactly what he'd promised Dylan he would do. He kissed her, stealing the complaints right off her lips as her sweet flavor once again filled his head. She was intoxicating, and he was drowning. Over and over again, he plundered the velvety depths of her mouth as her tongue twirled and twined around him.

Then the sweet, little miss tightened her lips and sucked his tongue in deeper, making Brandon slam her up against the wall as his dick drove him forward. It throbbed and ached, and he would probably have fucked her right there if he hadn't been consumed by an even more desperate desire.

Tearing himself free of Kristen's kiss, Brandon fell straight to his knees as his hands fisted in her skirt. He ripped it upward and didn't even bother to remove her panties before he was nudging the wet, silken crotch aside to dine on the sweet, heated cream coating her swollen folds. She tasted divine and he was instantly addicted, forgetting completely just where they were.

All that mattered to him in that moment was fucking his tongue up into the tight, heated clench of Kristen's sheath. She moaned, her fingers coming to clutch at his head as her hips arched upward, offering herself up for his feasting. Brandon's hunger was insatiable.

Again and again he teased the rippling walls of her cunt as he screwed his tongue deep into her honeyed depths only to retreat and lap at the hard bud of her clit. Kristen's groans grew into whimpers as her hips began to pump with a demand Brandon didn't have the will to deny.

Still it took all his self-control to rip himself away from the pussy melting all over her mouth and rear back up onto unsteady legs. Brandon's hands went immediately to his belt buckle and he'd have had the throbbing length of his dick freed and buried in Kristen's tight cunt if a rather annoyed voice hadn't broken into their heated embrace.

"Deputy Hammel, Miss Harold, I'm sure you have something better to do on taxpayer time."

* * * *

It was the mayor!

Kristen quickly jerked free of Deputy Hammel's hold, feeling her face go up in flames as she found herself facing the mayor, who did not look pleased.

"I'm sorry, sir," Kristen managed to get out as the deputy turned around and frowned. "We were just—"

"I know what you were doing, Miss Harold," the mayor cut in. "Now if you don't mind stepping out of the way."

"Oh, yes. Sorry, sir." Kristen quickly scurried out of his way, but the deputy moved at a slower pace.

He didn't seem the least bit concerned about getting caught in such an embarrassing situation. In fact, he appeared kind of annoyed. Kristen didn't know what right he had to that emotion. She was the one who should be upset... She just couldn't remember why.

Kristen frowned as she tried to sort through her scattered thoughts, but the deputy was quick to remind her what they'd been arguing about before he'd kissed her.

"You're right. Dylan and I share, and we treat women to the kind of pleasure that you can't even imagine, and when you grow up and want to actually know what it feels like to be a woman, you know where to find me."

Kristen gaped up at him, amazed that he could be so bold as to accuse her of not being grown up, but the deputy wasn't concerned by her building outrage. He was too busy storming off. He wrenched open the door and paused to cast her a soulful look.

"What is between us is special. Don't throw it away."

With that, he was gone, leaving Kristen confused and strangely saddened. Her thoughts were not friendly or cheery as she spent not only the rest of the day but the following day as well trying to figure out what she should do, what she wanted to do, and reconciling those two choices.

The two deputies gave her the room to think things through, which only added to her mopiness. A part of Kristen just wished one of them would kiss her, but that was the cowardly way out. They knew they couldn't make this decision for her. Neither could lust. She had to make it herself.

Though a little advice from a friend wouldn't hurt. That was just what Kristen received when, by Wednesday, she still hadn't recovered or come to any decisions. Cybil had asked several times if things were all right, but after lying for two days, Kristen broke down.

They were at the Bread Box, Janice and Cindy having gone to gossip at another table while they all waited on their food. As usual, neither Deputy Hammel nor Singer was there that day, and she'd so been hoping to get another look at them. Kristen missed seeing them, a fact that must have been apparent on her face because Cybil just shook her head sadly at Kristen.

"You look like somebody drowned your puppy. When are you going to put an end to this silliness?"

"You don't even know what's wrong," Kristen protested, not really offended by her friend's comment. She felt as though somebody had drowned her puppy.

"I know it has something to do with those two deputies you keep looking for every time somebody comes in," Cybil countered. "And I bet I can even take a guess as to what's wrong."

"I doubt it," Kristen muttered, but she was wrong.

"They're a packaged deal, aren't they?" Cybil smirked as Kristen gaped over at her. "I'll take that as a yes."

"How did you know?" Kristen whispered, her mind already leaping to one horrible conclusion.

"Oh, it's not like that." Cybil appeared to read her thoughts again and waved them away. "They're Cattlemen. They all come in twos or more."

Kristen blinked that in, not certain what Cybil was really saying. "I don't know what that means. They're Cattlemen? What are Cattlemen?"

"I mean they belong to the Cattleman's Club," Cybil explained.

"Isn't that a golf club?" Kristen scowled. She'd heard a few people whisper about Cattlemen but assumed it was some kind of men's lodge, which apparently it was, just not a golf-club kind.

"No." Cybil shook her head and frowned. "It's more like a sex club."

Kristen started feeling as if she'd just been poleaxed. A sex club? Her deputies belonged to a sex club? They could be out there screwing right now. Oh no. She was going to be sick.

"You know how you asked me about love and lust a while back?" Cybil asked, but Kristen didn't have the ability to speak. She could only nod. "Well, honey, if it was just lust, you wouldn't look like you were about to lose the lunch you haven't even eaten yet. So, let me give you a little advice. If you don't do them, somebody else will."

Kristen blinked that in, latching onto it as an anchor in a world that was spinning. Cybil was right. She had to decide whether or not she was willing to fight for what she wanted, and she hadn't moved out of her parents' house because she was a coward.

Deputy Hammel was right, too.

It was time she grew up and gave Brandon and Dylan her decision. First, though, she might need to take care of a few details.

"Cybil?"

"Yeah?"

"You wouldn't happen to know anything about else about the Cattlemen, do you?"

* * * *

Kristen learned later that night that waxing was painful. The attendant said it wouldn't be that bad. Cybil said it only stung a little. They lied. She hurt in embarrassing places, and it had her wondering if she wasn't making a colossal mistake.

It was a colossal decision. That was for sure.

She was going to have sex. Just the idea made her giggle and flush like a schoolgirl, leaving her wondering if she wasn't being a tad too optimistic about how things would go. After all, she was going to have to show a man her naked body…and let him touch her.

That idea alone was overwhelming, but then she'd remember that it was two men and that had her wanting to turn and run. There were moments when she was certain she couldn't do this. Moments when she couldn't wait to do it.

Kristen was that torn, but she was also that determined. No matter which way her thoughts went, she forced herself to move forward. After hair removal, tans, and even a quick stop by the mall to pick up a nice, attractive bra and panty set, Kristen even shelled out a few bucks that Cybil lent her to buy a nice dress.

This one wrapped around her body, hugging to the curves that the new set of underwear helped her create. Cybil even loaned her a necklace that hung down between her breasts and drew attention to her cleavage. A set of matching earrings and the woman looking back at her in the mirror was nearly unrecognizable.

"Oh my God, what are you planning?"

Kristen turned from the full-length mirror tacked to the back of the closet door to find her cousin smirking at her from the doorway to the bedroom. It was Thursday night, and Gwen was supposed to have a meeting, but Kristen guessed it got cancelled.

"No, wait. I can guess." Gwen held her hand up, forestalling any response Kristen might have made. "This is about those two idiots, Brandon and Dylan. Right?"

Kristen blush was her agreement, and Gwen's laughter was her response.

"Yeah, I should have known." Gwen smirked and shook her head. "You do realize you can do a lot better than them, right? I mean, they barely ever have any money because they spend it all on the stupid house."

"I like their house," Kristen objected. "And the fact that they are willing to spend their money there instead of on alcohol or women speaks highly of them."

Gwen grunted at that. "Trust me, they spend money on booze and pussy, too."

"Must you use those kinds of words?" Kristen flushed, annoyed with Gwen and bothered by the use of such crude language, especially when her cousin was talking about Kristen's two deputies.

That was how she thought of them now. Brandon and Dylan. They were hers, and the reminder that they had ever been anybody else's was not pleasant. Gwen didn't get the message, though. If she did, she chose to ignore it.

"Oh, please. If you're going to do them, you might as well know who you're doing, and those two idiots have gotten more ass than most towns have toilet seats."

Kristen refused to believe that. Even if it was true, it was coming to an end because they were hers now, and she wasn't going to make the mistake of leaving them on the tree for some other woman to pluck. They were hers, and she was going to fight for them. She would also stand up for them.

"They're not idiots."

"They're not any good either," Gwen muttered. "Trust me on this. If you want good, I can hook you up."

"I don't want good," Kristen snapped, inadvertently conceding the point, though she didn't agree with her cousin at all. It didn't matter. Gwen wasn't listening.

"I know this guy. He does this thing with his tongue and...oh." Gwen's eyelashes fluttered as a wicked smile curled her lips upward before she sighed. "Of course, he can't do that with his dick."

"Gwen!" Kristen felt her face going up in flames, completely uncomfortable with this line of talk. "That's enough. I told you I don't want...good. I want..." *To be loved.*

Kristen didn't have the courage to say that. She didn't need to. Gwen seemed to know what she meant, and it had her cousin sighing again.

"You really are hopeless. You know that?"

Kristen was half tempted to respond that at least she wasn't pregnant but bit the words back and simply shook her head at her cousin.

"And I wished you would realize that you're a beautiful, capable woman. You don't need all those men." Kristen only wished her cousin believed it, but it was clear that she didn't.

"Now you sound like your mother, except for the nice parts." Gwen groaned. "Has it never occurred to you that I like all those men?"

"But don't you like one more than the others?" Kristen asked, knowing her cousin did. Gwen liked the sheriff, but he must have hurt her something bad because her expression didn't grow wishful. It hardened.

"No." Gwen finally answered with an unnerving quietness. "There is one I hate more than all the rest."

Kristen's heart ached for the pain she sensed lying beneath that confession, but she knew how her cousin would respond to any hint of pity. So she straightened up and offered Gwen the sound, firm advice she needed.

"Hate is not going to get you anywhere."

That had Gwen cracking a smile that held little warmth. "Oh, Kristen, hate is going to take me everywhere."

With that, Gwen turned and disappeared down the hall, leaving Kristen staring at the door and wondering what her cousin meant by that. Actually she had a feeling she knew. As much as she tried to avoid the memory, Kristen couldn't help but recall the conversation she'd overheard between Gwen and her male friend and knew her cousin was up to no good.

Of course, her mother would have said the same about Kristen if she could read the thoughts swirling through her head lately. They were hot and exciting and beyond embarrassing, but that wasn't going to stop her.

Taking off her dress and packing up her outfit, Kristen washed up and headed to bed, only to lie there and count the clicks of the clock as the seconds slowly piled up into hours. She was too nervous to sleep. Tomorrow was Friday. Tomorrow was the day she would ask Brandon and Dylan out on a date.

Just the sound of their first names in her head had Kristen wanting to giggle with a strange glee, and she knew that tomorrow was the beginning of a wonderful adventure.

Chapter 15

Friday, May 23rd

"I don't know why I ever listened to you," Brandon grumbled for only about the millionth time.

That was just that day. It had to be like the gazillionth time for the week, and Dylan was getting tired of hearing him complain. He just knew nothing was going to stop him. So he just sat there listening while he glanced between his radar gun and the road it was aimed down.

Brandon's was pointed in the opposite direction. They had their cruisers pulled up side by side, their windows down so they could chat as they waited for the even traffic to pick up. Right then, the road was quiet, even if Brandon wasn't.

"This waiting is killing me."

"That's because you're obsessing," Dylan pointed out, earning him a dark look from the other deputy.

"I'm obsessing because you ruined my life," Brandon snapped back, making Dylan groan. This is what came from talking to his friend lately.

"I didn't ruin your life," he said, defending himself half-heartedly, knowing there was no real point in that either.

"There is no way a woman as sheltered and innocent as Kristen is ever going to agree to *both* of us. We should have drawn straws."

"And if you had lost?" Dylan asked, knowing the answer already.

"Still," Brandon insisted, pointedly ignoring Dylan's question. "If one of us had seduced her, we could have lured her slowly into the idea of multiples and domination."

Dylan didn't think that would have gone any better. It probably would have gone a whole hell of a lot worse. "Start as you mean to go on. There has to be honesty if you want a real relationship."

Brandon snorted at that. "Like you know anything about relationships."

Dylan defended himself. "I know what they're not. Besides, I'm not the one who invited Rachel to a fictional pool party, and I know if you're trying to date one woman, you're not supposed to ask another one out."

"Screw you, Dylan, you know I just did that because Adam *begged* me to."

"Yeah, he was desperate." Dylan could agree on that. "But you're only one step behind him, buddy."

Brandon snorted at that. "Please."

"You're just upset because she turned you down." Dylan smiled at that.

It was all so stupid. Adam and Killian were still trying to convince their girl to take them back, but Rachel was having none of it. So those two idiots had decided to surprise her with a romantic dinner. That wasn't the worse idea Dylan had ever heard, but then things had gotten weird.

For some reason Rachel thought Brandon lived with Duncan. Of course, Adam hadn't wanted to deal with Duncan's bullshit so he'd asked Brandon to invite her to Duncan's house for a party that had taken place a week past. It had all been in a vain hope to lure Rachel to Duncan's for a private, romantic dinner Adam and Killian had planned. It was supposed to be a surprise.

What would be a surprise, though, would be Dylan finally getting his own pool.

"I'm still thinking of the pool," Dylan admitted. "You think we can get it in by the end of the summer?"

"Pool? What pool?" Brandon acted as if the word was new to him. "We're not getting any pool."

"Oh, for God's sakes," Dylan muttered. "You know you can be a real ass sometimes."

"And you come by it so—oh, look at that." Brandon's attention caught at the sight of a massive sedan busting the speed limit as it hauled ass down the road. "I'm sitting right here!"

"That's thirty above," Dylan murmured, somewhat impressed by the numbers flashing on Brandon's radar. "You've got to hit that."

"No shit." Brandon was already clicking on his lights.

"You want backup?"

"I'll call if I need it."

Then Brandon was gone, his siren breaking up the quiet of the late afternoon and gaining an immediate response from the speeding car. It braked hard, assuring Dylan that there was no chase coming. No other cars, either.

Sighing as he glanced at the time, he hoped somebody came his way soon. He was bored. It was looking to be a long shift, or it was until the radio started crackling and Duncan was hailing him. Dylan pressed the call button on the mike clipped over his shoulder.

"Hey, man," Duncan called back, dropping police procedure and assuring Dylan this was a personal call. "You'll never guess who just came into the station house."

"Mickey Mouse?" Dylan shot back, smiling as he imagined Duncan's expression going sour with that sharp retort, but Duncan was quick on the return as always.

"Not that kind of mouse. Try Kristen Harold instead."

"Kristen?" Dylan perked up, his heart doing a double beat at all the reasons she might have stopped by.

"Yeah." Duncan drew the word out with a smugness that assured Dylan he was amused. "And she was looking for Deputy Hammel or

Singer and blushing about as red as a tomato. I think you boys are about to get lucky."

"Screw you, Duncan."

"She's headed home, if you want to go make a traffic stop."

Dylan was already pulling off the side of the road. If Kristen had something she wanted to say, then he was eager to listen. Eager enough to put on the lights and speed fast enough that he managed to catch her putting down Main Street.

Pulling up behind her, he beeped his siren at her and just like the good girl she was, Kristen immediately pulled over. She was already off the scooter and turning toward him wearing a smile and a blush as Dylan hopped out of his cruiser and started sauntering up to her.

"Deputy Singer." Kristen greeted him with a hint of nervousness coloring the delight in her tone. "Was I speeding?"

"I somehow doubt it." Dylan couldn't help but chuckle over even the suggestion, but then again, that might have had something to do with the light feeling of joy that flooded through him whenever he was in Kristen's presence.

"I hear you're looking for me," Dylan pressed, too eager to wait for the conversation to develop naturally. "So, here I am, at your service. What can I do for you?"

"Deputy Singer," Kristen started, only to pause, lick her lips, and suck in a deep breath before beginning again. "Dylan, I was wondering if you might grace me with the pleasure of your company on Saturday night."

Dylan laughed. He couldn't help it. She was so adorable in her pink helmet, glancing up at him with a shy hopefulness.

"You really are too much, princess. You know that?"

"Is that a yes?"

Dylan didn't answer. Not with words. Instead, he stepped up to cup Kristen's jaw and lift her face up for his kiss. With a tender gentleness he'd never felt before, he tried to go slowly, rubbing his lips softly against hers in a chaste kiss Kristen immediately deepened.

Her mouth parted beneath his and almost instantly he was drowning in her intoxicating taste.

He wanted more. He needed it. Dylan had waited long enough for another taste of paradise, and he didn't have the reserves to fight against the lust all but consuming him. Over and over he plundered the sweet, velvety depths of Kristen's mouth until she was moaning and leaning into him.

Who knew where that would have led if a car hadn't sped by? It honked its horn as some twit hollered a "woo-hoo" out the window. That destroyed the moment, and Kristen and Dylan broke apart, each taking a moment to catch their breath before Kristen met his gaze once again. This time there was a sparkle glittering in her gray eyes.

"That was definitely a yes."

"It was." Dylan paused to frown, remembering that he and Brandon. "Only Saturday is no good. Brandon and I are volunteering to help out at Camp D. We're participating in an obstacle course and will probably be pretty late."

"Oh." Kristen looked crestfallen for a moment before perking back up. "Well, you could join me and my friends tonight. We're going dancing again."

"I wish I could, princess, but I've got to work." Dylan scowled, feeling kind of a like a toad for turning her down twice in a row. "But we could do church and brunch on Sunday again."

It was as if he'd offered her diamonds. Kristen's face lit up with such happiness Dylan wanted to kiss her again. Then he did, though, this time, he forced himself to keep it short. Short and sweet, just like Kristen.

"Sunday then."

"Sunday," Kristen repeated back with a nod before casting him another hesitant glance. "Will…Brandon be joining us?"

"Always."

* * * *

Sunday couldn't come soon enough for Kristen. The time ticked by so slowly it was torturous. Friday night alone was a nightmare. She was so giggly and bubbly with the knowledge that, on Sunday, she was going to spend time with both Brandon and Dylan again. Some of that time they'd probably spend kissing.

The memory of how good their kisses could be made her blush and all the more eager to get kissed again. That thought had her watching the other men at the bar and wondering if any of them could kiss like her two. She didn't think so. She didn't think any other man could make her feel the way Brandon and Dylan did.

They made her feel special.

Kristen snuggled that feeling close and clung to it all night and all of Saturday until her cousin came home raging and busted Kristen's bubble of bliss.

Kristen was in the dining room, working on making a quilt out of the leftover scraps from her tailored wardrobe, when Gwen came slamming into the house. She was cursing and ranting into her cell phone. It was impossible, given the pitch of her tone, to avoid hearing what Gwen had to say.

"...Not right! That was supposed to be an all-male event. What the fuck was Heather doing there?"

Kristen cringed at her cousin's choice of words but focused in on the one word that explained a lot.

Heather.

This had to be about the sheriff. Kristen had learned enough over the past couple of weeks to put the picture all together. Gwen and the sheriff had obviously had a thing, but he had a real thing for Heather Lawson. That had broken Gwen's heart and made her bitter.

"You're so full of shit. There's no way Miss Goody-Two-Shoes would ever get it on in the bathroom of a boy's camp. I don't believe it...it's a lie. No, it has to be....Ahhh!"

Gwen screamed, prompting Kristen to hop immediately up and rush toward her. She made it in time to see Gwen chunk her phone on the ground and stomp it to death. She belted out one obscenity after the other with each smashing pound of her foot before she wore herself out and collapsed in heaving sobs on the couch.

"Oh, honey." Kristen was beside her in an instant. Throwing an arm around Gwen's shoulders, she tucked her cousin into her side and began to rock her. "It's all going to be okay."

She repeated that mantra until Gwen had calmed down enough to jerk back. She leapt off the couch and turned to pin Kristen with a pointed look.

"This never happened."

Kristen had no idea what she meant by that, but before she could ask, Gwen was storming off to her room. She disappeared down the hall, and a moment later, her door slammed, leaving Kristen sitting there wondering what had just happened.

She didn't really know, but it left her disturbed and with an uneasy feeling that her cousin was spinning out of control. She felt a need to do something but didn't know what to do. So she went reluctantly back to her sewing but wasn't able to find happiness in the effort as she had earlier.

Instead, she worried over Gwen. That was, she worried until Brandon called to arrange a time to pick her up in the morning. He said he was looking forward to seeing her, that he'd missed her, and Kristen went to bed holding on to those sweet words and woke smiling with them still ringing in her head.

She took her time showering and getting ready for church, wanting to look her best for both Dylan and Brandon...and God, she quickly reminded herself, not wanting to think what He'd have to say with her dating two men at the same time. Hopefully, He'd understand, though she knew her parents never would, but this wasn't their life.

It was hers, and she was going to live it.

Kristen made that vow as she took one last look in the mirror. She heard the truck pulling up in the driveway and grabbed her purse, pleased that her men were punctual. It was an admirable quality, and so was patience, but Kristen was out of that.

She threw open the front door before Brandon even reached it and was waiting on the top step to the house's small front porch. He smiled up at her as he came bounding up the steps. Boy did he ever look good in a suit. She smiled, thinking he'd probably look good in anything.

"Good—"

Kristen didn't get a chance to finish her greeting as Brandon caught her cheeks in his hands and sealed her lips with a kiss. The heady, intoxicating flavor of coffee and cinnamon flooded through her as Kristen sighed and melted into his arms. This was what she'd been missing, what she was willing to risk her heart for.

She just hoped she didn't end up sitting on the couch, crying her eyes out. That grim thought had her pulling back and forcing her quivering legs to take her weight as she stared up at Brandon. He stole all the worry beginning to fill her with one simply whispered confession.

"I missed you."

"I missed you, too," Kristen whispered back, feeling her heart grow soft and heavy as her words brought a smile to his lips.

"Come on, we better get before I ravage you right here on the front porch." Brandon held a hand out to her, his eyes twinkling with merriment and a heat that assured her he wasn't entirely kidding.

Kristen returned his smile and slid her hand into his. "Just think what my parents would say if we skipped church to spend all morning kissing."

Brandon blinked and shot her a funny look. "It wouldn't be only kissing, Kristen. You know that, right?"

"We shouldn't talk about that," Kristen responded as her face flamed at even the implication they'd be having sex. If that was what it came to, that was what it came to, but she wanted it to evolve naturally…without any discussion. Brandon, apparently, did not agree.

"Don't you think we should?" He paused to open the cab door, and Dylan caught his question. He was waiting in the driver's seat to greet her with another bone-melting, heart-pounding kiss before blindsiding her with a question.

"Don't you think we should what?" Dylan asked as Brandon joined them on the bench seat and shut his door.

"Talk about sex."

"Deputy Hammel!" Kristen felt the searing heat flush across her cheeks, but they weren't laughing because they weren't kidding.

"No," Dylan cut in as he began to ease the truck back out of the drive. "He's right. We need to come to a few understandings."

Kristen didn't want to understand anything. She wanted out of this conversation but feared the only way to the end it was to go through with the discussion. "Like what?"

"Well, like birth control," Dylan began pointedly before making Kristen squirm with even more embarrassment as he bluntly continued on. "I'm assuming, given your never-been-kissed status, you aren't on any."

Kristen should just let that lie, but neither man was filling the silence, and finally she caved. "I am."

"You're on birth control?" Both men seemed honestly shocked by that admission, but Brandon recovered first, frowning down at her. "Why?"

Kristen couldn't meet his gaze but focused on her hands as she tried to politely explain what she didn't want to explain. "It's a female thing."

"A female thing?" Dylan snorted. "What the hell does that mean?"

"I'm…not regular."

"Birth control has something to do with bowel movements?" Dylan frowned.

"Don't be absurd," Kristen snapped, out of patience with his prodding. "I'm talking about menstruation!"

"Oh." Both men breathed out that word as they nodded and then fell awkwardly, blessedly silent. That only lasted for a moment, though, before Brandon was turning back to the second most uncomfortable conversation she had that day.

"Well then, that's great. No condoms needed, right?" He glanced down at her hopefully, and Kristen didn't even know what to say. Dylan did.

"I assure you we're both clean, so you don't have to worry about diseases."

"What? Do they test you down at the club?" Kristen shot back, more than eager to turn the conversation from something humiliating to her toward something that should have humiliated them, though neither one of them looked particularly embarrassed.

"I was wondering if Gwen told you about that," Brandon muttered, no doubt thinking mean thoughts about her cousin.

It probably wasn't right to let him think Gwen when it was Cybil who had actually told her, but she didn't want him thinking mean thoughts about Cybil either.

"We're quitting."

"What?"

"What?" Brandon echoed Kristen's stunned amazement as they both turned to stare at Dylan, who made his position perfectly clear.

"I don't need all those women, princess. Not if I have you." He sealed that vow by reaching out to lace his fingers through hers and give them a squeeze. "And I'll kill any other man that touches you...besides Brandon. Understand?"

Kristen could only nod, dumbfounded as she continued to gape up at him. Brandon recovered quicker and took her other hand to draw her attention back to him before making a similar solemn vow.

"I've been in love with you since I first laid eyes on you, so try not to break my heart. Okay?" Brandon offered her a small smile, and Kristen felt the tears spring into her eyes.

This was more than just lust.

Leaning up, she sealed that vow with a kiss that almost had them getting caught by her parents as they pulled into the church parking lot. Dylan saved them from an embarrassing mistake when he gave a quick whistle.

"Parental unit alert," he called out. "At least they looked happy."

Happy wasn't the word for it. Her mother was fairly glowing, and it soon became obvious why. Dylan was back, and her scooter wasn't. Her daughter was dating a deputy, and Marissa was strutting like a peacock showing off every feather as she introduced Dylan to almost every member of the congregation.

It was embarrassing, but no more than when her mother started hinting that she was ready for grandchildren. Dylan handled the moment well, assuring her mother that he did want children, one day. That comment struck Kristen as she wondered what she wanted.

She had a whole long hour of church to think about it. The only conclusion she could come to was that she wasn't ready for children. Kristen would have to find the courage to explain that to her mother. It became apparent she was going to have to find it soon, though.

That became clear after her mother invited the three of them to a baked ham lunch. Dylan and Brandon were agreeing before Kristen could warn them that her mother's ham was kind of like her tea—rotten. They learned that soon enough and made Kristen smile when they cleaned their plates.

After then it was off to the living room with the men. No doubt so her father could grill her suitor while her mother grilled her in the kitchen. It started innocently enough, but Kristen knew exactly where her mother was headed when she commented on what a nice gentleman Deputy Singer seemed to be.

"He's lovely," Kristen agreed, thinking that no real gentleman could kiss the way Dylan did.

"He's got a stable job," her mother pointed out as she began washing the dishes. "A stable, respectable job."

"And dangerous one," Kristen added on as she scraped another plate clean over the trashcan. "Deputies get shot at, you know."

"Hush, Kristen, or you'll invite the devil." Her mother waved away that talk with her usual rejoinder.

Normally she thought her mother was being overly dramatic, but this time she could see her point. Kristen feared she might already have invited the devil into her thoughts because she hadn't considered that point until right then. They really could be shot. Then what would she do?

"Oh, now you're frowning." Her mother shook her head at her. "And don't think I don't know why, but you shouldn't start crying until there is something to cry over."

That was true. With a deep breath, Kristen reminded herself that she couldn't stop the future. So she might as well enjoy the present.

"Thanks, Mom." Kristen gave her mother a quick side hug and a peck on the cheek before turning to the ham. "You want me to wrap this up."

"Sure, but first let's cut you off some." Her mother quickly moved to fetch a knife. "You know you should come over some time and let me teach you how to make a ham. I think your deputy liked it."

Chapter 16

Kristen held back her giggles until she was safely encased in the cab of Dylan's truck, her parents' house fading into the background. They pealed out though as she looked to find Brandon staring down at the plates of ham her mother insisted he and Dylan take. The expression on his face was priceless, and she felt compelled to lean up and give him a quick kiss on the cheek.

"Thank you for being so nice to my parents."

"Him?" Dylan snorted. "He wasn't the one being glared at by your father. I don't think he likes me."

"I'm sure he loves you," Kristen countered, though she wasn't really sure. What she was sure of was that she was grateful. Leaning up, she dropped a quick kiss on his cheek. "Thank you, too."

"If you really want to thank me, you would—"

Whatever lewd thing Dylan had been about to say got cut off as Kristen laid her finger across his lips. "Don't ruin the moment."

"Yes, ma'am," Dylan agreed after she'd lifted her finger.

"Why do I get the feeling your agreeableness is just a trap?" Kristen eyed him suspiciously. Dylan was smiling, a no-good kind of smile.

"It's not a trap," Brandon assured her, making Kristen realize he was wearing a very similar grin. "It's more like an afternoon surprise."

"A surprise?" Kristen blinked in delight. She hadn't known what she expected, but she'd hoped they'd plan to spend the afternoon with her. "What kind of surprise?"

"The kind that requires shorts and T-shirts." Brandon paused to cast her an amused look. "You do own a pair of shorts and a T-shirt."

She didn't, and he knew it, but Kristen wouldn't give Brandon the pleasure of telling him he was right. "I can borrow something from Gwen."

Her cousin wouldn't mind. In fact, she'd probably be thrilled. Gwen still made little comments about Kristen's clothes, and she knew it drove her cousin nuts that she wasn't more fashionable. Still, she wasn't sure how fashionable she had to be when Dylan added on that she might want to wear her bathing suit.

That comment unnerved Kristen.

"I'm not going to get tossed in any more pools, am I?" She glanced nervously from man to man, but both had the same response.

"Definitely not."

"Not this time...but you might get wet," Brandon warned her, leaving Kristen even more confused on what they planned, but they weren't spilling any more details.

No matter how much Kristen probed and prodded, they only teased her back. In the end, it really didn't matter. Kristen knew, whatever they planned, she'd have a good time. After all, she'd be with them.

First, though, they dropped her off home with the promise that they'd be back in an hour to pick her up. That gave Kristen more than enough time to get ready. Just as she'd expected, Gwen didn't mind lending her an outfit. The hard part was making sure she didn't go off the deep end and leave her half-naked. The bikini she had no intention of showing off did a good enough job of that.

Of course, if it were just Dylan, Brandon, and her, she might change her mind. Just the thought of being that close to naked with them had her remembering how good it had felt to feel Brandon skin-to-skin when he'd kissed her at the pool party. It had been electrifying.

And he'd said it wouldn't just be kisses.

A sense of such excitement flooded her with such strength she couldn't help but giggle. This was going to be the best day of her life. She could just sense it.

"Oh God. Look at you. You're glowing." Normally that would have been a compliment, but the way Gwen bit out the words, it was clear she was disgusted. "You've really got it bad for those two idiots, don't you?"

"They're not idiots," Kristen countered, allowing her defense of them to say it all.

She did have it bad, bad enough to consider dating both men at the same time. Kristen wasn't sure how it would all work out, but she was willing to try and to trust that Dylan and Brandon would know how to manage things.

"You are in for quite a shock," Gwen warned her. "Men are only in love for as long as they're hard."

"I wish you wouldn't be so cynical." Kristen frowned at her cousin. "There is reason to hope."

Gwen shot that down instantly. "No. There isn't. Men are never loyal. It's against their nature."

"That's not true. Just think of my father," Kristen insisted, certain her father had never strayed. He was an honorable man, a family man, but Gwen's smile sent a cold tendril winding through her.

"Yeah, look at your daddy."

"What do you mean by that?" Kristen demanded to know, puckering up instantly in defense of her father, but before she could lecture Gwen on her father's finer attributes, a knock echoed through the house.

"Your lover boys are here." Gwen's smile turned more mischievous as she slipped back out of Kristen's bedroom and headed for the front door.

Kristen raced after her, worried her cousin might ruin her date, again. She got distracted, though, by the sight of Brandon in his shorts as Gwen opened the front door. They hung down low along with his oversized shirt, but there was no hiding the power of the muscles beneath. He was long, hard, and so damn hot he made her knees weak.

"Gwen." He greeted her cousin with a scowl that lightened immediately as his eyes skipped over Gwen to settle on Kristen. "Hey, beautiful. You ready?"

"Where you guys headed?" Gwen asked as she slipped past Brandon. "Oh, I see. It's lake day, huh?"

That question drew Kristen's attention past Brandon to where Dylan's truck idled by the curb. There was a fast-looking boat hitched up behind the truck that left Kristen unnerved.

"It's a perfect day," Brandon shot back, his smile growing as his eyes remained locked on Kristen. "But any day with my princess is bound to be perfect."

"Oh please." Gwen groaned as she fished out a pack of cigarettes from their hiding place behind the sconce that hung near the door. "You're going to make me sick."

Kristen blinked, her attention turned by the sight of her cousin snapping the pack against her wrist. "You're still smoking?"

"Yeah." Gwen paused to cast Kristen a pointed look. "Why wouldn't I be?"

"Because…it's not healthy." Kristen quickly caught herself before she revealed the truth.

Gwen still hadn't mentioned her pregnancy, and Kristen didn't know what she intended to do about the matter. Still, smoking was a horrible habit that she didn't approve of, whether Gwen kept her baby or not.

"Please." Gwen snorted. "Next you'll be nagging me about not going to church."

"Well, I'm sure Pittsview has some lovely churches," Kristen insisted, telling herself that wasn't nagging.

"Yeah, Gwen, maybe next Sunday we could all go check out First Citizens Baptist," Brandon suggested a little too eagerly, causing Kristen to frown up at him.

She knew her parents were a little much, but he didn't have to be so gleeful about trying to avoid another service with them. A second later Kristen realized that wasn't his intent.

"I'm kind of wishing we'd gone there today." Brandon directed that at Kristen, but she could tell by the sparkle in his eyes he was taunting her cousin. "After all, there was quite a spectacle with the sheriff and Heather Lawson all but announcing their engagement. Everybody is talking about it."

Kristen froze as those words trickled out of Brandon's mouth. She felt gut-punched and could only imagine how Gwen was feeling. Actually, she didn't have to imagine. Gwen's response was instantaneous.

"Bullshit!"

"Sorry, Gwen." Brandon apologized wearing a smile that made a mockery of his words. "The sheriff is officially off the market."

"No way!" Gwen chunked the pack she was crushing in her hand down, and Kristen would have loved for her to stomp on it, but Gwen stepped over them as she wagged a finger at Brandon. "No fucking way! You're lying!"

"Maybe you better go make a few calls," Brandon suggested, but Gwen was already shoving past them.

Only Kristen, though, saw the tears in her eyes. The door slammed shut a second later, and Kristen felt torn. She knew just who to blame for that. Turning a frown on Brandon, she glared at him hard enough to have him holding up his hands.

"She was going to find out sooner or later, beautiful, so don't give me that look."

Kristen figured he had that right, but that still didn't excuse his smile. "Yes, well, you didn't have to enjoy it so much, did you?"

"Yes, I did," Brandon answered honestly, grabbing on to her hand and beginning to tug her down the steps. "And since you're on the wrong side of the door to slam it in my face this time, you might as well forgive me and agree to come and have some fun."

"Yes, well, I should probably still go check on her," Kristen murmured, glancing back at the house as Brandon all but pulled her across the small yard.

"Don't waste your time. I can tell you how that conversation would go." Brandon paused by the truck door to shoot Kristen another quick smile. "But I wouldn't want to offend you with the obscene language your cousin is spewing right about now."

He was probably right on that point. Gwen was no doubt raging, and when she finally calmed down, she'd either lock herself in her room or go out. There really was nothing for Kristen to do, so she let Brandon lift her up into the cab, but that didn't mean she stopped worrying.

"Hey, princess." Dylan greeted her with a smile as Brandon followed her into the cab. "What's with the frown?"

"Gwen's upset," Brandon answered for her.

"Oh." Dylan didn't sound as if he cared, but Kristen did.

"And Kristen, being such a sweetheart, is upset for her," Brandon tacked on.

"It's just a...delicate time for Gwen." Kristen hesitated over her words, not certain if she should be honest about Gwen's condition.

It really wasn't her business and certainly not her business to tell, but she wanted to talk about it, wanted to know what her men thought, and she could trust them, couldn't she?

"Delicate? Gwen?" Dylan snorted over each word and shook his head. "Honey, you're wearing some seriously rose-colored glasses if you buy that crap. Gwen is as hard as most nails."

"She's pregnant."

Those two words popped out without permission from her mind, but Kristen didn't regret them. She knew this was a big step, but if she was willing to give them her heart and body, she might as well risk her secrets would be safe along with them.

"Holy shit!" Dylan's jaw dropped as Brandon started shaking his head.

"No way." Brandon rejected her words without any hesitation. "Gwen knows better than that…unless, of course, it was intentional."

Brandon and Dylan shared a look over her head that had Kristen frowning.

"Pity that fool," Dylan muttered, and Kristen started to pucker up.

"There is no reason to pity a man for having to share a child with my cousin. Gwen may be a little wild, but she's got a good heart."

"And you got a big one if you believe that," Dylan shot back.

How was Kristen supposed to argue against that? "Okay then, but it was an accident."

"You're certain?" Brandon asked, clearly not in agreement.

"If Gwen was going to get intentionally pregnant by anybody, then it would be the sheriff," Kristen pointed out. "He's the one she loves, and clearly it's not him."

"That's for sure." Dylan nodded. "Alex wised up a long time back. He hasn't touched Gwen since."

"What do you mean? Wised up?" Kristen demanded to know, ready to defend her cousin once again, but she was blindsided by Dylan's next revelation.

"She had the sheriff, okay? She had her chance," Dylan corrected himself. "But then she tried to play one of her games, tried to make him jealous by sleeping with those idiots, Killian and Adam."

"That was so stupid," Brandon grumbled with a roll of his eyes. "I don't know why women think stupid games like that will get a man to admit to loving them. If a man loves you, he'll tell you."

There was a grim finality to those words that had Kristen glancing up at him in wonder. "But you said you'd fallen in love with me."

Brandon's face lit up with the kind of smile that shined pure warmth straight into Kristen's soul. Then he was kissing her, a gentle rub of his lips at first, but as usual, things spun a little out of control, and it was only the need for air that finally broke them apart.

Their lips were still almost touching as Brandon's thumb rolled slowly across her cheek in a sweet caress that had her leaning into the hard strength of the palm cupping her jaw.

"I do love you, beautiful," Brandon whispered. "You're funny and sweet and innocent, and yet you have the strength to stand up for what you want, for what you think is right. Your light shines from within, Kristen, and I am captivated."

He said the sweetest things, and she felt the tears flood her eyes. She choked on a breath that she didn't dare release for fear it would shatter this dream. Then she feared her silence would kill it. Kristen wanted to tell him she loved him, but something just wouldn't let her.

Brandon seemed to understand. He smiled, a slight hint of sadness tinting the twist of his lips as his thumb rolled across her cheek once again. "I know. It's okay. I can wait."

That was the sweetest thing any man had ever said to her. Overcome by the moment, Kristen leaned up to brush a kiss across his lips before pulling back and giving him all that she could in that moment.

"I never dreamed I'd meet a man like you."

"And what about me?" Dylan broke in, causing Kristen to glance back over at him. He might have sounded a little sullen, but he was wearing a grin that left no doubt of how good he was actually feeling. "You ever dream about me, princess?"

"Wouldn't you like to know," Kristen retorted tartly, not about to confess to the silliness of her own dreams.

"You can show me later, princess." Dylan shot a wink in her direction as he pulled off the road and into a landing that was already maxed out with trucks and trailers. "Right now we've got something more important to teach you."

"How to swim?" Kristen took a guess, not thrilled by the idea at all.

"Swim?" Dylan snorted as he began to turn the truck around, backing the boat toward the drive that led down into the lake. "Please, this is much more important. We're going to teach you how to fish."

Chapter 17

Fishing turned out to be fun, despite Kristen's hesitation to actually keep the fish. It wasn't as though she didn't like eating the fish, but she felt a little sad for them as they banged around in the cold storage. Dylan had the cure. He just turned the music up in a gesture that touched her heart.

They did a lot of that through the afternoon. The first was when they'd tucked her safely into a life vest and made her swear not to take it off. Then they'd produced a cooler full of Popsicles and juice, which was just perfect for her.

What else was perfect for her was Dylan and Brandon.

They made her laugh. They made her think. Sometimes they even made her frown and argue. Most of all, though, they set her free. When Kristen was with them, she felt unrestrained, allowed to express her feelings and thoughts without censure or worry that she'd draw disapproval from either of them, even when they disagreed with her.

They didn't do that much, all three of them seeming to like and dislike the same kinds of things and holding similar opinions, though both Dylan's and Brandon's tended to be harsher than hers. That just made things more lively as they battled to corrupt her and Kristen fought to remain open-minded.

The afternoon flew past in a wave of laughter and conversation that ended up with her agreeing to dinner at their place. Dylan was going to grill up the fish that Kristen had caught. That had actually been fun, but there was something a good deal more to the day than that.

Kristen couldn't exactly describe it, but as she sat out with Brandon on the back porch watching Dylan work his magic at the grill, all she knew was that she felt at home. This was where she belonged, where she wanted to stay. The only problem was she thought that about every moment.

Catching the fish, laughing and running as Dylan tried to gross her out when he cleaned them at the dock, picking vegetables with Brandon, and now, right then, sitting in the warm glow of the candlelight and the stars above, there was no moment she didn't savor, even the walk they took after dinner as all three of them strolled hand in hand around their neighborhood.

It was one of the older neighborhoods, with big lots and various styles of homes. It was a place people settled down to have children and grow big, happy families. In that moment, Kristen knew that was what she wanted, only she wanted to go slowly and enjoy every day of the fantasy.

Kristen could guess at what fantasy her men were planning to make true come that night. The moon had risen high into the sky, lighting it up enough that the stars had faded from view when they finally turned back for home. Brandon's thumb had started a slow roll across her palm that Dylan's mimicked, sending a bolt of pure pleasure radiating up both her arms and enveloping her in a bubble of pure bliss.

How then could she turn down Dylan's kiss when they finally reached the back porch door? And how could she not but thrill in wanton ways as Brandon pressed his body close behind her, his lips coming to nuzzle the sensitive arch of her neck. Kristen moaned into Dylan's mouth and melted between them, unconcerned, even as Brandon trailed a series of nibbling kisses to the strap of the tank top she wore.

She hadn't had the nerve to remove it all day, but as Brandon's hands slid down to her waist and began slowly ease it up, Kristen found the courage to pull back from Dylan's kiss and hold her arms up so Brandon could pull the shirt completely free. Instantly, Dylan's eyes dropped to her breasts, and there was no denying the heat that filled his gaze as his hands came up to brush aside the small cups of her bikini.

Kristen trembled, feeling a strange warmth fill her as she waited for what came next as his head slowly dipped. Still, her breath gasped out of her in shock at the first electric touch of his velvety lips as they broke over the sensitive peak of her nipple. Her breasts swelled in a rush as the pleasure of his kiss had her all but collapsing with a heady rush of delight.

She might very well have fallen over if Brandon's strong arms weren't there to hold her. He was still nibbling on her shoulder, sending delightful thrills of heat spiraling downward. The sensation soaked through her as his rough voice murmured in her ear.

"Kiss me, beautiful. Show me how much you enjoy what we're doing."

Kristen obeyed that command without hesitation, turning her head to meet his lips and give life to all the pent-up lust churning inside of her. Her tongue dueled and danced with his, even as Dylan's toyed and twirled around the hard pebble her nipple had puckered into. Then his lips clamped down tight, and he sucked on her, making Kristen cry out into Brandon's mouth and arch not only into Dylan's kiss but also into the hands following the quivering trail of delight right down her stomach and dipping below the waistband of her shorts.

Gwen was a little more rounded than Kristen, and the shorts hung a little loose, giving Brandon's callused fingertips the room to roam as they slid slowly down to cup the sensitive flesh that ached for the feel of his possession. She was hot, wet, and twisting in their hold, not able to focus on kissing Brandon as his hand slid beneath the panty of her bikini and laid claim to the molten folds melting into his hand.

She felt him part the lips protecting her intimate flesh, and then he was touching the most magical spot on her body. This thumb settled over the pulsing bud she could feel blossoming as he began to roll and pump it. With every motion, another bolt of tension twisted through her, dragging her toward an explosion she could only pant and plead for in broken breaths as Brandon began to stretch her sheath wide around the plunge of his thick fingers. Over and over he fucked them deep and fast into her until Kristen was coming apart in a shower of such exquisite ecstasy she didn't even have the strength left to stand as both men pulled back.

Brandon caught her before she fell over as Dylan chuckled, a little unsteady sounding himself. His hands worked quickly, though, as he stripped her down until she was wearing nothing but shivers and a blush. Before embarrassment could take hold, though, Dylan was kissing her, robbing her of the ability to think, much less worry.

There was nothing to worry over because there was no way this could be wrong. It was too good, too perfect. As Dylan swept her up into his arms and began carting her back into their house, she let go of all her reservation and inhibitions. They wouldn't hurt her.

Not ever.

That confidence dimmed a little as Dylan carted her into a bedroom, Brandon fast on their heels and shedding his clothes as he went. Kristen was admiring the show, amazed at how strong and sexy his arms looked. His chest, his stomach, they were ripped with such power that he made her mouth water, but when finally he shoved his boxers down and kicked them aside, her thoughts soured.

He was huge!

And kind of angry looking.

Kristen's nose wrinkled at the sight of his penis jettisoning out from its nest of coarse-looking curls. It stared back at her with an unblinking eye that tipped the swollen and flushed head. His entire length was flushed, a vein protruding that made her cringe at the thought that he might be in pain…or about to cause it.

Brandon caught her staring and smiled, a devilish twist of his lips as he reached down to stroke his own length in a hard-looking fist.

"Yeah, beautiful, this is what you do to me, but don't worry, it just wants to be your friend."

"I have a feeling it wants a good deal more than that," Kristen retorted tartly, not about to buy into that line.

Dylan and Brandon both laughed as Dylan settled down on the bed, still holding her and fully clothed. He adjusted their position until he was leaning back against the headboard, Kristen settled against his chest. Then he used those thick, big knees of his to force her legs wide, leaving Kristen completely exposed and blushing as Brandon began crawling up between her knees.

This was not exactly how she expected things to go.

"I think there are a few things we need to explain to you, beautiful," Brandon began, his eyes twinkling with delight. "First off, this is your pussy."

Brandon reached down to cover her folds with his fingers, making her flush all the hotter, though not with embarrassment this time. This time she was moaning and arching as he discovered that hidden magical spot once again and treated it to a quick caress.

"That's your clit," Brandon murmured before leaning in close enough for his lips to brush hers as he gave her one simple warning. "And I'm going to devour both."

With that, he sank down, capturing her pussy with his mouth and doing just as he promised. It was as if she was being branded, only the flames sizzled with a rapture so searing that Kristen didn't even have the breath to cry out. All she could do was pant and writhe as she found herself trapped between her two lovers once again.

* * * *

Brandon lost all control at the first taste of Kristen's cunt. She was soft, wet, and so damn delicious he could have dined on her forever. Forever was too long of a wait, though, for his dick. It pulsed angrily, wanting a taste of Kristen, too, but Brandon ignored its painful threats.

He wasn't going to rush this. Not Kristen. This was her first time, and he didn't want it marred by anything. So he drove her from one climax to another, stretching her cunt wide as he fucked his tongue up the velvety wall of her sheath over and over again.

She cried out, finally burying her hands in his hair as she pressed him tighter against her spasming flesh, and he knew she was lost in the pleasure. It was time, but Brandon's needs went deeper than mere lust. He wanted something more.

He wanted total possession.

So, he crawled back up Kristen's sweaty and trembling length to meet her tear-soaked gaze and demand the words he needed to hear. He held her gaze as he slowly lowered his hips until his dick was being branded by the molten feel of her cunt lips. They enveloped him in a wet, suckling kiss that had him grinding down into her heat, her softness.

Over and over again, back and forth, Brandon pumped himself through Kristen's sodden folds, watching as her eyes darkened and the flush brightened in her cheeks. Slowly, her hips began to move with his, and he knew he had her in his thrall.

It was time. He felt his heart seize with the knowledge as his hips instinctively lifted, dragging the throbbing head of his dick down to lodge against the clenched muscles guarding the entrance to her body. Kristen's heavy lids fluttered up, her eyes clearing for a second as the two of them locked gazes.

"Tell me to fuck your pussy." Brandon growled over the words, straining beneath the need to pound forward, but he held back, waiting for her to obey, but Kristen couldn't get the words out. All she could do was whimper and twist in Dylan's hold.

"Please," she pleaded softly, but Brandon wanted more.

Dylan seemed to understand. His hands covered Kristen's breasts, toying and teasing her as he coaxed her into giving in.

"Come on, princess, tell him what he needs to here," Dylan murmured in her ear, nibbling on the lobe and making Kristen moan anew as she turned to offer her neck up. Dylan kissed his way down the graceful arch, peppering each one with words that had Kristen lifting startled eyes back to Brandon.

"Brandon didn't lie. He loved you first. He gets to have you first. Tell him what he needs to hear. Tell him to fuck your pussy."

The air thickened with a sweet tension as Kristen licked her lips and slowly said the words.

"Fuck me."

That's all Brandon needed to hear and he was claiming her mouth even as he claimed her body. It was like sinking into heaven, and it took every bit of strength and willpower Brandon possessed not to jerk forward. Instead, he allowed Kristen's body the time to adjust as it melted around him, slowly easing his path forward until finally he settled his full length deep inside Kristen's hot, tight sheath.

Beneath him, Kristen moaned and twisted, her eyes fluttering closed as her cunt pulsed and clamped down around him. Brandon's balls were full and tight, his dick throbbing in agonized pleasure, and every instinct he had was screaming at him to move, but he held still, allowing Kristen to savor the moment. His arms quivered, his thigh muscles twitched, and the strain became nearly unbearable as the seconds ticked by, but soon he was rewarded for his patience as Kristen finally murmured a breath and began to twist beneath him.

Slowly, with more tenderness and care than he'd ever shown any woman, Brandon began to move, shifting his weight back and forth and teasing them both with what was to come. The slight motion set off a ripple of fireworks that shot blazing sparks up his spine as Kristen gasped, her hands coming out to clutch at him.

The sharp bite of her nails along with the sudden thrust of her hips was his undoing. He cried out to her, praying that she forgave him as the reins of his control snapped and his hips started to lift and surge in a rhythm as old as time.

* * * *

Brandon needn't have worried. Kristen was too lost in the glory of the moment to notice even the slightest pinch of pain as he began to pound into her with increasing demand and strength. Each thrust of Brandon's hips ignited a new and boldly more intense burst of delight that had her legs lifting and twining around his waist as she offered herself up to his savage loving.

They were not alone in the moment. Dylan's strong arms held her close, the thick ridge of his erection grinding into the small of her back as his hands continued to torment the sensitive peaks of her breasts. Then he was dropping one, allowing it to slide down over her sweat-slickened side and curve around the flushed globe of her bottom.

Kristen's eyes damn near bulged out of her head as Dylan let his fingers slide down the crease of her rear to touch her where nobody had ever touched her before, not even the gynecologist.

"Shh," Dylan murmured softly in her ear as she tensed slightly in his arms. "Just relax and enjoy."

That sounded like an impossible task, but it was a command easily obeyed as Brandon grunted above her, driving into her now with a relentless speed that blinded Kristen to all else but the pressure building up inside of her. That pressure grew twice as thick and powerful as Dylan slowly screwed his fingers deeper into her, making everything that much more intense.

Then the world was exploding around her, Brandon was roaring as he convulsed, and the hot flood of his seed washed through her. His hips pounded hard against her, grinding his balls against the soft flesh of her pussy until he collapsed beside her on the mattress.

Before Kristen could even catch her breath, much less touch back down from the starry wonder she was flying through, the room was spinning around her, and suddenly she was being pressed into the bedding right beside Brandon's shoulder as Dylan reared up behind her.

A second later the release sizzling through her caught fire once again as Dylan slammed the thick length of his dick deep into her pussy. Kristen gasped, her breath catching as he set up a fast pace, even as he apologized for using her so roughly.

"Sorry, princess, I can't...stop."

She didn't want him to. Despite the slight tinge of pain marring each of his thrusts, the pleasure far outweighed the pain, and she found herself responding once again as the delight bloomed within her. Over and over he drove himself deep into her body, making her toes curl and her drool pool into her mouth, but it was the feel of Brandon's palm coming to brush the hair back from her face that had her eyes fluttering open to meet his loving gaze.

There was something so erotic, so wanton about watching one man as another laid claim to her body. It combined with the wicked sensation of Dylan's clothes rasping against her ultra-sensitive skin as he loved her with hard, pounding thrusts, but Kristen only came apart when he dipped his fingers deep into her ass and began fucking her in two indescribably delicious ways.

Kristen came with a scream, her whole body bucking beneath the avalanche of ecstasy that tore through her, leaving her a sweaty mess, strewn across the bed. Dylan followed her over the edge, slamming into her one last time as his dick pulsed and unleashed another hot wave of cream deep within her body. Then he was collapsing beside her, his hands still holding her hips, assuring that her ass stayed buried in his lap, his dick tucked deep inside her still spasming sheath.

It was all so perfect, so splendidly perfect, and the bubbles of joy percolating through her popped out as giggles as Kristen gave in to the soothing rush of bliss that filled her.

Chapter 18

The sound of Kristen's laughter sent a bolt of pure sun-lit joy through Dylan, making him smile and his heart swell. Nothing had ever felt that good before. Nothing compared to the overwhelming sense of satisfaction that filled him as he lay there by her side, held warm and tight within her body.

He'd found his home.

With that thought, Dylan's arms tightened around Kristen's slender form, pulling her in close so he could lay kisses across her shoulder and whisper to her the truth filling him in that moment.

"I love you, princess. Now and forever."

Kristen tensed, her laugher falling silent as her head whipped to the side, her eyes widening in shock. "What did you say?"

"I'm yours," he vowed. "Body, heart, and soul."

Tears filled her eyes, and her little mouth worked to speak, but nothing came out, and he knew what she couldn't say. She loved him, too. She just wasn't ready to admit it, but there was no denying the evidence. Kristen wouldn't have given her body to them if she hadn't already given her heart.

Now it was time to take care of her.

Dropping a quick kiss on her swollen lips, he braced himself, pulled free of the clinging clench of her cunt, and rolled off the bed. With quick motions, he shed his clothes and reached for her as Brandon finally roused himself and headed for the bathroom that connected his room with Dylan's.

He already had the water going by the time Dylan carried Kristen into the shower. She whimpered slightly as he finally set her back onto her feet, and Dylan couldn't help but smile, guessing she was a little sore.

"You okay, princess?" he asked, lifting a hand up to her warming cheek as the spray of hot water enveloped them.

She smiled shyly and nodded, assuring him that she was growing embarrassed by the memories of the passion they'd just shared, but Kristen had nothing to be ashamed of. She was a sensual, beautiful creature that had branded him with her innocently uninhibited responses.

"I'm sorry I was so rough." Dylan wasn't really. He was feeling way too good for guilt to intrude on his mood, but he knew he'd feel bad later when he wasn't still glowing with the aftereffects of loving Kristen.

"I liked it," Kristen finally whispered back, her gaze dropping. A small smile still lingered on her lips. "It was perfect."

"That it was," Brandon agreed as he stepped into the shower stall behind Kristen.

The stall wasn't small, but it was tight with three people, and there was no way to avoid rubbing up against Kristen. Not that Dylan tried. He was still hard, still hungry, but this time he savored the moment, taking the washcloth from Brandon and cleaning Kristen with a slow thoroughness that had her panting and twisting in Brandon's arms as he held her up, his big hands covering her breasts.

Kristen's head arched back into Brandon's chest as her whole body lifted in an invitation Dylan didn't have the will to resist. Dropping the washcloth he sank to his knees and into the warm, humid scent of Kristen's blossoming arousal. Her cunt lips were swollen and dripping with something more than water, beckoning Dylan to lean forward and lick his tongue over their pouty edges, inflaming his own sense with the intoxicating taste of her heated cream.

He wanted more. Needed it and didn't know he wasn't alone as Kristen's hands twined into his hair and guided his head back to her cunt. It was the sexiest thing he'd ever experienced, made even more so as her legs shifted, opening her pussy up to him as she whimpered out a soft plea.

"Please. Kiss me."

Dylan was lost. He gave in to her demand, sinking his tongue into her velvety heat and losing himself in her taste.

* * * *

Kristen was lost in the splendid wonder of being held by one man while the other man kissed her in the most intimate of fashions. They both loved her. It was her fantasy come true. They were better than she'd ever imagined.

She was strung out on the pleasure, twisting between her two lovers and panting as her tired muscles tensed once again with a sweet tension that exploded into another firestorm of delight. Kristen was left weakened and feeling as if she was floating, anchored only to the world by Dylan and Brandon, who tempted her with even more wicked suggestions.

"Dylan and I, we want you bare," Brandon whispered in her ear. If Kristen had any doubt over his meaning, Dylan made it clear as he cupped her pussy in his broad palm and trapped the heat of her recent release against her still weeping flesh.

"Let me shave you," Dylan murmured as he ground his palm against her mound. "Let us have you this way."

How could she deny them? She'd almost done it to herself, but waxing sounded too painful. This moment was far from that.

"Yes." Kristen closed her eyes as that word slipped out of her lips, embarrassed even by the sound of it.

She shouldn't have been. This was Brandon and Dylan, and they loved her. Kristen reminded herself of that fact as Dylan sank back to his knees, this time with a can of shaving cream in one hand and a razor in the other. He took his time, going slowly, methodically until she felt every drop of water falling from the showerhead against her newly naked skin.

It felt sensual and naughty, just like the hot wash of Dylan's breath as he covered her cunt in a series of kisses that had her mewing with renewed want. It never seemed to go away or die down. This need that was redefining her entire world held her captive, a demand she could not help but yield to, and one that she knew how to make her men cave in to.

"Fuck me." Kristen needed to feel that full pressure again, and she reached down to cup Dylan's cheek and tilt his gaze up until it connected with hers. "Please, fuck me."

She didn't have to ask twice. Dylan was on his feet in an instant, his hands gripping her hips. Then she was being lifted up, her legs twisted around his hips as Brandon held her secure. Then the thick head of Dylan's cock was pressing against her opening. He paused for a moment to meet her gaze once again and offer her a smile before he slid in, making the world spin once again.

The hard length of his cock stretched the sensitive walls of her sheath, setting off tendrils of pure ecstatic delight. Her body demanded more, her hips lifting and pumping in time with Dylan as he began to move. He set a fast pace that had Kristen crying out within minutes.

Then it was Brandon's turn as he shifted her weight to Dylan's arms. Kristen was still moaning over her release when she felt him thrust deep into her, taking up a pounding rhythm that had her clawing at Brandon's back and bucking as wave of rapture too intense to be endured crashed through her, blackening out the world and sweeping her away on a tide of pure, molten ecstasy.

* * * *

Brandon felt Kristen come apart as her tight cunt rippled around him. Her sheath clenched and milked him, making Brandon's eyes all but roll back in his head as his balls almost exploded with the pleasure. It was too much, and he slammed into Kristen, holding on to her tightly as his dick pulsed and unloaded.

He'd never before taken a woman without wearing a condom. Never before felt the slick flesh of a pussy spasm around him or known the feel of the heated wash of his lover's release cocooning him in a warmth so deliciously hot that he felt as if his dick was on fire. Then again he'd never loved a woman, not like he did Kristen.

Brandon might have been Kristen's first lover, but she was his first everything else. The first woman he'd ever carried back to bed and snuggled down with. The first woman he held, unable to go to sleep because he didn't want to miss a second of this night. This was the first night with the love of his life.

As Brandon lay there, visions of their future started to dance through his head. He'd always thought he'd just want a kid or two when the day came, but that night he found himself envisioning a whole messy brood. He could even imagine himself adopting. Why not? They were going to build a life worth being shared.

"I think I should be the one to marry Kristen." Dylan's soft whisper broke into Brandon's fantasy like a sour note, and he frowned.

"I loved her first." That should mean he got to marry her. Kristen was going to be a Hammel. Not a Singer.

"And I let you have her first," Dylan countered.

"So you should get to marry her?" Brandon lifted up onto his arm to glare over Kristen, careful not to disturb her while she slept. "Was that your plan? You gave me first dibs because you thought you could guilt me into letting you have her for the rest of her life?"

"We're both going to have her," Dylan shot back in a furious whisper as he lifted up slightly to meet Brandon's glare. "That's not even up for debate."

"Kristen is going to be a Hammel."

"What if she wants to be a Singer?"

Brandon didn't doubt that she would agree to be a Singer, but he wanted her to be Hammel. He knew she wouldn't agree to be either, though, unless both of them were all right with the final decision. That could be tricky.

"Maybe we should make her a Hammel-Singer," Brandon suggested, thinking that split the baby nicely, but Dylan didn't seem to agree.

"She can be a Singer-Hammel, but she can still only legally marry one of us."

He had a point, though, Brandon hated to admit it. This was going to take some thinking. He settled back against the mattress to do just that. There had to be some way out of this mess.

* * * *

Kristen held herself still, waiting to see if the men continued to argue. She couldn't even believe they were arguing in the first place. Arguing over who was going to get to marry her. That notion both paralyzed her with fear and filled her with such a joy that she thought she might float away.

They really did love her…and she really wasn't ready to get married.

Kristen had just started to live. She wanted to enjoy this time, with just them and the freedom to discover all the beauty their relationship had to offer. Then there were her dreams of going to school. Kristen might not know what she wanted to be, but she knew she wanted to be something.

Perhaps they could have a long engagement, though she suspected Brandon and Dylan were already several steps ahead of her and thinking about children already. Well, Brandon probably was. He was such a worrier, but Dylan was a little more laid back. He was probably still planning his pool.

Kristen cringed away from that thought, still unnerved by her one dip into one. It had not been pleasant, but what came after certainly had. That was until she'd brained Brandon. She wondered if he still had the stitches in his head. If he did, they certainly didn't seem to bother Brandon, which was unusual.

Not much seemed to bother Dylan, though, which was one of the reasons he was so special. Special to her. Brandon was just as special, though he clearly tended to overthink things and become obsessed about them. Sort of like his garden.

Kristen smiled at that thought, imagining just how he'd be with kids. They were going to be smothered, and if they had girls, he'd probably end up being just like her dad—interrogating them in the living room. Except Kristen suspected Brandon would be better at it.

He was so big and strong and hers. Unable to resist a peek, Kristen lifted her lashes so she could gaze down the hard planes of Brandon's chest. He'd tucked her into his side with Dylan pressing in behind her so that she could feel him but only marvel at Brandon's cut form.

Even lying down in bed, totally relaxed, he still looked tense and ready for battle. Each line ripped across his stomach held a sense of power that Kristen knew well. It all uncoiled and unleashed when he…fucked her.

She felt the heat sear across her cheeks at that crude thought but enjoyed the burn. There really was no better word for what had happened. Brandon and Dylan may have loved her, but they hadn't spared her the hard edge of their lust or the pleasure it brought. It had gone far beyond simply making love into a whole new realm of desire.

Kristen couldn't deny that she craved another taste. It was like an ache in her bones that she didn't think would ever truly be appeased. She marveled at its power as her gaze dipped down to where Brandon's penis lay. He still looked semi-aroused, a condition she might have mistaken before as fully aroused. Kristen now knew he could grow even bigger, even harder, wonderfully so.

Shivering with the memory of what it had felt like to have him pounding into her, Kristen reached a tentative hand out toward his penis, fascinated by the knowledge of what he could do with it. It looked so funny, and it thumped at the first touch of her fingertips, that blind eye lifting right up as if he could see her hand about to grip down.

Kristen jerked her arm back, startled and uncertain but still curious. With her heart pounding and her palms beginning to sweat, she slowly reached back down but didn't have the courage to touch him, not until Brandon's hand lifted to cover hers and guide her motions downward.

In a hushed silence that was its own form of intimacy, he taught her just how to stroke and pump his long, thick length, making it grow and flush hot beneath her hand. Kristen watched in amazed fascination as all of Brandon's muscles truly tensed and began to quiver. She had done that, her touch had done that, drawn him to a tight bow.

As the blind eye glaring at her began to weep, Kristen was overcome with a need to taste him just as he had tasted her. She could only hope that he would know the same kind of satisfaction he had shown her earlier. Fascinated that she might have such a power, she dipped her head slowly downward as Brandon's other hand came to twine itself in her hair and guide her motions.

He didn't rush her, though. He gave her the room to start slowly with just one tentative lick across the flared head straining to reach her lips. Instantly, Brandon groaned and flexed, his hips pumping up through the fist he forced her to tighten around his shaft. Emboldened by his response, Kristen treated him to another lick and then another, becoming drugged on the heady, salty flavor of his desire.

She could have lapped at him all night if Brandon's fingers hadn't tightened over her head and forced her lips lower until she was kissing that blind eye. Kristen might be innocent, but she wasn't totally naïve. She knew what came next and parted her lips to clamp them around his bulbous head and suck, earning herself another groan and jerk.

Then there was no more patience left in him. Controlling both the tempo and speed of her head and fist, he taught her how to fuck him in a whole new way. Kristen couldn't deny that she enjoyed the lesson, taking to it with an enthusiasm spurred on by her own ever-growing desire.

She was wet and ready to be filled but having too much fun to stop. Thankfully, she didn't have to. Thankfully, she had Dylan to help ease the burn of her own enflamed lusts. With a mutter, he shifted behind her, dragging her leg over the thick bulge of his own and stuffing the head of his cock into her aching opening with a rough motion Kristen loved.

Then he was holding her still with a tight grip on her hips as he began to pound into her with a merciless frenzy that had her going wild and fucking Brandon with the same enthusiasm. It didn't take but minutes before her whole world started to come apart at the seams.

Kristen came in a hard, orgasmic explosion that had her bucking and convulsing with the avalanche of rapturous delight flooding through her. Brandon and Dylan were right there with her, grunting and straining as they both went tense. Then Kristen had to swallow quickly as both men came with echoing roars.

Then Dylan collapsed, sandwiching Kristen in a hot, sweaty oven as she ended up plastered against Brandon's heaving chest. Kristen's breasts lifted in rhythm with his as she gasped in rough, ragged breaths, trying to calm the rapid fire of her heartbeat, but only time could slow it down.

The seconds dripped past as the euphoric cloud that had bloomed through Kristen finally began to recede, allowing her to catch her breath and become increasingly aware of how sticky she was. It was time for another shower, and a shower meant it was time for another round.

Kristen didn't think she was up to that. Even as she began to squirm for freedom, she felt the ache down below had taken on a strange soreness that left her moving with a little hesitation. Thankfully neither of her men commented as they released her, rolling away from each other and starting to rise to their feet.

"I can't." Kristen blurted that out with a blush as she took note that neither man was what could be defined as soft. "I'm sorry."

"Oh, princess, you don't have to apologize," Dylan quickly assured her as he held a hand out to her. "I promise. No more."

"Though it should be noted that you started it the last time," Brandon tacked on before offering her up a firm warning. "So, if it's a no-go, keep your hands to yourself."

Kristen bit back a smile and nodded. "I'll keep that in mind."

"Then I think you better grab a shower alone," Dylan suggested, not bothering to disguise his own smug smile. "We wouldn't want to tempt you."

Kristen laughed at that and allowed him to pull her off the bed. The two men went to the other bathrooms that were tucked in on the enormous top floor of their house, leaving Kristen to shower alone and retreat back to bed, where they soon joined her. Once again she found herself tucked in between them, surrounded by the warm musk that lulled her to sleep.

As she was drifting off, she heard Dylan offer up another point in what appeared to be Brandon and his ongoing argument.

"That's another first I let you have," he grumped as Brandon yawned.

"Oh, shut up, Dylan."

Chapter 19

Monday, May 26th

Kristen woke up feeling better than she ever had. The sun shined brighter, the birds tweeted louder, and she ended up needing another shower before she made it out of bed. Hell, Brandon and Dylan started before she'd even fully woken up. They roused her from her sweet dreams into a world of erotic heat, making her moan and twist and beg for their fucking.

Then they gave it to her, each man playing with her tight rear entrance as they pumped into her, driving her insane with whispered promises of what was to come and making her ache for it in a way that almost had her begging for both of them at the same time.

She wasn't ready for that and was still a little embarrassed by their intimate touches. They seemed to know not to push, allowing her the time and room to adjust to their intentions. Unfortunately they didn't have the time to give to hers as she asked them over breakfast if they would care to join her at the festival Cybil's church was holding that Memorial Day.

Kristen wasn't surprised when they said they had to work. They were, after all, dressed in their uniforms. Still, she felt it was only polite to ask, and it also opened the door for them to counter with an invitation to dinner and the suggestion that she might want to bring some work clothes just in case she decided to stay over.

They made it sound as if they were giving her an option, but Kristen knew the truth. They had plans for her that night. How could she turn that down? She didn't think there would ever be anything she could deny them, and hoped that there never was.

She also hoped that Gwen wouldn't be around when Brandon and Dylan finally dropped her off back at home, but her wish wasn't granted. Kristen could see her cousin's car parked in the driveway. Worse, there was a pickup truck behind it.

Uncertain of what to expect, Kristen opened the front door tentatively. She saw the next few minutes going either one of two ways. She could be about to walk into an intimate moment between her cousin and a male friend, or she could be about to be teased by her cousin for clearly spending the night with her own male friends. Either way it would an awkward moment, and Kristen simply hoped to get to her bedroom without any unnecessary embarrassment.

What Kristen hadn't expected was to be greeted by the thunderous roar of an outraged man. The sound gave her pause and then had her rushing toward Gwen's bedroom, where she could hear him yelling. Kristen came to a hard stop, though, as his words finally penetrated.

"...do this? What the fuck were you thinking? Sneaking into the sheriff's bed?"

"He told me the door was always open!" Gwen cut back, clearly on a tear herself.

"Yeah, when you were dating!"

Kristen recognized that voice. Gwen's mysterious Dean had returned.

"The door was unlocked!"

"So you just decided to strip naked and crawl into his bed?" Dean sounded justifiably outraged by that suggestion. It was so outrageous even Kristen was having hard time believing it. Gwen didn't deny his accusation, though.

"You don't understand. When Alex wakes up next to a naked woman, he just rolls over and does her."

"Oh, for God's sake, Gwen! That's idiotic."

That was beyond idiotic as far as Kristen was concerned. It was almost downright weird and desperate. She'd read about pregnant women who went crazy and couldn't help but wonder if her cousin wasn't turning into one of them.

"It would have worked."

"It didn't."

"That's because that fat bitch *Heather* showed up," Gwen snapped before starting on a rant that had her calling Heather everything from dumb to worse.

Kristen cringed at her cousin's language, wishing she would just take a breath and calm down. Certainly all this carrying on wasn't good for the baby. Of course, neither was planning a murder.

"She's got to go."

"Gwen—"

"No! I mean it. I know you know people who can handle the matter. I want Heather Lawson gone, *for good!"*

Kristen's eyes widened at the firm determination in her cousin's tone. It countered the voice in her head saying Gwen didn't mean it. She was just upset. Once she calmed down, she'd realize that she was talking crazy.

She would, Kristen swore to herself. She would.

"Even if you get rid of Heather, Alex isn't coming back." Dean argued, earning Kristen's respect for being willing to battle the crazy that was coming undone in Gwen's bedroom. "He had you arrested, Gwen. *Arrested!"*

Before Gwen could respond to that or Kristen could absorb it, the shrill ring of a phone cut through the air, shattering the illusion that this was all just a horrible dream. In a split second, Kristen was rushing to her room as she heard footsteps pounding toward Gwen's door.

Kristen made it to her safe sanctuary, managing to close the door before her cousin slammed open her own. With her ears cocked to the sounds of Gwen answering the phone, Kristen quickly ripped off the shirt and shorts she'd worn home. The bathing suit had gotten left behind, but before she could reach for a fresh pair of underwear, Gwen was pounding on her door and making Kristen dive for her robe as she threw it open.

"Phone is for you."

With that abrupt pronouncement, Gwen stormed back off to her room, leaving Kristen shaken and uncertain of what to do besides answering the phone. Cinching her robe's belt around her waist, she darted quickly across the hall to pick up the receiver, only to find that it was Cybil calling to confirm that she was on her way.

That left Kristen no time to get ready. She was hopping down the hall as she fumbled with her shoes and tried to answer the door all at the same time. Thankfully, whatever was going on in Gwen's bedroom, she and Dean had turned down the volume, assuring Kristen didn't have to explain anything to Cybil.

Her own curiosity, though, was churning. Over the next week, it burned brighter as her cousin started acting weirder and weirder. It came to a head the following Sunday. Kristen had spent almost every night at Brandon and Dylan's, a fact that had not gone unnoticed by the good citizens who shared their neighborhood and their love of gossip with just about everybody else.

While Kristen wasn't ashamed of her blossoming relationship, she was unnerved by the curious looks and speculative whispers. There was one way she knew to get them to stop. It was time to go to church in Pittsview. Churches in small, rural Southern towns were basically like families, and only families attended. Going with Brandon and Dylan would solidify that they were not just fooling around but committed, even if their relationship had some peculiarities.

So Sunday morning she got dressed in her finest clothes after taking a titillating shower with both her men and headed off for the First Citizens church. The way took them past the small, run-down motel that had been built decades past on the outskirts of town. Only the most disreputable sorts stayed there.

Sure enough, as they cruised past, Kirsten's eyes lit on the sight of her cousin racing through the parking lot wearing next to nothing and chasing the sheriff. It was too much to hope nobody else caught the spectacle Gwen was making. Brandon certainly did, slamming on his brakes and coming to a stop to gawk at the sheriff as he ducked into his cruiser. Gwen was only a few steps behind him, and she began beating on his windows. Kristen could hear her screaming across the street.

"Oh my God," Dylan breathed out, cracking into a smile that was downright wicked. "You don't think the sheriff—"

"Nope." Brandon shook his head and hit the gas. "If you don't want to end up working on the night shift, you didn't see anything either."

"I think I now know why she's going crazy," Kristen murmured more to herself than anybody else, but neither Brandon nor Dylan were one to leave that comment alone.

"Who? Gwen?" Brandon asked as Dylan chimed in.

"Why?"

"Yes, Gwen," Kristen responded before casting a glare out the back window where she could see the sheriff easing his cruiser out of the motel's parking lot, leaving her cousin screaming in the background. "He's driving her to it."

"Who?"

"The sheriff?" Dylan once again echoed Brandon's question with one of his own.

"Of course." Kristen sniffed as she gave the sight of the sheriff coming up behind them a cold shoulder. "He's playing with Gwen's affections."

"Gwen has affections?" Dylan laughed at the very notion, causing Kristen to pucker up, but before she could say anything, he was kissing the reprimand right out of her head.

They did a lot of that. Picked on her a little, teased her sometimes, and then kissed the mad away before it ever had a chance to catch on.

Kristen would have suspected them of playing with her emotions, but she knew that it just tickled them that they had that kind of power over her concentration.

That, apparently, wasn't the only kind of power they wanted to yield. Kristen discovered that later that night after they'd finished off another dinner of fresh fish that she'd caught that afternoon. Once again, Dylan cooked, grilling the fish along with the fresh vegetables Kristen and Brandon had picked from his garden.

The dinner was perfect, and so was the mood. With the night sky blooming with stars that matched the flickering glow of the candlelight, Kristen couldn't be blamed for misunderstanding the moment when Brandon picked up her hand and announced they had something they needed to talk to her about.

"I don't want to get married," Kristen blurted out in a rush of panic that she was about to be cornered.

"What?" Brandon blinked as Dylan scowled.

"What do you mean you don't want to get married?" Dylan's tone mirrored the same sullen look he shot her as he retreated slightly in his seat. "I thought you loved with us."

Kristen had never said the words. She'd felt them, but something had made her hesitate. That something melted beneath the hurt she saw reflected in his eyes.

"I do," Kristen vowed softly before adding on her own plea. "And if you ask me to marry you, I would say yes, but I'm not ready. I want to go to school and...I don't know, figure out my life first. Do you understand?"

"Perfectly." Brandon nodded. "Believe it or not, Dylan and I go to school. In fact the summer semester out at Troy started this week. We just got distracted and forgot to enroll, but maybe you'd like to join us."

"I'd love to." Kristen smiled wide, thinking of just how perfect her two men were for her. What she didn't see coming was what Brandon had to say next.

"Good, but we still have something to talk about," Brandon informed her. "Dylan and I want something from you."

"What?" Kristen blinked, thinking there was nothing she wouldn't give them.

"Total submission." Dylan smiled, promising he had plans with what he was going to do with her. "At our complete mercy."

"Aren't I always?"

Kristen lifted a brow, thinking she never really had any control when they were around. All they had to do was give her a look, and she grew flushed and itchy, willing to do whatever they asked. Just like right then.

"We're not just talking about following our lead, princess," Dylan warned her. "We're talking you obeying without hesitation or question. If you don't…punishment."

The way he savored that word assured Kristen that Dylan was looking forward enough to that to assure she violated some rule. She probably should have been indignant that he would suggest such a thing, much less savor the idea, but the heat flooding through her had nothing to do with outrage.

"I…I…don't understand." Not what they wanted. Not how her body was reacting to the situation.

"Then let us show you," Brandon suggested as he rose up to extend a hand to her. "Give us this one night to teach you everything we know."

Kristen swallowed, wondering if she was ready for everything but too afraid to pass the opportunity up. After all, everything they'd taught her so far had been absolutely amazing. She trusted them, loved them, and couldn't say no. Instead, she lifted a hand up to slide it into Brandon's and allowed him to pull her to her feet. He hesitated before leading her into the house to offer her one simple instruction.

"If, at any time, you want to stop, simply say Godiva."

"Godiva," Kristen repeated.

She was certain she wouldn't need to use it, and followed him willingly. He led her through the kitchen and up the stairs to the master bedroom they'd started using as their own.

It hadn't been renovated yet, but Dylan had big plans. Right then, she suspected he had even bigger plans for her. Conscious of his size and heat as he followed behind her, Kristen felt his hands settle on her hips, all but guiding each one of her steps and making her wonder if the fun had already begun.

It had for her. Kristen felt her heart rate pick up, her nerves growing into excited tingles as they reached the bedroom and both men stepped back to rake their gazes over her. She knew those looks, knew what thoughts were running through their heads. Instinctively, her body responded, warming and swelling with a welcome that had her breathless by the time Brandon broke his silence.

"We want you naked, beautiful." His tone might have held a loving edge, but that didn't mask the determination ringing in his command. "Strip."

Kristen hesitated for a mere second before her hands curled around the edge of the T-shirt she'd borrowed from Gwen's closet. She really needed to go shopping, but she'd been kind of busy all week. Kind of busy and kind of naked, strangely enough never self-conscious about that fact.

How could she be when Dylan and Brandon looked at her with such want and love shining in their eyes? She couldn't help but enjoy the moment. Both men watched her with growing tension as she slowly eased her shirt upward.

"You weren't told to tease, princess," Dylan ground out in a tone she'd never heard from him before. It sent a wild thrill racing down her spine as his lips kicked up in a wicked grin she did know very well. "That's one."

"One?" She blinked, not completely certain she knew what he meant. "One what?"

"Talking back, that's two," he warned her.

"Punishments?" Kristen asked, knowing she was right by the way his lips twitched.

"Are you asking for three?"

"I think you just want to give me three."

"And now you have four," Dylan stated as he held out his hand. "The shirt, princess. You've got five seconds, or it will be five punishments."

Kristen felt like sticking her tongue out at him, but instead, she had seconds to finish pulling her shirt off and toss it at him. She didn't dare say a word but simply lifted a brow as Dylan dropped her shirt onto the floor.

"That's six, princess," Dylan informed her, assuring her he'd been counting the seconds, too. "Now the rest or we'll go for an even dozen, and it'll be a long time before you get to come."

That was a threat worth respecting.

Kristen made quick work of shedding the rest of her clothes until she was standing there naked with her men starting to circle around her. She wasn't left to wonder what they were thinking either. Brandon and Dylan were all too ready to share their opinions on just about anything.

"We need to get you some nicer underwear," Brandon murmured. "Make you put on a little show."

"I'm not wearing a thong," Kristen warned him, drawing a line in the sand when it came to have a string up her butt crack.

"That's a dozen," Dylan warned her.

"Oh, hush up." Kristen shushed him, only to end up gasping as Brandon laid a sharp slap across her ass.

"You don't talk unless commanded to," he instructed her, not that Kristen was paying him much mind.

She was still on fire from that first spank. It hadn't really hurt, but it did ignite a rush of heat that had her flushing and dancing a step forward. The blossoming pleasure was a surprise, but the second spank wasn't.

"You're to say, yes, sir, when receiving commands," Dylan explained and then promptly spanked her again when she failed to respond.

"Yes, sir," Kirsten quickly gasped out, feeling her face flame along with her ass.

"I still detect a hint of attitude," Brandon murmured close to her ear as he crowded in behind her. "I say we make her punish herself. What do you say?"

Kristen licked her lips and bit back a giggle, trying to sound properly intimidated instead of wantonly amused. "Yes, sir."

"Hmm." He eased back. "Definitely a hint of attitude. On the bed, beautiful. It's time to teach you what domination is all about."

Kristen forced herself not to smile at that threat, certain she already knew what it was all about. It was all about them bossing her around. She didn't doubt it fed their natural machismo, but what they didn't know is that it fueled her own raging desires.

Of course they were determined to know it, ordering her to settle up against the headboard with her legs spread and her pussy open for them to enjoy. In that position, there was no hiding the arousal glistening on her lips and making her intimate flesh swell with heated longing. Kristen felt her pussy blossoming beneath their looks, and the urge to touch herself and taunt them almost overwhelmed her.

That was just what they wanted.

"Pet yourself, princess," Dylan ordered her with an eager note lighting his words. "We can see your little pussy is begging for some attention, so give it some."

She ached to, but Kristen had never touched herself like that before and hesitated, a little embarrassed by the idea altogether. Hesitations, though, were not allowed, and this time, Brandon cracked his hand right over her intimate folds, making Kristen squeal as a bolt of white-hot rapture shot straight out of her clit and left her buzzing with delicious, wicked delight.

"Now, beautiful, pet yourself or get spanked…choice is yours."

She wanted to be spanked, but more than that, she wanted revenge for that smug offer. She knew just how to get it.

Chapter 20

Brandon held Kristen's gaze for a long moment as her eyes began to sparkle and her hand began the slow slide down over her stomach to settle over the swollen folds of her pussy. The plump and glistening lips parted beneath her touch, revealing the sweet flesh beneath and making him crave a taste.

Since this night was about indulging every craving he had, Brandon caught her hand and held her gaze as he lifted her fingers up to his lips and sucked them dry. He watched her eyes darken with a desire that assured him Kristen was enjoying this just as much as Dylan and him.

Dylan, though, was a man with a plan, and he caught Kristen's hand as Brandon released it to slap a brand-new dildo into it, one he'd gone down to Dothan to purchase along with a few other items.

"It's time to stop playing, princess, and start fucking," Dylan informed her as he released her hand, but it didn't fall back.

Instead, Kristen's eyes remained glued on the toy as if she'd never seen one before, which she might not have. She should still be able to figure out how to use it. That was just why Brandon spanked her cunt again.

"No hesitation, remember?" he reprimanded her as she gasped and flushed, lifting into his palm and telling him without words how much she enjoyed being paddled. He rewarded her with another quick slap as he barked at her.

"Get one of those hands on those tits and the other in that cunt. You heard Dylan. It's time to start fucking."

Brandon knew just how his crude words affected Kristen. He could see the proof in the way her nipples puckered and her breath shortened. This time she didn't hesitated to drop her hand back to her pussy. Without any delay, she fitted the flared head of the plastic cock to her tight opening and shoved it in, making her moan and twist upward as her other hand came to toy with her breasts.

Kristen still managed to defy them, though, when instead of fucking herself with the toy as commanded, she left it buried deep inside of her and lifted her fingers to capture her clit. She began to torment the swollen little bud, driving her flush to a fever pitch as she began to twist about with her pleasure.

She was such a squirmy little thing, but he and Dylan had the solution for that. With a nod from Brandon, Dylan moved off to gather the velvet ties he'd purchased that afternoon. He passed one over to Brandon, and they both waited until Kristen had herself so strung out on pleasure that her legs instinctively snapped shut.

That happened a lot. There really was nothing like feeling her thighs clamp tight around his hips as she lifted and came all over the length of his dick. Right then, though, he wasn't distracted by the feel of her release and managed to keep a level enough head to match Dylan's motions and latch onto her ankle.

With a yank, they pulled her down the bed, forcing her legs wide until each one could be bound to an opposing corner post. That had her squealing and releasing her own molten flesh as her eyes blinked up to gaze up at them with lusty confusion. Brandon smiled down at her as Dylan retreated back to his newly purchased bag of goodies.

"You were told to fuck yourself, beautiful, not play with yourself."

"But…but…but…" Kristen couldn't seem to get the words out as she gasped over the sight of Dylan returning, two floggers in hand. "You're not going to *whip* me, are you?"

Brandon and Dylan just shared a smile, not responding to that with words as Dylan passed Brandon a flogger. They lifted their hands into the air as Kristen let out a preliminary shriek.

"Can't we talk—"

No, they couldn't. They'd rather show her. That was just what they did. Dylan aiming for her breasts as Brandon allowed the velvety tassels of his flogger to dance over Kristen's cunt, leaving red streaks in their wake and making her cry out and arch into their lashing. In seconds, she was begging for more, not less, as her hands clawed at the sheets.

She was twisting and moaning, turning into a siren before Brandon's very eyes and making both his heart and dick swell. He really did love her, but he'd feared that she wouldn't be able to handle Dylan and him like this. Brandon was never more grateful for being wrong.

Proving she was, indeed, prefect for them, Kristen blossomed beneath their punishments, taking to them like a bird did to flight. She was a sensual, wanton vixen who arched into every lash of their whips as her skin flushed and her muscles tensed. Brandon sensed that she was on the verge of coming and dropped his flogger to reach down and take hold of the end of the dildo still stretching her cunt wide. He began to pound it in and out of her, riding her right over the edge until she was lost, too lost in the ecstasy to notice when he pulled the toy free and slid it down to the clenched opening of her ass.

He screwed the already lubed dick slowly into her as Kristen stilled, her eyes flying open and mouth falling limp beneath her gasp. Their gazes connected and locked, Brandon couldn't help but smile down at her as he changed speed and pumped the dildo deep into her.

Kristen cried out, her whole body lifting up in a graceful bow as her ass clenched down around the toy, holding it still. Brandon gave her the moment but not much else as he retrieved his flogger and nodded toward Dylan. Once again they laid into her, and this time, she came all that much faster and all that much harder.

Brandon couldn't resist. He wanted her. Even though he knew Dylan had more plans for the night, he took control of the moment, climbing between Kristen's splayed thighs before Dylan could stop him. Then he was pushing into the tightest heaven he'd ever tried to fuck. Brandon could feel the hard plastic of the dildo packed in her ass as he slid slowly into her sheath and knew that he was pushing Kristen harder than they ever had before, but he couldn't stop.

* * * *

Kristen didn't want him to stop. She'd known this day was coming, known what they'd intended, but she'd never guessed it would feel like this. Her body was inflamed with a volatile mixture of pleasure and pain, of pressure, and the sweet sensation of fullness that made everything she was feeling only more intense.

What she was feeling was amazing.

Her nails dug deeper into the mattress as Brandon fed her another hard inch. He was sweating and grunting above her, his arms beginning to tremble, and Kristen knew how much it was costing him to hold back. She appreciated his effort but ached to feel him unleashed, only Kristen couldn't get the words out.

She couldn't make a single sound, especially not as Dylan came to kneel beside her, his hand twining in her hair and guiding her head toward the thick cock weeping for her attention. Kristen didn't even hesitate. Not only had she grown good at sucking dick, but she'd also grown to enjoy it.

In those few minutes when she had them completely at the mercy of her kiss, Kristen felt all-powerful and so damn sexy that her confidence simply bloomed. That night, though, she was at their mercy, and she'd never felt more desirable. Dylan fucked her mouth with a savagery that was the perfect counterpoint for Brandon's slow thrusts.

He teased himself and her, grinding this thick dick along the sensitive walls of her sheath, only to angle himself with every inward thrust to tease the sweet spot hidden deep within her body. With every magic press against that special spot, Kristen's world lit back up with another bolt of pure sunshine that had her whole body clenching and tightening around both cocks buried inside her, along with the one pumping into her mouth.

It was all too much and yet not nearly enough.

Kristen started to buck with that contradiction, trying to force Brandon into a faster rhythm. Her attempts succeeded in snapping his control and reducing him down to a creature of relentless need just as he'd stripped her down to nothing but pure lust. They moved together, their body's lifting and surging in one perfect rhythm as the rapture built into a blinding ball of pure ecstasy.

It consumed her whole, taking Brandon and Dylan with her. Both men came with matching roars that left her penetrated and full of seed. Kristen swallowed quickly as Dylan blasted his release down her throat before he fell over on his side, Brandon collapsing on top of her.

They did this a lot. Spent themselves, collapsed, and then five minutes later, they were back to ravaging her. Her men had stamina, sort of. Kristen smiled at that thought, loving this moment just as much as she loved all the others.

She ran her fingers through Brandon's sweaty tresses, gently massaging his scalp and making him moan and turn into her touch. It was a simple moment but one made all the richer thanks to the bliss still pumping through her veins. It filled her with a sweet joy that still throbbed with a deeper, darker need.

Her ass was on fire, throbbing with the strain of still being stretched wide over the dildo. Kristen felt her cheeks heat as her whole world began to narrow back into a pounding ache that had her shifting and Brandon's head lifting. He blinked lazily and smiled down at her.

"Something wrong?"

His tone held the rough, husky undernotes of amusement that assured Kristen he knew just why she was twitching, but she didn't give him the satisfaction he was obviously looking for with her agreement. Instead, she dared to boldly lie with a lift of her chin.

"You're getting kind of heavy."

"Is that right?" Brandon lifted himself back up onto his arms before raising a brow. "Is that better?"

He knew it wasn't. He had to know that his new position had buried his hardening dick deeper inside her, which made Kristen only squirm all the more. Still, she refused to give him the answer he so obviously wanted.

"A shower would be better."

"Is our little princess trying to make demands?" Dylan butted in as he stretched and lifted back up onto his feet.

"She's getting sassy, that's for sure," Brandon agreed.

"Well then, maybe we ought to show her the renovations we made to the bathroom," Dylan suggested with a smile that warned her he'd been up to no good.

"What an excellent idea," Brandon agreed, pulling out of her with a quickness that left Kristen grasping.

It became clear as both men turned to work the ties around her ankles free that they planned on leaving the dildo packed into her rear. That had Kristen torn between embarrassment and a pleasure too wicked to be voiced. Instead, she bit her lip and endured the wondrously forbidden delight buzzing out up her spine as she took Brandon's hands and allowed him to pull her up onto unsteady legs.

He held on to her hands for a moment too long, and Kristen realized she'd stepped into a trap. It was too late, though, to do anything about the matter as Dylan stepped up to snap a cold, metal bracelet around her wrist. Before her amazed eyes, the man actually handcuffed her and then grabbed onto the chain links connecting the two cuffs to drag her behind him like some common criminal.

Kristen really should have objected, but she didn't have the voice because, from that first fumbling step, the dildo still tucked inside her began to shift, causing ripples of a pleasure so intense they bordered on painful to dance up her spine. It didn't help either when Brandon decided to give her a firm spank, making her all but trip over her feet as she gasped with the sheer delight.

Brandon laughed as Dylan tugged her into the bathroom, allowing her to come to a stop and admire his handiwork. He'd removed the door to the shower stall and installed a handheld head that was aimed out toward where a hook came down from the ceiling.

"That's never going to hold." Kristen blurted out the very first thought in her head. She could figure out that they meant to hang her from that hook, but all she could envision was the ceiling falling in on her head.

"Sure it will," Dylan assured her, releasing Kristen's wrist to step into the stall and reach a fist up to grab the hook. He spun around in a circle, his feet coming off the ground. "See. It can hold me."

Kristen smiled. She could see him, and he looked good naked and dangling there. It made her mind pop with all sorts of forbidden thoughts.

"Hey," Brandon snapped, giving her bottom another swat. "Keep it moving."

Kristen's lashes fluttered with the rush of pleasure that swamped through her and stumbled forward.

"That's it, princess," Dylan coaxed her as he released the hook to take command of her cuffs once again. "Come right over here and let's get you tied up and ready for your bath. You know, I think we're going to have to shave tonight."

He wasn't going to take the dildo out for that either. That was clear as Dylan stretched her hands high over her head and caught her cuffs on the hook. She could still reach the floor but only if she stood perfectly straight, and doing that caused her ass muscles to clench tighter around the dildo.

The next half hour passed in a torturous, sensual haze of a pleasure so thick it steamed the mirror and had Kristen mewing for breath. Both men cleaned her with gentle strokes that covered her body as their lips followed the trail of their washcloths, leaving her panting and twisting beneath their loving touch.

They lulled her into a sense of complete security, allowing them to shave her as they had only a week ago. This time was different, though. This time she wasn't rewarded for her submission with a kiss but, instead, felt her folds being parted by the cool, bulbous head of another plastic cock.

Her eyes fluttered open, but the darkness didn't dissipate. That was when she realized she'd been blindfolded and was in real trouble now.

* * * *

Dylan stepped back to admire his handiwork as he watched Brandon fit the vibrator into Kristen's cunt. Her pink folds split wide around the wide purple cock as she danced up onto her toes, and he could imagine just how stuffed she was feeling.

It was only the beginning.

Once he tore out this bathroom and built it back up into the perfect sex chamber, they'd be having all sorts of fun. The fun was only beginning for Kristen. She gasped and squirmed as Brandon clicked on the vibrator. Then came the butterfly.

By the time Brandon finished strapping her into the little toy and turning it on, Kristen was dancing around on the tips of her toes, a fresh sheen of sweat beginning to make her skin glow as she flushed a pretty pink color. Dylan smiled, enjoying the sight.

Brandon stepped back to join him in admiring his handiwork before wiping the grin from his face and issuing a hard-cut command.

"This is your punishment. Do you remember why you are being punished, beautiful?"

Kristen didn't answer fast enough, and Dylan had the pleasure of smacking that sweet ass once more. Kristen immediately squealed and danced forward as Brandon repeated his question, and this time she was quick to answer.

"Yes, sir."

"Very good." Brandon stepped up to drop his tone to a low murmur as he all but whispered in her ear. "This is your punishment, so I suggest you use that time to remember the rules."

As if that's going to happen, Dylan snorted to himself. He wasn't even completely certain Kristen had understood Brandon's threat, but she couldn't escape it. She hung there gasping and twisting, clearly enjoying her punishment but not enough to satisfy the cravings beginning to drive her breathing to a frantic pace, and then she was begging, pleading, using all the dirty words that Dylan and Brandon had taught her.

It took an immeasurable amount of self-restraint not to give in to her cries, and after about a half hour, Dylan's control began to snap. It wasn't like she had watch on or could measure time by anything other than the rapid pound of her heartbeat. It was beating fast. Dylan checked, making her whimper as he pressed his fingers into her neck.

Kristen turned into his touch. Her tears had soaked through her blindfold and left a streak across his fingers as she tried to whisper kisses across them as her words murmured out in a broken, husky plea.

"I love you, Dylan. I need you. Please."

He didn't know how she knew it was him, but Dylan knew he'd never felt the way he did in that moment. Kristen completely undid him, and he didn't care what Brandon said. Dylan was definitely going to be the one to marry her.

He sealed that silent vow with a kiss that had Kristen twisting into his body and rubbing her own against him as she teased his with the swollen feel of her breasts, the hard tips of her nipples, and quivering softness of her stomach. It was too much. He needed her now.

The last threads of Dylan's self-control snapped in that instant as his hands flew toward her hips, only to find Brandon's already there and pulling the butterfly off of her. The vibrator was next. Then Brandon was reaching for the dildo, but Dylan slapped his hand away.

He was going to be Kristen's first at something.

With that thought, he latched onto the base of the dildo and began slowly fucking her with it, making Kristen gasp and break free of their kiss as her body began to sway in beat with the motions of the dick pumping into her ass. Dylan wanted to be that dick. He was done waiting. She was ready.

Still, Dylan found himself hesitating, and he pulled the dildo free and stepped into the shower stall to take his position behind her. He brought the throbbing head of his cock to the tight entrance still clenched and barred against his entry and paused. Gripping Kristen's hips, he held her still as he pumped his heated length up and down the heavenly crease of her ass, teasing her with what was to come, even as he asked for permission.

"I love you, Kristen," he whispered out, his own voice broken by the need clawing through him. "And I want to love you this way. Say yes."

For a long second, Dylan held his breath before Kristen finally answered.

"Yes." Despite the tears, despite the strain of pleasure so clearly gripping her, despite even the magnitude of the moment and the step she was taking, Kristen managed a small smile as she tacked on a "sir."

Dylan couldn't help but laugh, feeling a lightness flood his soul that had him nipping at her ear. "You'll pay for that attitude, princess."

* * * *

Kristen didn't think so. She figured she'd already paid. Now she was about to be rewarded. Kristen's breath caught as Dylan slid the thick length of his dick slowly back so that the flared head of his cock pressed against her virgin entrance, and she couldn't help but tense in preparation for his penetration, but Dylan hesitated.

"You need to relax, princess," he warned her, nothing but love and want thickening his voice.

"I don't think I can," Kristen whispered back, knowing she couldn't.

She was too strung out on the pleasure to be able to relax even the slightest bit. The need clawing through her echoed out of her cunt and throbbed out of her ass, the two sensations combining into an intense whirl of delight that had only bloomed higher and thicker. There seemed to be no end in sight.

Kristen didn't need to explain. Her men knew. They knew her that well and treated her even better as Brandon sank to his knees, his big, broad hands coming to press her thighs open. The hot wash of his breath over her already sensitized flesh was like a stroke of pure, searing heat, leaving her whimpering as she knew what he intended.

Brandon didn't disappoint her, covering her pussy in wet, suckling kisses that quick evolved into deeper, longer strokes of his tongue as he alternately teased her clit before dipping down to fuck his velvety length into her pulsing sheath. With a speed and mastery she'd come to know and love, he drove her right to the pinnacle of the greatest release she'd ever dared to reach for and flung her body and soul into the devastating explosion of her own climax.

In the rush of rapture that tore through her, she felt her muscles relax for just a second. A mere breath of time, which was all Dylan needed to pound the thick, full length of his cock deep into her ass.

Kristen swallowed a hard breath, but there was no stopping the avalanche of delight that bloomed out of her ass as Dylan began to move, fucking her with slow, loving strokes that had her twisting in delight as her release collapsed into the next one building inside of her, warning her that this time her climax just might be her last.

Surely nothing could ever compare.

That was Kirsten's last rational thought as Brandon rose back up to his feet and fitted the bulbous head of his cock against the weeping opening of her cunt. Then he was sliding in, making her eyes all but roll back into her head as the pressure inside of her twisted into a tight knot of throbbing need.

Dylan was still pumping himself in and out of her ass as Brandon joined in, setting a rhythm that had Kristen writhing between them. She bucked and flexed her own hips, trying to force them faster to match the frantic beat of the need inside of her while sometimes they delighted in holding back, making her beg and plead and cuss as she used words that would have shamed her mother.

That wasn't all that would have shamed her mother, but Kristen felt no guilt in being caught between the two men she loved and the two men who loved her. How could anything they did be wrong? If this pleasure was wrong, then Kristen didn't want to be right. She didn't want to be taunted either.

Now was not the time, and her two men seemed to understand that as they picked up speed until both Brandon and Dylan were grunting and staining against her. They were pounding into her, driving home one bolt of rapture after another until Kirsten was squealing and shattering into a million pieces as she heard them roar. They came together in one glorious release that left Kristen limp and dazed.

She was dimly aware of being released from the cuffs and then carted off to another bathroom for a shower that had their hands working over her body in a soothing massage before they finally carried her back to bed and tucked her safely between them. Kristen was just drifting off when she heard Dylan murmur a warning to Brandon.

"Kristen is marrying me."

"In your dreams."

Kristen smiled, thinking that they were certainly in hers.

Chapter 21

Friday, June 6th

The rest of the week flew past in a delirium of sexual delights Kristen had never believed could exist. Brandon and Dylan kept her up all night and yawning all day. It seemed now that she'd agreed to indulge their need to dominate they couldn't get enough of her.

The truth be told, she couldn't get enough of them. Kristen might have blushed whenever she thought about the things she let them do, but she didn't regret a single one. Just the opposite. She craved more.

Unlike Cybil's dire warning about things that burned hot burning out, there seemed no end to either her or her men's need. In fact, it seemed to only grow, which was why she was a little irritated to get a call from her mother informing her that her dad was demanding to see her that night.

It was Friday, and they were supposed to go dancing, but Kristen knew better than to disobey her parents, even if she knew what they wanted to talk about. No doubt her dad was concerned about her dating and her mother distressed that she hadn't come to church the last Sunday.

Her independence was a difficult notion for them, and Kristen knew that avoiding the lectures and nags coming her way would only entice them to panic even more. So, she informed both Brandon and Dylan that she would be having dinner with her folks and they would have the night off.

That didn't sit well with either man, and both vowed to wait up for her. Kristen didn't have the heart to turn either one down, promising that she'd come back to their house when her dinner was over, even though that would mean she hadn't spent even one night at her cousin's house.

Not that Gwen seemed to notice. Every time Kristen ran across her cousin, Gwen remained silent and sullen. Kristen figured things were not going her way, especially given the sheriff's engagement had turned out to be a reality and not a hoax. While Kristen felt bad for Gwen, she couldn't help but notice that every time she saw the sheriff at lunch, he was smiling now.

The man was clearly happy, and she suspected a Cattleman, given the rumors that Heather hadn't just taken up with the sheriff but also with his best friend. Kristen couldn't cast a stone at that rumor, especially not when she knew there were ones circulating about her.

It turned out that the problem with riding a pink scooter was that everybody knew exactly where she was, and it hadn't gone unnoticed that she had been parking it in Brandon and Dylan's drive every night. Cybil even asked her about it, but Kristen could only grin. Her relationship wasn't anybody's business anyway.

Not even her parents', but that certainty was tested Friday night.

Kristen knew she was in trouble the moment her mother opened the door. Marissa looked worried. More than that, she looked afraid and her father sat at the head of the table, clearly steaming through the whole meal.

Worse, neither one of them asked her about Dylan, which meant he was likely the source of their agitation. Kristen couldn't help but wonder if the rumors had reached them down there in Dothan as she followed her father into the living room, leaving her mother to clear the table and cast fearful glances after them.

"Shut the door, young lady, and have a seat," her father commanded as he settled into his normal seat. "We need to have a talk."

That didn't sound good, and Kristen hastened to obey, unnerved by the tone in her father's voice. It was one she very rarely heard, and one that warned her he was beyond mad. Dylan would have said he was pissed, but Dylan had a potty mouth.

"I received this in the mail the other day," her father began as Kristen settled down onto the loveseat.

She watched him reach for a large vanilla envelope resting on the side table next to his chair. While she couldn't guess at what was in it, she couldn't help but feel the ominous weight of dread as her father passed the envelope to her. Her father's steady look didn't help, and she pulled back the flap slowly, certain she didn't want to know what was inside.

There was no way to avoid it, and the truth turned out to be worse than anything she could have imagined. Kristen felt herself flush and start to tremble as a set pictures fell out into her hands. They were of her and Dylan...and Brandon locked in an intimate embrace on their back porch. There could be no denying what they were doing or how the snapshots had ended, or her father's reaction to them.

"To say I'm disappointed would be an understatement," her father began in a strained tone as he continued to glare at her in disapproval.

"I...I..." Kristen didn't know what to say. What was she supposed to say? Her father didn't suffer from that dilemma, and his command came instantly.

"You'll be moving home, obviously."

Kristen just gaped at him. Move home? She couldn't do that. She couldn't go back to living her life in a shell. She had dreams. She had plans.

"And never seeing either one of those men again," her father continued on, seeming completely oblivious to Kristen's internal battle.

It was instinctive to obey her father, but everything he said had her shaking with a rush of pure panic. Never see Dylan and Brandon again? She couldn't do that. She loved them. She wanted to build a life with them. She'd never give them up. She couldn't.

"God willing, Mr. O'Leary will be willing to accept you as you are now and—"

"Accept me?" That insult snapped Kristen out of her stupor, and she found herself instinctively puckering up. "I don't need Mr. O'Leary to accept me. I don't accept him."

"Now, young lady—"

"And I'm not moving home." Kristen rose up with that proclamation, feeling as if she were shedding a set of shackles that had weighed her down for far too long. "I'm sorry you are disappointed, Dad, but this is my life. I have to live it my way."

"How dare you." Her father rose up slowly, his face flushed with his outrage. "Your mother and I have provided for you for twenty-two years, and this is the respect you show us? The gratitude?"

"I am grateful," Kristen insisted, clutching the photos to her breasts as she held on to them as tightly as she wanted to hold Dylan and Brandon. She wished they were there to give her strength, but she refused to buckle without them.

"I'm my own woman," Kristen said aloud, needing to hear it almost as much as her father did. "And my personal business is mine. Now, I love you, Dad, but I can't live my life for you. I have to live it for me."

With that, Kristen lifted her chin and headed for the door. This conversation was over. Permanently.

"You walk out that door, young lady, don't you think you can walk back through it," her father warned her, making Kristen's heart break. She paused to look back at him.

"You know my door is always open," she assured him softly and then fled.

She flew past her mother and made it out of the house before she started crying. Kristen didn't let those tears stop her, though. Neither would she allow the shaking to keep her from moving forward. She fumbled with her helmet, securing the envelope with the pictures in her purse before mounting her scooter and heading back for home.

Home, where Dylan and Brandon were. She needed them now more than she ever had before. She needed their strength and assurance that she had chosen wisely. That struck her hard as she putted back down the main highway toward Pittsview, leaving her to wonder if she'd simply replaced her father's authority with theirs, but then Kristen remembered all the little ways they catered to her and gave her the freedom to do as she wanted and knew that their relationship was something more. Something special.

Something somebody had tried to destroy.

Somebody who knew how her parents would react, and there was only one person Kristen could think of who knew all of that—Gwen. That bitch. After all the times Kristen had stood up for her, she couldn't believe her cousin would betray her like that. She needed proof, needed to confront Gwen and hear it from her cousin's lips why she'd do something like this.

Determined to get that answer, Kristen aimed her scooter for Gwen's place, only she wasn't there by the time Kristen arrived. It was dark out, and she knew Gwen probably wouldn't be back for hours. She also knew Dylan and Brandon were probably growing anxious, but Kristen didn't pass by Gwen's dark house and keep on going. Instead, she pulled into the driveway, intent on tearing Gwen's house apart until she found the proof she was looking for.

It didn't take her long, and she certainly didn't have to go through the whole house. Kristen stumbled into a nightmare within five seconds of starting her search. She began, as seemed appropriate, in Gwen's den and her precious desk. Two drawers down, she found the files that proved Gwen was capable of anything.

Kristen stared at the pictures of her cousin in all sorts of intimate poses and embraces with more men than Kristen had ever realized. There were at least twenty of them, and she recognized more than one face. There was a journal stored with the files, and as Kristen flipped through the pages, everything just clicked and she knew what she was looking at.

Her cousin's blackmail ledger and the evidence she was using to force her subjects to pay.

It was horrible, and very real. What was she supposed to do now? Turn her cousin in? She couldn't do that. Even after what Gwen had done to her, she couldn't destroy Gwen's whole life or that of her marks. She couldn't do that, but neither could she stay there any longer.

Tucking everything back into the desk drawer, Kristen told herself it wasn't any of her business, but those men weren't exactly innocent victims either. They were married men, respected pillars of the community, many elected to office. They didn't deserve her sympathy, and she didn't deserve to carry this weight.

The more Kristen thought about it, the more she came to realize that there was only one solution to her problem. She had to walk away from this situation. That was just what she did. She walked slowly down the hall to her borrowed bedroom and began packing everything up. She didn't have much, and it didn't take long, but she still couldn't cart it all up to Brandon and Dylan's on her scooter.

Kristen was left with no recourse but to call them and ask for help. She didn't doubt for a single moment that they would come, but they arrived faster than she'd thought, and she was still lugging suitcases and bags out onto the porch as both men jumped out of Dylan's truck and came rushing toward her.

"What is all this?" Dylan frowned, pulling to a stop as Brandon wove his way around her luggage to swoop her up in his arms.

"It's okay, beautiful," he murmured, crushing her in a bear hug as he seemed to instinctively know that something was very wrong. "Whatever it is, we'll get through it."

Kristen knew that was true, but his words still helped her believe in that truth. Pulling back, she met his gaze with her own, unable to mask her worry as she finally greeted him.

"My parents know about us." Kristen didn't have the heart to tell them what Gwen had done and didn't think it necessary.

"Oh, princess." Dylan sighed and looked pointedly at her luggage. "Please tell me you didn't agree to move back in with them."

"No." Kristen hesitated, for the first time feeling a little awkward about her plan, but that didn't stop her from pushing through. "I was thinking I'd move in with you two."

"Is that right, beautiful?" Brandon cocked a brow, his amusement betrayed by the twitch of his lips. "Are you sure you are ready to make that kind of step?"

"I'm sure I love you, and I've been spending every night with you...so...you going to help me move or not?"

"Of course, princess," Dylan instantly assured her. "All you had to do was ask."

Epilogue

Sunday, July 20th

Kristen fell silent as it dawned on her that she might have revealed too much, but Wanda simply patted her hand and smiled.

"It sounds to me like you made the right choice."

"I don't know." Kristen sighed, not doubting that she'd made the best decision ever when she'd decided to move in with Brandon and Dylan but unable to escape the guilt at having abandoned her cousin. "There was a break-in a few days later, and then Gwen was dead."

"And you feel bad because she died while you were still angry with her," Wanda concluded, amazing Kristen with her perception. Even Dylan and Brandon hadn't figured out the secret she'd been harboring.

"I should have tried to help her more," Kristen whispered, thinking of all the things she could have done but hadn't.

"She probably wouldn't have let you." Wanda smiled slightly, a sad twist of the lips that held way too much sorrow for her emotions to have only been touched by Gwen.

This was a woman who knew about those poor souls who lost their ways. Kristen had a feeling Wanda knew how to guide them back to the right path. If only Gwen had had that chance. The thing Gwen had a chance at now was justice, not that it would do her any good.

"Did you tell Dylan or Brandon any of this?" Wanda drew her attention back to the moment, back to the one subject that ate at her. Kristen had no choice but to slowly shake her head.

"No. I…I didn't want them to do anything to Gwen—"

"Like arrest her?" Wanda cut in, taking an accurate guess at Kristen's motives.

"Yes," Kristen admitted with a slow nod. "After she passed, I was afraid that…"

"Somebody might think you were guilty because of the pictures she sent your parents?"

"Yes."

"Did you ever wonder if maybe somebody else sent those pictures?" Wanda pressed, causing Kristen to frown.

She never really had. "Who would have? Why?"

"I don't know." Wanda shrugged. "Just a thought, and here's another one, you better tell those boys of yours what you know before they find out you know it some other way."

Kristen knew she was right, had known what she had to do for weeks now. It was just cowardice that had made her hesitate. Things were going so well between them, but more than that, she just didn't want everybody to think of Gwen as a blackmailer…even though she was one.

"Did you see your parents at the funeral?" Wanda asked softly, touching on a subject Kristen couldn't help but cringe away from.

"My parents didn't attend the funeral," Kristen stated firmly. "They didn't approve of Gwen's life."

They didn't approve of her either. They weren't technically speaking to Kristen, but her mother was writing letters. She knew eventually her mother would come to accept the situation. Her father, she feared, never would.

"I'm sorry to hear that." Wanda paused as somebody passed to close to their table before she continued on in a softer voice. "And I want you to know that you have helped me, and I'm going to help find the bastard that hurt your cousin. She will have her justice."

Kristen gazed over at the other woman, sensing her determination and nodded. "I don't doubt she will, and I'm glad I could have helped. If you need anything more—"

"I know where to find you." Wanda nodded.

Kristen left her sitting there, thinking over all the things they had talked about. It was strange, but her conversation with Wanda had been very therapeutic. It felt as if a weight felt had been lifted from her shoulders, and now she was ready to tell her tale to Dylan and Brandon.

They were out fishing, as was their Sunday after-church tradition. Normally Kristen joined them, but that day she had chosen to have brunch with Wanda. Though it turned out she wasn't the only one who had decided to handle other business that day.

That became clear as Kristen pulled up the driveway to find a massive pink Cadillac parked at the top. It was huge with tail fins, and it had a trunk that could damn near have fit her scooter into it. A convertible with a pure white interior, the car was a classic beauty and clearly for her, given the words written in cursive over the back of the trunk.

Pink Princess.

"Hey, princess!" Dylan hollered from the back porch as Brandon appeared in the back door. "Guess what we got you?"

Both men came rushing down as Kristen dismounted from the scooter. By the time her hands were reaching for the strap on her helmet, Brandon was there to brush her hands away and take care of the latch for her.

"Hey, beautiful." He smiled down at her, dropping a quick kiss on her lips before stepping back to allow her to admire the Cadillac. "What do you think?"

"I…think it is so cool." Kristen broke into a massive grin, feeling her smile wipe away what little worry clung to both men.

"It's for you," Dylan explained as if she hadn't already figured that out. "We figured you'd like it better than a ring."

"A ring?" Kristen blinked, her heart seizing. "Is that today?"

"No, beautiful," Brandon murmured. "We know you need time, and while you're taking it, we want you to be safe. So, with all respect, we're asking you to give up your scooter."

"We're swapping with you." Dylan wagged his brows at her. "So what do you say?"

Kristen hesitated to look over at the scooter. She loved her little bike. She'd bonded with it. She'd also bonded with her men and loved them too much to allow them to worry. It was clear from the car before her that, despite the fact that they hadn't been nagging her, they had been worried.

That more than anything made up her mind.

"Yes."

Dylan let out a whop and lifted her right off her feet as he spun her around. Kristen laughed as she clutched him, infused by his excitement and forgetting for a moment she'd come home to talk to them about Gwen. That conversation got put off as Brandon insisted they all pile into her car and take a drive down to the lake.

The thing was big enough with bench seats that they could have all fit into the front, but Dylan hopped into the back as Brandon tossed her the keys. Then they were hitting the road. With the top down and the sunlight shining on them, it felt as if the whole world were celebrating with them.

They ended up down by the lake, parked under the shade of an old oak, and they strolled along a stretch of sandy beach hand in hand. It was a perfect afternoon. Kristen hated to ruin it, but her thoughts drifted back toward her conversation with Wanda, and she found herself unable to hold them in.

Slowly, with a sinking feeling that she was ruining the mood, Kristen told them the whole long, sordid tale. They remained silent through it as she revealed the truth about Gwen's pregnancy, her blackmail scheme, and how it was that her parents came to find out about them.

In the end, they didn't shout or yell, or tell her they were disappointed in her. They simply hugged and kissed her and explained that it was time to go to the station house. Kristen had a statement to make.

* * * *

Wanda wouldn't have been surprised to know that Kristen had gone home and spilled her guts. She'd known and met enough people to recognize that Kristen's innocence went deeper than a simple hymen. It sounded as if her men were actually just as decent. If Kristen confessed everything, they'd make her give a statement.

How could they not?

The real question was whether the cops already knew about Gwen's scheming. They must have searched her house by now, and if they had, they'd have found the blackmail material...unless, of course, somebody had removed it. That would be an interesting question to find the answer to, and a pivotal one because if somebody had removed the evidence they'd likely done it for a very obvious reason.

They'd killed Gwen.

Wanda didn't allow that thought to push her ahead of herself. She'd run enough investigations to know that all questions had to be answered before any conclusion could be made. Kristen's tale certainly brought up a lot of questions.

The most obvious one being, what was Dean's real role in Gwen's life? He was clearly the closest to her, but there was more than that. He'd been the one Gwen had turned to help her with her schemes, which meant he wasn't to be trusted. Wanda would need to know the answers to the questions she asked him before she interrogated the man. That would be the only way to know when he was lying to her, and in those moments, he'd reveal his true motives.

Wanda didn't even want to begin to guess at what they were, not until she had more of the story. Thankfully, Kristen's tale had pointed her in an obvious direction—the mayor.

How had the mayor known who Kristen was?

Kristen hadn't mentioned meeting him, and it wasn't as though her position would have warranted his notice. What would was the fact that she was living with Gwen, but that was only if the mayor was doing Gwen. That didn't seem like a far stretch to make, and it was the only lead she had.

Kristen had not given her the names of any of her cousin's marks. Wanda hadn't pressed for them, knowing when and when not to force an issue. She didn't need Kristen to tell her the details, anyway. Wanda would find them out. She planned on starting work on that task right away, and as luck would have it, the very person she wanted to talk to walked into the bakery.

THE END

WWW.JENNYPENN.COM

ABOUT THE AUTHOR

I live near Charleston, SC with my two biggies (my dogs). I have had a slightly unconventional life. Moving almost every three years, I've had a range of day jobs that included everything from working for one of the world's largest banks as an auditor to turning wrenches as an outboard repair mechanic. I've always regretted that we only get one life and have tried to cram as much as I can into this one.

Throughout it all, I've always read books, feeding my need to dream and fantasize about what could be. An avid reader since childhood, as a latchkey kid I'd spend hours at the library earning those shiny stars the librarian would paste up on the board after my name.

I credit my grandmother's yearly visits as the beginning of my obsession with romances. When she'd come, she'd bring stacks of romance books, the old fashion kind that didn't have sex in them. Imagine my shock when I went to the used bookstore and found out what really could be in a romance novel.

I've working on my own stories for years and have found a particular love of erotic romances. In this genre, women are no longer confined to a stereotype and plots are no longer constrained to the rational. I love the anything goes mentality and letting my imagination run wild.

I hope you enjoyed running with me and will consider picking up another book and coming along for another adventure.

For all titles by Jenny Penn, please visit
www.bookstrand.com/jenny-penn

Siren Publishing, Inc.
www.SirenPublishing.com

Lightning Source UK Ltd.
Milton Keynes UK
UKHW02f1001090418
320733UK00006B/912/P